W9-CET-099

The Husband School

This Large Print Book carries the
Seal of Approval of N.A.V.H.

THE HUSBAND SCHOOL

KRISTINE ROLOFSON

THORNDIKE PRESS

A part of Gale, Cengage Learning

Farmington Hills, Mich • San Francisco • New York • Waterville, Maine
Meriden, Conn • Mason, Ohio • Chicago

GALE
CENGAGE Learning

LIBRARY OF CONGRESS CATALOGING-IN-PUBLICATION DATA

Rolofson, Kristine.
    The husband school / by Kristine Rolofson. — Large print edition.
      pages ; cm. — (Thorndike Press large print clean reads)
    ISBN 978-1-4104-7654-8 (hardcover) — ISBN 1-4104-7654-5 (hardcover)
    1. Cowboys—Fiction. 2. Dating shows (Television programs)—Fiction.
  3. Large type books. I. Title.
  PS3568.O5428H87 2015
  813'.54—dc23   2014042269

Published in 2015 by arrangement with Harlequin Books S.A.

Printed in Mexico
1 2 3 4 5 6 7 19 18 17 16 15

Dear Reader,

I'm so happy to be writing again! I took some time off from my computer to plan weddings, experience the thrill of being an adoring grandmother, travel and learn to play the violin. I even went to Blue Grass Camp! I also sewed twenty-eight quilts (but who's counting?).

The Husband School was inspired by a stop in a small Montana town during one of my husband's and my annual cross-country road trips. Combine our love of small Western towns with the memory of running a café ourselves *plus* the many "what if" questions a writer naturally generates, and with a little luck and a whole lot of time, a story was born. This story. About a little town trying to save itself and its way of life.

I once lived in a town so small that when I went to a yard sale, the woman running the sale knew what I was going to buy before I got there. She was right!

I hope you enjoy Willing, Montana, and the people who live there. The world needs more love stories, good neighbors and happily-ever-after romance.

Love,
Kristine Rolofson

www.KristineRolofson.wordpress.com
www.WelcomeToWillingMontana.wordpress
.com

To Sharon Winn and Patricia Coughlin, who listened and helped. I owe you more than all the dark chocolate and blueberry cake in the universe can repay.

CHAPTER ONE

On a typical Monday, Owen MacGregor would have never set foot in Meg Ripley's restaurant. He would have done what he always did, which was drive up to the Java Hut, order a tall black coffee from dour Esther Grinnell and drive the final eighty miles home. But on this bleak October morning, when the sky looked as if it was about to unleash a wild storm on his corner of Montana, Esther's coffee shack was inexplicably shuttered and Owen needed food. Boo nuzzled his collar and Owen reached up and scratched the dog's chin.

"You hungry, too?" That was a dumb question, since the little mutt was always ready to eat. When he wasn't sleeping. Or sprawled on the couch watching television. Owen had found the skinny stray hanging around the barn weeks ago. He'd brought him inside, fed him and named him. Content with his new living arrangements, Boo now had little use for the outdoor life.

Owen hesitated at the flashing red light at the intersection of Highway 10 and Main. Two blocks to the right, at the north edge of town, was a hot breakfast with his name on it, along with bacon for the dog gazing out the window and wagging his tail. Boo was looking for McDonald's, his favorite place in the world, and expected a treat whenever he rode along in the truck. But Owen hadn't had an appetite two hours ago after his weekly trip to Hopewell Living Center, and had sped past the cluster of Great Fall's fast food restaurants next to the highway. It had taken some time for his mood to lift and his hunger to set in.

And now the thought of breakfast was strong enough to make him consider stepping into the Dirty Shame Café. Oh, the sign in front of the building read Willing Café, but folks born and bred in the area knew the place as "The Shame" and probably would always call it by its original name. He'd heard Meg had changed the name on the menus, but he also knew she couldn't fight history.

Boo whined and wagged and licked his ear, but Owen didn't smile. He rarely smiled these days. . . . His own fault. He'd spent most of his adult life in an office, dealing with politicians and lawyers. He had a gift for dealing with difficult people, and he'd turned a law degree into one of the top environmental firms in the country.

And yet he rarely felt any degree of happiness.

Owen turned the steering wheel and stepped on the gas. The world wasn't going to come to an end if he walked into Meg Ripley's restaurant and ordered a couple of fried eggs.

With luck, she wouldn't be there.

With luck, she'd ignore him.

With luck, he'd be able to ignore her.

Owen didn't imagine his luck, meager as it was this morning, would hold. For one thing, he assumed Meg would be working. He also assumed she still lived in one of the original cabins adjacent to the restaurant. And ignore him? Well, that was the best he could hope for.

She was thirty-two, unfortunately young enough to remember their disastrous summer together, unlike his irate mother, who this morning had demanded he apologize for sitting on her cat even though she hadn't owned a cat in two decades, and he'd made the mistake when he was nine. His mother's memory had become increasingly faulty, her confusion more apparent this past year. He

11

hadn't told her about his temporary move to the ranch; she assumed he was still working in DC and so far it hadn't occurred to her to question his weekly Sunday visits, though on the rare times she mentioned his work, he'd told her he'd taken some time off. She hadn't seemed to understand, which was just as well. Explaining he'd used the settlement of the ranch property as an excuse to leave an increasingly boring career would not have been easy. His mother had no love for the Triple M.

Boo whined again as Owen drove past the restaurant to find a parking spot in the lot next door. The dog believed "stop" equaled "food," and he was usually right.

Owen took a couple of minutes to stretch while Boo trotted over to a half-dead bush and lifted his leg. Then the dog hurried back to jump in the front seat, knowing he would be rewarded with food after guarding the truck while his owner was inside the building doing whatever humans did before they brought food to their loyal canines.

"I'll be back," Owen promised. He was talking to his dog a lot more often lately, which was the behavior of a man who had settled into a solitary lifestyle. No, he told himself, he wasn't going to turn into his late uncle, a grizzled loner who preferred

dogs to people and rarely bathed. He didn't
want to end up dying alone, freezing to
death next to a barn, his body discovered a
week later by a UPS driver. That was not a
lifestyle Owen would willingly choose.
Although lately he'd begun to wonder if
he'd started down the "eccentric bachelor"
path without being aware of it.

Damn. Hungry and lonely was a tough
way to start the day.

"Do you think she'll marry me?"

"Of course not." Meg placed a plate piled
high with bacon, eggs and hash browns in
front of the hopeful suitor. She had no
intention of coddling Joey Peckham, who
was at this moment looking depressed,
despite the fact that she'd just refilled his
coffee and served him breakfast. "You must
be out of your mind. She's not going to go
out with you, so leave her alone."

"You serious?"

"Deadly serious," she assured him.

"Aw, you're breaking my heart." He picked
up his fork and, ignoring the paper napkin
she'd slid next to his coffee cup, stabbed a
chunk of fried egg. "And ruinin' my day,
too, if you want to know."

"I'm not ruining anything. She danced
with you once, at Pete's party," she re-

minded him. "It wasn't exactly a relation-ship."

"It could be. If she'd let it. If you'd talk her into giving me a chance." He spoke with his mouth full, so Meg turned away. Joey was six years younger than she was, but acted about fifteen instead of twenty-six. He needed to find himself a real, live girl-friend, the sooner the better, and stop imagining himself in love with every woman who two-stepped with him. Especially not with Lucia Swallow, who baked the restau-rant's pies and was single-handedly raising three children since her husband had died in Afghanistan.

"You're hallucinating. Lucia is too old for you," she stated one more time over her shoulder, knowing as she said it that the only thing Joey wanted to hear was that she would support his romance.

Which she wouldn't. Lucia was a friend and Joey was an idiot.

"You don't know what it's like to be in love," Joey muttered.

"Maybe, maybe not. But I'm sure it's overrated."

"You have no heart," he said, looking down at his eggs again. "That's your prob-lem."

"One of many," Meg agreed, trying not to

laugh. "Really, Joe. Lucia's not the woman for you. And you're too young to be a father to those boys of hers."

He scowled down at his plate. "How come you know so much and you don't even have a boyfriend?"

"They're overrated, too." She gave in and laughed, all too familiar with comments about her private life. There were few secrets in such a small town. "And if you don't stop griping, I'll tell Lucia you have fourteen cats."

"That's my uncle. Not me."

Meg shrugged. "She'll think that kind of crazy runs in the family."

"We have dogs," Mr. Fargus interjected from his perch on the neighboring stool. "Two poodles. Do you know my wife lets them dogs in the bed the minute she hears the back door slam shut? Every morning. None of them can wait for me to leave."

Meg could understand that. Ben Fargus, at the age of eighty-six, was a man who liked the sound of his own voice. Meg was accustomed to his opinions; they piled up like dirty dishes all morning long. She often wondered how his wife put up with him, but they'd been together for more than sixty years. By choice or habit, Meg had no idea, but poor Mrs. Fargus obviously had a lot of patience. Or was really good at pretending he didn't exist.

"Women," Joey said, shaking his head. "They're difficult."

"So are poodles," Fargus stated. "Real smart, though."

"Huh," Joey said, letting that information sink in. "Meg, do you think Lucia would like a dog?"

What Lucia liked or didn't like wasn't any of Joey's business, so Meg pretended she didn't hear the question and poured more coffee into the half-full mugs lined up in front of the five retired men seated in their usual places at the counter. For many of her customers, breakfast at Willing's was a tradition only broken because of vacations, hospital stays or death. Despite such loyalty, Meg was always worried about making it through the winter.

"How's everyone doing? Martin, you need more half 'n' half?"

"I'm set, thanks."

"George?"

"Please."

It was a typical morning; the L-shaped room, as familiar to her as her own little house, was comfortably packed with the usual crowd. The mayor was holding his monthly meeting to discuss town business.

16

The council members had pushed a couple of tables together in the back corner and from all appearances were involved in a serious discussion. Mondays were busy, but this morning had been almost hectic. There was something about the snow flurries and the gray sky that seemed to make folks want to get out and about while they still could, before a long, blizzard-filled winter began in earnest. And few seemed to be in any hurry to leave the snug warmth of the restaurant and head out into the wind.

Meg moved down the counter and dispersed coffee. The slender man on the last stool put his hand over his cup. "Thanks, Margaret, but I've had enough. Should be getting home, I guess."

"Okay." She paused in front of Mr. Ferguson, her former algebra teacher, who'd long since retired, and set his check on the counter. "How's Janet? I haven't seen her in a while."

"She's been busy getting ready for the quilt show. She's been in her sewing room for weeks." He smiled the indulgent smile of a man who loves his wife. "She says it's going to be quite a show."

"I'm looking forward to it," Meg said, knowing the annual event would give business a boost. "I bought an ad in the program. It's on Saturday, right?"

"Yes." He frowned, trying to remember. "Sunday, too, I think."

"I hope I can get over there to see it." She'd have to remember to ask one of the high school girls to fill in for her for a couple of hours after the noon rush. The quilt guild would be selling coffee and desserts during the show at the senior center, but Meg hoped a soup-and-sandwich special at the café would bring in a little extra business.

"What are they doing over there?" Fargus gestured toward members of the town council huddled around a large table at the far end of the room.

"Planning to raise taxes, I'll bet," George grumbled. "I'm getting damn tired of taxes."

"You could move to Florida," Martin said. Meg hid her smile. George, a creature of habit who had been born in Willing, didn't even like going to Billings.

"There's something going on," Fargus declared. "We'll hear about it soon enough. Jerry's got some idea. I can tell by the look on his face."

They all stared down at the far end of the room. Sure enough, the mayor seemed excited as one of the town elders read aloud from a sheet of paper.

"If they're raising taxes, then they're trying to figure out how to get blood from a stone," George grumbled. "I've half a mind to go over there and tell them so."

Fargus snorted. "Like that would do any good."

"Maybe I should get on the town council," Joey mused. "Women like men with power, right?"

Meg noticed John Ferguson and Martin Smith exchanging an amused look before John grabbed his cap and stood to leave.

"Thanks for breakfast, Margaret." He set six dollars by the empty coffee mug. "Guess I'll get home before the snow starts for real." He turned as the door jangled to announce another customer.

And it wasn't just any customer, either, because the sight of this one made Meg's stomach tense and her mouth go dry.

Owen MacGregor, master of all he surveyed, was a tall, imposing man. A down vest, unzipped, covered most of his wide chest, and he wore the typical Montana outfit: jeans, boots and plaid shirt. He politely stomped his feet on the worn doormat and removed his hat, but before he could move toward a seat, a white-haired man called his name. Meg watched as he greeted the Burkharts, an elderly couple in the process of holding each other up as they made their way across the room. Owen MacGregor played the gentleman and opened the door for them, allowing another burst of cold air in. If she didn't know better, she'd think he was the best thing to ever walk into the room. Even Mr. Ferguson looked pleased as the two men talked for a minute before the teacher disappeared out into the cold.

"Well, this is a surprise," Martin declared quietly to his cronies at the counter. "Didn't think he remembered where he came from."

"With Eddie dead and gone, I don't think there's anyone to run things," George said. "Guess that forced his hand."

"Irene's in a nursing home in Great Falls now," one of the other men informed them. "I heard she gets confused easily. My daughter-in-law works there, says the boy visits her every week."

Yes, Meg thought. *He was always a devoted son.* She'd assumed the old witch would live forever, queen of all she surveyed. She couldn't picture the regal Mrs. MacGregor incapacitated in any way. The last time Meg had seen her was after the funeral, and the widow hadn't let Meg in the house. Still, it was sad to think of Irene MacGregor in a nursing home.

She watched Owen slide into an empty

booth and shrug off his jacket. He set his gloves on the table and picked up a menu. Which meant she was supposed to scurry over there with coffee and take his order, just as if they barely knew each other?

This was true, actually. He was a stranger now, far different from the young man who'd told her he loved her and given her his grandmother's sapphire ring.

Meg still remembered the day she heard he'd left town. She'd cried in her mother's arms for hours.

"You'd better get on over there," one of the men said. "MacGregor doesn't spend much time in town, so this is a special occasion."

"You're right." She managed a cheerful smile. "And I need all the customers I can get."

Well, she could handle it. No problem. She'd give him a minute to read the menu, and then she would saunter over and pretend they were friends.

This morning Owen MacGregor looked a little the worse for wear. Oh, he was still handsome, with that lean, lined face and thick, dark hair. She knew he wore contacts, hated shrimp and had named his first horse Pumpkin, much to his father's dismay. He was secretly afraid of heights, crazy about

21

animals and had broken his nose twice in one summer, causing his mother to faint both times.

At the moment he and his nicely healed nose were absorbed in the menu.

"Hey," she said, approaching the table with a carafe of coffee.

"Hey." He tipped his mug right side up and Meg filled it for him. "Thanks."

"You're welcome. What can I get you?" She used her best cheerful-friendly-waitress voice, as if he was a tourist she'd never seen before. He frowned just a little.

"It all looks good," he said, copying her tone. "How about the Hungry Man Special, with scrambled eggs and bacon? And with an extra side of bacon to go, please."

"Sure." This wasn't so hard. She could do this. Meg didn't write down the order for fear her fingers would shake. Silly, but she had her pride.

"So how've you been?" He took a cautious sip of coffee and looked at her with real interest. As if he actually wanted to know the answer.

"Just fine. And you?"

"I'm good." He kept looking at her, studying her face until, still gripping the handle of the carafe, she backed up a step. She was conscious of how she must appear to him, dowdy Margaret Ripley in her apron, worn jeans and thick athletic shoes. "Well, I'll go put your order in."

"Thanks."

With that she turned and headed toward the kitchen. She returned the carafe to the coffee machine, wrote up the order before handing it to Al and, on the pretense of checking supplies, escaped to the back room. There wasn't much privacy in either the town or the restaurant, but there was a tiny alcove behind the walk-in freezer that provided the perfect place to hide for a few minutes. Meg leaned against the gray wall, took a deep breath and eyed the calendar tacked to the wall. October was here already, with a long winter ahead.

She should be over it. She was over it. She was a grown woman, capable of running a business and running her life. She had friends. And a home. She dated when she wanted to, though she seldom wanted to, and rarely ever thought of the eighteen-year-old girl who had fallen foolishly in love with a young man she could never have. His presence here couldn't upset her if she didn't allow it to, but she hoped he wouldn't make breakfast at Willing's a habit. They'd each become so good at pretending the other didn't exist, so why stop now?

■ ■ ■ ■

"And so we have to ask ourselves — what do women want?" Jerry Thompson desperately needed to know the answer. He tapped his pen against the empty page of the legal pad spread before him and studied the yellow-lined paper as if the solution to his problems would magically appear. When he looked up, the six members of the town council stared back at him.

Bachelors all, they were a varied group. On his left sat Les Purcell, a young cowboy who had been injured on the rodeo circuit and now lived with his grandparents. Seated next to Les was Pete Lyons, a nice enough guy who looked as if he slept in his clothes.

"Now, there's one heck of a question," Les muttered. "Anyone who has the answer to that can write a book, go on *Dr. Phil* and make a pile of money."

"It's a valid question," Jerry, recently elected mayor — because Art Woodhouse died and no one wanted the job — and full of ideas, looked across the table at the owner of the only auto-repair place in town. Hank Dougherty was likely too busy to watch much daytime television.

"What's Dr. Phil got to do with it?" Hank asked.

"Nothing. Just that he knows everything."

"Or thinks he does," Les said.

Jerry took a swallow of coffee. Obviously this was going to take more time than he'd thought. "Let's not get off track. I'm serious about this. We need to know what women want and then we have to give it to them." He ignored the spurt of laughter that followed this declaration and frowned. "I'm trying to get something going here. We're talking about publicity. About money coming into town. About *women* coming into town."

"Women? What kind of women?" This question came from Jack Dugan, who Jerry figured had no problem getting dates.

"Single women," he replied, as if he was talking to a bunch of first-graders. Not that he had any idea what it was like to talk to schoolkids. But this group, the city council and various other men who enjoyed free coffee once a month at the town meetings and sat around a couple of pushed-together Formica-topped tables, was about as dense a bunch of men as he'd ever met. No wonder they didn't have women of their own, or at least a date once in a while. Not that he himself was much different. He'd had two dates since he left Los Angeles three years ago and neither one had been what anyone would remotely call a success.

Pete, a thirty-something rancher who also drove the school bus, leaned forward. "How old are these women gonna be? And they're not gonna be from a foreign country, are they?"

"Like the Russian mafia and the mail-order brides," Mike Breen, the town treasurer who ran the county newspaper, added. "Saw it on *Law & Order* last night. Scary stuff."

This was quite the suspicious group. Jerry took a deep breath and started over again. "No, Mike, they're not going to take your money and kill you when you want to divorce them." He'd seen that episode himself. "Look," he said, eying the six bachelors who comprised the council. They weren't a bad-looking bunch. They could be cleaned up, their shirts ironed or, better yet, replaced. They had a rugged appeal he knew some women were attracted to, but he had severe doubts that his constituents had the skills to keep a woman interested past the first date. Heck, most of them couldn't make it further than a getting-to-know-you bottle of beer. "I have a friend in Los Angeles who's putting together an idea for a reality show."

"Like *Survivor?*" Hank perked up. He was fifty-five, widowed, with two grown daughters and a decent property in town. He might appeal to an older demographic, maybe the over-forty women.

"More like *The Bachelor.*"

Jack, who worked at the feed store, grinned. "Man, that's a great show, that *Bachelor.* I never miss it." The crowd grumbled their displeasure, but Jack didn't waver. "You should see the women," he insisted. "They act crazy, and they're gorgeous and they sit in a lot of hot tubs with the bachelor. Everyone tries to get a date with the guy and lots of times he can't tell the crazy ones from the ones who really like him."

Jack was young and good-looking, struggling to keep a small cattle outfit afloat while working in town. He picked up odd carpentry jobs and was careful with his money. And, Jerry thought, he'd look perfect on TV.

"That's right. Hot tubs and hot women in bathing suits." Now he had their interest.

"The only hot tub in the county belongs to MacGregor," Gary Petersen, retired from the co-op, whispered. "And he just sat down behind you, Jerry, so you might want to keep your voice down."

Jerry restrained himself from turning around to see if Gary was telling the truth. He'd never met Angus MacGregor's descendant but he'd read a lot about the family history. They'd practically invented cattle ranching in Montana.

"Thanks, Gary, for pointing that out." Jerry wrote *hot tub* on his paper. "I'll bet the TV production would spring for something. Either that or maybe we could use some town funds and buy one ourselves." Everyone looked at Mike, who shrugged.

"Money's hard to come by these days," he declared.

"Yeah," Pete muttered. "And so is a sex life."

"We're not talking about sex," Jerry felt it necessary to point out, though the lack of women was one of the biggest drawbacks to living in rural Montana. "We're talking about attracting single women to our town. We're talking about publicity, about attracting businesses, about letting people know we live in a beautiful part of the country where people care about one another. We're talking about expanding the population, saving the school, making Willing a great place to raise a family again."

"Quite a speech, Jerry. You're starting to

sound like a politician," Hank said, chuckling. "You're not running for governor, are you, son?"

"Not yet," Jerry said. "Now, do any of you have any objections to getting married?"

"Well," Hank drawled, "I did it once."

"And?" Jerry prompted.

"It sure beat being alone."

Not exactly high praise. Jerry fought the urge to bang his forehead on the table. Instead he gave each man a long look. "You're all lonely and miserable and you know well enough that if a woman gave you as much as a nod you'd be signing a marriage license and following her around the IGA with a grocery cart."

No one denied it, so Jerry figured they'd all just voted yes. Yes to inviting Hollywood to Willing. Yes to encouraging a busload of single women to give Montana bachelors a chance to impress them. Yes to drumming up a little excitement for a change.

Speaking of excitement, Jerry looked down the length of the crowded room and waved to Meg. She picked up a carafe and made her way toward his table. As far as Jerry was concerned, Meg Ripley was an important person. She knew everyone in town and he had no doubt she could run against him for mayor and win in a landslide. He'd been told she was thirtyish, single and straight, so Jerry had asked her out to dinner a month after he'd moved to town. They'd quickly become friends, though Meg politely refused any dates that could be construed as romantic.

He actually preferred blondes, but dark-haired Meg was attractive in a no-frills, low-maintenance way. He'd never seen her in anything but jeans, but she had a cute figure and a nice smile. In a town overpopulated by men, she mysteriously remained single, though he'd heard plenty of stories about broken hearts. As far as he could tell, Meg kept to herself and didn't go out of her way to break anything.

"Meg," he began, "how many times have you been proposed to?"

"I really don't think —"

"Seriously," Jerry said. "It's important."

She took a step back. "I'm not going to —"

"Eighteen," Jack declared. "Last time we did a count, it was eighteen."

"You've kept count?" Meg shot him a horrified look and Jack shrank back into his chair.

"It's posted at the Dahl," Hank pointed out. "It's not like it's a secret or anything."

"P-posted?" Meg sputtered. "I never saw it."

"Men's room." Les whispered to Jerry, "Lucia Swallow's up to eight and Patsy — you know, Patsy Parrish at the Hair Lair — she has seven." These were interesting statistics, but Jerry needed Meg involved in his scheme and these numbers weren't going to make that happen.

"Eighteen proposals of marriage," he mused. "I'm impressed."

"Don't be," she said. "I'm not." She set down the full pot and removed the empty one. "Every once in a while someone has too much to drink, waves roses in front of me and wants to get married. And don't get me started on Valentine's Day."

"There," he said, slapping his hand on the table. "You've proved my point exactly. Do you all see now how unbalanced and crazy this is?"

"Crazy? You think it's crazy that someone would want to marry me?" The look she gave him practically shriveled his manhood.

The council members sucked in their collective breaths. Jerry realized he was flying too close to the flame now, and any minute Meg would toss them all out of the restaurant, meeting adjourned. She wasn't a fan of personal questions and she didn't take kindly to discussing her love life, not that anyone thought she had one. He'd know if Meg had a boyfriend, probably because the news would make the front page of the local paper. Or at least the men's room of the Dahl.

For one agonizing moment Jerry feared she would fling the empty coffeepot across the room. He'd heard there was a temper beneath the cheerful smile, but up until now he hadn't believed it. He pulled out a chair and gestured toward it. "Look, Meg, I'm sorry. That's not quite what I meant. Join us for a minute, will you?" He kept his voice soft, used the persuasive tone he'd spent so much time cultivating. "We need your help."

She edged away. "No, thanks. I have breakfast orders —"

He wasn't about to let her off the hook. He needed a female perspective and he needed it now. And he didn't care if it came from an overly sensitive woman who had a bad attitude or a bad boyfriend or just disliked men. "Meg. Please. Just tell me, what do women want? You know, from men. We need to know."

"Excuse me?" The question obviously surprised her, because she paused in midflight and stared at him.

"I'm serious," he repeated, his pen poised.

"Tell me what women want. It's important. I'll take notes."

"Jerry," she said, backing up. "You don't have a big enough piece of paper."

CHAPTER TWO

Owen paid no attention to the yammering of the town council until Meg approached their table and got all huffy. Then, his attention caught by the curious discussion going on behind him, he overheard Jerry's question and the laughter from Meg's reply.

She'd been proposed to eighteen times? The official count was more likely to be nineteen, because Owen doubted that their teenage romance was public knowledge, so his own proposal wouldn't be on the list. Had every man in town tried to hook up with her these past years? Now, that was an unpleasant thought. No wonder Meg was kind of prickly about the subject. That kind of attention would embarrass her — or at least would have embarrassed the shy girl he'd once known.

He watched Meg — who, surprisingly, had acted as if they were nothing more than acquaintances, which he supposed was exactly what he'd hoped for — hurry to the counter, where a couple of old guys waited to pay their bills. She looked good in those jeans. And kinda cute in the red-checked apron, too, so he couldn't really blame the local guys for trying.

"Mr. MacGregor? I don't think we've met." Owen turned to see the redheaded man standing next to his booth and holding out his hand toward him. "Jerry Thompson. Mayor."

"So you're the brave man who wants to know what women want? Nice to meet you." Owen stood and shook the hand offered to him, which prompted a flurry of greetings from the others at the table. There were condolences about his uncle, surprise that Owen was still in town and introductions made to the younger men Owen didn't recognize.

Jerry grinned. "I guess Meg's keeping it a secret."

Owen, who'd had a few eye-opening experiences of his own since growing up and venturing off the ranch, knew what women wanted. He uncharacteristically shared the knowledge. "Women want your money, your attention and your soul." That got a burst of laughter. Owen frowned and added, "And that's just the beginning."

The mayor's disappointment was obvious. "Don't tell them that. I'm trying to get something done here."

"You're awfully bitter for a young man, MacGregor," Gary Petersen pointed out.

"Yeah, well, women have a way of doing that to you." Owen returned to his seat in the booth and picked up his coffee mug. "Sort of gives you a different perspective."

"So you're not lookin' to get married any time soon?" another guy asked. Pete . . . Pete Lyons was his name.

"I don't have anyone in mind, Pete." He'd played football with the guy in high school, he remembered.

"It's a generational thing with these kids. They're all that way," another said.

"No, we're not." Jerry looked insulted. "Not all of us. I've been looking around for the right woman. It just hasn't happened yet."

"And when it does?" Owen asked the question of Jerry while the others looked embarrassed. "Will you live happily ever after?"

The mayor blushed. "I sure hope so. I want a relationship, a wife, kids, a family. The whole enchilada."

"I don't think it's that easy."

"It should be."

"Yeah," Owen said, "it should be, but I've never had much luck."

Jack's face fell. "Well, if you can't get lucky, there's no way the rest of us can."

The conversation was fortunately interrupted by the arrival of Owen's breakfast. Meg set three plates in front of him, one with five strips of bacon, another with three hotcakes and the third with eggs and hash browns. It was everything he'd hoped for.

He attempted to change the direction of the conversation. "I heard there's snow —"

"Hard to believe some gal hasn't moved herself into your place by now," Pete declared. "Unless you've got someone in the city that you're not telling us about."

He quickly looked up to see if Meg had overheard that comment, but she seemed to have hightailed it out of there as fast as she'd delivered his meal. "It wouldn't be a secret," he replied as quietly as he could, "but no, there's no one out at the place right now but me." Not that it was anyone's business, but that didn't seem to stop the men's questions.

"There will be when the TV cameras show up," the annoyingly cheerful mayor assured him. "They'll probably want to see a working cattle ranch. You know, for atmosphere."

"TV cameras?" Owen picked up a slice of

bacon and bit into it. Hot and crispy, it smelled and tasted great. Everything, from the buttered toast to the fried potatoes, smelled great. "What exactly is it that you have going on, Mayor?"

"We've just voted to bring some new business into Willing," Jerry told him proudly. "It definitely has possibilities for population growth and prosperity."

"He's bringing women into town," one of the younger ones said. The bull rider, Owen thought. "For us."

"Beautiful women," another interjected.

Jerry correctly interpreted the look on Owen's face and hurried to interject. "For a TV show. A friend of mine from L.A. is looking for a remote Western location with lots of local color."

"Local color," Owen repeated, picking up another slice of bacon. "I assume that's all of you?"

"What do you think?"

"About you bringing in a TV show?"

"Yes."

"Why bother? Don't you still get your fair share of tourists in the summer?"

"For two months, maybe three," Jerry said. "It's not enough."

"Our hyperactive and ambitious mayor has come up with a way to increase the year-round population of Willing and save the town," Gary explained. "It's a bold plan. I'll give him credit for that."

"Save the town from what?" Owen hid a smile behind his coffee mug. "Plague? Pestilence? Space aliens?"

Jerry wasn't amused. "From certain death. Literally. I have a study, with future growth projections and analyses of trends. According to the experts, Willing is going downhill."

Owen thought about that for a long moment. He glanced out the window and didn't see much going on. The main road into town was empty, but October was a quiet month. And winter was a quiet season. He couldn't blame folks for worrying about the future, but Willing had never seemed to change much, let alone go downhill. It occurred to him how little time he spent here, how little he knew or cared what went on. His life was elsewhere, and had been for many years.

"What kind of trends?" Mike wanted to know. "I like to keep track of advertising prospects," he explained.

"I have copies of the report for each one of you," Jerry said. "As I said earlier, if we don't start attracting businesses and families, there's not going to be any reason to support a school. Or the money to do it. And once we have no school, we're finished." Jerry was obviously getting revved up.

"And the solution is a television show?"

"The solution is *publicity,* and lots of it."

"And women," Jack interjected. "Don't forget the TV show is about women."

"We could make this town come alive," Jerry said. "Unless you're willing to stand by and see your heritage evaporate, Mr. MacGregor, Willing will be a ghost town one of these days."

Owen wasn't sure he wanted the town to "come alive," whatever that meant. What should have been a quick stop on the way home had turned into the possible annihilation of his descendants. "What's wrong with things staying the way they are? And how does not having a school mean the demise of Willing?"

Jerry slid a sheaf of papers across the table. "Take a look at these and see if you think things can stay the same. As I've explained to the council, we need to become proactive."

"I'll look at them. While I eat." Owen turned back to his meal. Because he'd said he would — and because he knew the town council would watch — he studied the report. Sure enough, doom and gloom were on the horizon, but it didn't spoil his appetite. He methodically worked his way through his meal — and the pages of information — until all three plates were empty. Meg left him alone, as did everyone else. The illustrious members of the town council quietly discussed the weather, the price of cattle, football and the new season of *Survivor.*

When he was finished eating the best breakfast he'd had in years, Owen pushed the plates aside and moved his coffee closer. Across the room, Meg worked the cash register while two elderly men took turns handing her money and getting change. She looked the same as she had in high school, except her hair was shorter. She had the same warm smile he remembered being directed at him when he'd spent a lot of time hanging out in the summer kitchen, flirting with the shy girl with the big brown eyes.

"All right," he said, turning around again to face the council. "I see your point."

Jerry nodded. "I thought you would."

"But I guess I can't imagine your friends in California would be interested. We're not exactly Bozeman."

"That's the hook. We're small-town guys."

He waved his arm toward the rest of the men. "The fantasy is moving to small-town America."

"Whose fantasy?"

"Well, people who don't live in small towns, of course." Jerry picked up his notepad and leafed through the pages until he found the one he wanted. "Let's move on to preparation. We're going to need to form some committees. Owen, can I put you down for locations? You know more about this county than anyone, and Tracy — the producer of this thing — will be looking for local color."

"I don't —"

"Meg!" Jerry called as she approached to clear Owen's table of dishes.

She wiped her hands on her apron. "I am not going to answer any more ridiculous —"

"This is about catering." Jerry flipped to another page. "Tracy will need a price list for the crew. That is, if we get the gig. Can you put something together? Meal ideas? Costs? They're going to need to use as much local help as possible, which is good for you, since you're the only game in town aside from Chili Dawgs, and who can eat chili dogs every night?"

Pete raised his hand. "I can."

"I can put a menu together," she said slowly. "What's going on? And who's Tracy?"

Les leaned forward in his chair. He was a likable kid and Meg felt badly that the rodeo career hadn't worked out for him. "Jerry's friend. Hollywood's coming," he said, giving Meg a shy smile.

"That's the plan. Sit down and I'll explain everything." Jerry gestured toward the seat opposite him.

"Okay. I have a few minutes," she said, surprising Owen by sitting. "Before the lunch rush starts."

Owen watched Meg's expression change from tolerant to skeptical as the eager mayor launched into his dying-town, we-need-women-and-families spiel. He wound up with, "What do you think? Can we make it work, get our single guys fixed up with some city women?"

"Well." Meg looked at the men gathered around the table. Except for Jerry, they were not a sophisticated group, but she clearly didn't want to hurt their feelings. "I guess that's up to, ah, Tracy."

She glanced at Owen.

"Don't look at me," he said, raising his hands in surrender. "I'm not going on a television show."

"Of course you're not. I'm sure you have plenty of women already," she agreed, which made it sound like an insult. Owen didn't have "plenty of women," but he wasn't going to deny it. Let her think he slept with someone other than Boo. She didn't need to know that he'd read *War and Peace* last summer and talked to his dog more than his friends.

"You're a fine example of the Western man," Jerry said. "We'll need your help."

Owen frowned at him. "I'm a what?"

"Fine example of a Western man," Meg repeated, obviously trying not to laugh. "That's quite a compliment."

Owen opened his mouth to protest, but closed it again. Jerry Thompson was one strange character. Jerry scribbled something on his pad. "Can I put you on the education committee, too?"

"No."

Jerry acted as if he hadn't heard Owen. "We'll drive Tracy around and you can explain the history of the place and show her some picturesque spots for dates."

"Picturesque spots?" Meg chuckled. "Like watching bears at the dump?"

Jerry bristled. "It's a transfer station now. Very contained."

Gary grinned. "We conceived our oldest

daughter, uh, 'watching the bears.' Had to get married three months after that."

"Too much information, Petersen," the town treasurer said.

"But romantic," Jerry interjected.

"Well, it was at the time." Gary looked around the table. "I'll bet I'm not the only one who went bear watching."

Jack blushed and hurried to his feet. "I have to get to work. I told the boss I'd be in before noon."

"I'll walk out with you," Hank said. "Got to put a new transmission into a Buick. Meeting adjourned?"

Jerry reluctantly nodded. "I'll email everyone with your committee assignments. And I have your approval for an emergency town meeting?"

There was groaning, but Owen noticed no one actually protested. Jerry continued to make notes, Meg remained in her seat and the three youngest members of the town council sat back as if they had nothing more interesting to do this morning.

"Well," Meg said to Jerry, "you have your work cut out for you."

"I know."

"No offense," she continued, glancing at the three younger men. "But when's the last time any of you had a date?"

Les raised his hand. "Last summer. She was backpacking —"

Owen's curiosity got the better of him. "Did you ask her out, put on a clean shirt and take her somewhere?"

"Like where?" The poor guy actually looked confused.

"To dinner," Meg prompted. "Or to the movies."

"Not exactly."

"That doesn't count as a date," Owen said.

Jack, one of the best-looking men in the county, leaned forward. "What about blind dates? Do they count?"

"If you asked her out, put on a clean shirt and took her somewhere," Owen repeated.

"Nope." Jack spread his hands out. "Got nothing."

"It's not like there's a lot to choose from," Les said. "I mean, I live with my grandparents."

"Which helps them out a lot," Meg assured him. "They're always telling me what a blessing you are to them."

"Well, blessings don't get dates. If it wasn't for Mexican Train dominoes and satellite TV, I'd go crazy."

Owen felt his pain.

"For heaven's sake," she muttered. "Iron

your clothes and go out once in a while."

"Go where?"

"The Dahl? Church? Billings?"

"Yeah," he grumbled. "With who?"

"This brings me to my next issue," Jerry interjected. "We all know there are very few single women in this town." He held up his pad. "I've made a list."

Meg rolled her eyes. "Why doesn't that surprise me?"

He looked down and read aloud. "In no particular order. Deb Walker, divorced. Lucia Swallow, widowed. Joanie Parker, divorced. I'm not counting anyone collecting Social Security or using a walker. For now I'd like to just concentrate on the under-forty age group."

"Under forty," Meg repeated. "That leaves Deb out."

"I'll cross her out, but she sure doesn't look forty," he said, studying his notes again. "Lucia, Joanie, Patsy Parrish, Aurora and —"

"Joanie is with Cam," Joey said.

"Nope. Broke up. I checked."

Joey brightened. "Really?"

"You're an efficient guy." Meg looked impressed. Owen wasn't. He figured Jerry Thompson was too damn nosy. Despite the gloom-and-doom population study and the lack of social events, hosting a television show was just about the strangest idea he'd ever heard.

Jerry looked up from his papers. "Cam drank himself into a stupor last night and Aurora had to take him home when she closed up."

"If Cam stopped drinking, he might still have a girlfriend," Meg declared. "The guy needs help."

"What's in it for you?" Owen asked the mayor. "You must have known when you moved here there wasn't much going on."

"Uh, yeah." He flushed, fiddled with his pen and avoided making eye contact with Owen. "I thought it was a great real-estate opportunity."

"Uh-oh," Meg said. "Broken heart?"

"Yes," he admitted. "Tracy — the producer. We, uh, had a thing. About five years ago. She wouldn't leave Los Angeles and I was having a really bad asthma problem. Smog," he added. "I thought, well, never mind what I thought. We still text." He glanced toward Owen. "Hey, it's a start."

He shrugged. "You do what you have to do."

"She'll be here in three weeks," he said. "She's coming for the weekend, before Halloween. She'll get a taste of our picturesque

Western town, meet the guys, see the sights and check out the festivities."

"Festivities?" Owen remembered parties for the kids at the elementary school, teachers dressed as witches and decorations on a few houses, but he wouldn't have described them as particularly festive.

"Big party at the Dahl the Saturday night before Halloween," Jerry said. "There's a raffle to see who gets to decorate the bear."

"Your grandfather's bear," Les explained, in case Owen had forgotten. "It's a big deal."

Owen tried to picture the massive stuffed grizzly in a costume but couldn't wrap his mind around it. He wondered if that was another one of the mayor's crazy ideas.

"The base is cracked," Jerry said. "We're going to have to raise money to repair it soon." He gave Owen a pointed look. "Unless you'd like to take care of that yourself."

"Back to the list," Meg said. "Who else do you have?"

"Maxine, rents a place out of town, has all those dogs. And then there's you, of course."

"Keep me off your lists." Meg frowned. "Wait a minute. Why *is* there a list?"

"Because I needed to point out to the council — and to the preproduction team — that we have a lack of women to, uh, you know, get together with."

"Like we didn't know?" Les, who might have been bucked off one too many bulls, looked confused.

"They wanted to make sure we were legitimately short of women. To keep things accurate, I also have a list of all the single men in the county," Jerry said, flipping through the notebook until he found the page he wanted. "I starred the ones who are between twenty-one and forty-five."

"This gets better and better." Meg leaned forward to peer at the names. "How many?"

"Forty-eight." He glanced at Owen. "I didn't put your name on here because, ah, it's not like you really live here."

"True."

"But I can pencil you in," he offered. "Have you ever wanted to be on television?"

"About as much as I want to sit naked in a pit of rattlesnakes," Owen replied.

"Well," said Meg, pushing back her chair, "that's an appealing vision. I'm going to go back to work now and let you future reality stars work out the minor details."

"Leave me out of this," Owen said, but Meg ignored him. Again. He watched her head toward the counter, where one lonely patron sat nursing his coffee and reading *People* magazine.

"Damn." Jerry closed his notebook and grimaced. "I wasn't finished."

"She used to be shy," Owen said. "Quiet. Sweet."

"No way," one of the kids said. "She's tough."

"Hard-hearted," another agreed. "Not like her mother. Loralee was always smiling and happy."

"And not the brightest light on the porch." Owen assumed Loralee, who was something of an airhead in the marriage department, had a lot to do with her daughter's lack of enthusiasm for the men around here. He dropped a twenty-dollar bill on the counter and scooped up the Styrofoam container of bacon for Boo.

"Gentlemen," he said, settling his hat on his head. "It's been a pleasure, but I'm heading home."

"I'll be in touch when I get this thing going." Jerry stood and shook Owen's hand, as did the other three.

"I'm afraid I'm not going to be much help." *Because I don't want to be on television, I don't want to help turn the town into a dating game and I think you're all pretty much insane.*

CHAPTER THREE

Meg stood behind the counter and fiddled with the money in the cash register as if it was the most important thing she'd done all morning.

She ignored the ringing phone, the clatter of dishes, the chatter between customers, and took a few moments to feel sorry for herself. There'd been times in her life when she wished she was drop-dead gorgeous, and this morning was one of them. She wished she'd been able to stun Owen Mac-Gregor with her beauty, make him secretly regret their breakup, see him surprised and awed by the elegant Meg Ripley.

But that would never happen. Meg slammed the register drawer shut and thought about cleaning the restrooms. No, that could wait. She would pour more coffee and take more breakfast orders and help Al prepare for the lunch rush.

Wowing Owen, the "fine example of a

Western man," wasn't going to happen. Meg was plain. She knew it. In fact, she'd been told as much from the age of four, when her pretty mother had no longer been able to hide her disappointment. Her daughter was, at best, nondescript. A shy child with brown eyes, brown hair, knobby knees and pink plastic eyeglasses, Meg wasn't exactly a Miss Montana hopeful, though her mother had assured her that someday she would blossom into a lovely young woman. She had never blossomed. Not really. And certainly not to her mother's expectations. She wore contacts now, but her eyes and hair remained a nondescript brown and she'd obviously inherited her decidedly nonvoluptuous body from her father's side of the family.

She was grateful for that, actually. Her mother, sweet and foolish, had enjoyed looking in the mirror and unbuttoning her uniform to show a little more cleavage. "You have to flaunt 'em if you've got 'em," she'd say, giving Meg a wink. Loralee believed in the power of blue eye shadow, underwire bras and high heels. And, despite having married five times, remained convinced that Mr. Right was just around the corner. The perpetual stack of romance novels next to her bed and her tendency to weep during made-for-TV movies led Meg to believe her mother would never, ever change. Despite Loralee's exhausting marital history and age — sixty-two was a rough estimate — she showed no signs of slowing down. Men still circled around her to admire and be admired. Loralee didn't disappoint.

"Meg!" Al broke into her self-pity. "Phone!"

She took the portable phone from him without looking at the caller ID.

"Willing Café," she said, wondering if she should get her hair highlighted.

"Sweetie," sang a familiar voice. "How's everything at The Shame?"

There was no use reminding her mother that the "Dirty Shame" was now the much more respectable "Willing Café." Loralee didn't listen. "Hi, Mom. Believe it or not, I was just thinking about you."

"You'll never believe what Joan and I did this morning! We played golf! Can you believe it? Golf," her mother chirped over the phone. "I've hit the mother lode."

"The mother lode of what?"

Loralee, too busy talking to answer questions, had continued, "I've taken up golf myself. There are men everywhere, Megs. Lovely men who enjoy talking to a woman once in a while."

Her mother wasn't a gold digger or an opportunist. She'd married men she'd felt sorry for, or thought she was in love with and could help with their drinking problem or their gambling issues, or, in one drastic case in 1988, a shy trucker who'd decided it was time to go straight. Men took advantage of Loralee, not the other way around.

"Be careful," Meg warned, feeling much too old to deal with another stepfather. "Don't even think about getting married."

"Honey, I'm done being young and silly," Loralee said. "But I'm not about to sit around this condo and watch Joan knit charity afghans."

"No," Meg said, "of course not. But maybe you could borrow some yarn and learn to —"

"And I don't like the casinos that much," she mused. "Joan does, though, so I go along to keep her company. We like the buffets."

Unlike her youngest sister, plump Aunt Joan had married a man who needed no fixing. She'd waited forty-one years to find the love of her life, which Meg thought was admirable. They'd been married thirty years when he died, leaving Aunt Joan with no financial worries and a spacious two-bedroom condo overlooking a golf course.

She'd begged her sister to move to Arizona. Loralee had flown down for a visit last year and showed no sign of returning.

"We're going to join a league, so we'll play almost every morning before it gets too hot. What do you think?"

"That sounds fun." In no universe could Meg picture her mother playing golf or, for that matter, being content to live with her much older, conservative sister. However, both women seemed pleased with the arrangement so far. Meg suspected that soon enough Loralee would find life with Aunt Joan a little tame and move back to Willing.

"We might drive up in the spring, make a road trip out of it. See a bit of the country. And you, of course, sweetie. Are you going to come down for Christmas? I'm on the internet right now, looking at flights. I can book it right now for you, what do you think?"

"I don't know about Christmas, Mom. Maybe I'll come down in January, like last year."

"You can't tell me that place is busy over the holidays. I know better."

"I can't travel if there's a storm —"

"There's always a storm."

"Yes." And it was difficult to drive to the airport in three feet of snow. "And I'd rather not get stuck in an airport when I could be home."

"You should move down here. Get out of the cold weather," her mother said, as she did near the end of every phone call to her daughter. "We sit by the pool every afternoon, you know. A little sun would do you good, brighten you up a bit."

"It sounds wonderful," Meg fibbed.

"You're at a nice age to find an older man, sweetie. You could get highlights, a bright red bathing suit — men love red. And a spray tan! I've been saving coupons —"

Meg punched the on switch on the empty food processor and raised her voice, "Static, Mom! I can't hear you!"

And feeling relieved and guilty, she hung up.

Loralee meant well, but she refused to accept her daughter's single lifestyle. *I want you to be happy. I want you to find a man and have babies. I don't want you to be alone every night.*

Fair enough. That all sounded good, but Meg had had a shot at all those things once, a very long time ago. Even then she'd known that dreams didn't always come true. In the years that followed, when she'd finished school and worked at her dream job, she'd assumed she'd meet someone special, someone who would charge into her world and fill her empty heart with massive amounts of love. Who would make everything good and right and perfect simply by taking her into his arms.

Just the way Owen MacGregor had.

But fifteen minutes ago she'd watched that particular man leave the restaurant and stride across the gravel parking lot. And she knew she'd given up on fairy-tale endings a long time ago.

Her one and only Prince Charming had left the building.

"It's the craziest idea I've ever heard." Owen pointed the truck west, out of town and toward home. Boo, busy chomping on bacon, didn't argue. He didn't even bother to lick the rancher's ear, which was the way he usually participated in conversations.

"Good thing I got out of there when I did," Owen muttered as he adjusted the heating vent. Amazing that by changing his Monday routine in the slightest way, he'd risked getting involved in the wackiest town project since the stealing of the grizzly from Dahl's.

That memory made him smile. The old man, with typical good grace, had thrown a welcome-home party for the bear once

Owen and his teammates had confessed and hauled the mangy thing back to the bar. Sean MacGregor had then grounded his son for two weeks, and the Willing Destroyers had spent a long weekend cleaning out cattle sheds.

Until the day he died, which had been just a few short years later, Sean had sponsored an annual "Grizzly Reunion" beer fest at the Dahl. And to his shame, Owen had no idea if that was still going on. The truth was, Willing was no longer his home and hadn't been since his father died. Ed, a recluse all his life, had moved in and taken over the cattle operation. Owen's mother refused to live in the big house alone and had moved to Helena, and then followed him to DC. Owen had switched his major from grassland management to environmental law and, until now, had never looked back.

He'd been proud of his family's contributions to the town — heck, his great-great-great-grandfather had named the stupid place — but he'd had no interest in Willing for many years. Cattle ranching, what he'd grown up expecting to do for the rest of his life, had lost its appeal after his father's burial in the family plot.

While his mother's relatives littered half of the state, there were no other Mac-

Gregors left. Ed was gone. Owen, temporary cattleman, had a pile of decisions to make.

And none of them involved television shows, dating, the mayor's Hollywood girlfriend or Margaret Ripley's boyfriends. But Owen thought about his father, the man he'd respected more than anyone else in his life, and looked for a place to turn around.

Shelly couldn't wait to get off the bus. She had to pee. And she'd been feeling queasy for about a hundred miles. Or maybe longer, like five months. Since she'd found out she was going to have a baby. If any news was guaranteed to make you want to stick your head into a toilet bowl, it was learning you were pregnant. Especially if you were eighteen and the baby's father was nowhere to be found.

Not yet, anyway.

Shelly resisted the urge to pat her swollen belly and instead reached into her bag for M&M's. If she sucked on them one at a time, until the coating evaporated in her mouth, she could make the rest of the bag last until the next stop. According to the driver, they were about fifteen minutes away from a quick breakfast stop at a café. He recommended the cinnamon rolls, if there were any left, and explained that the passengers were welcome to bring their hot drinks back on the bus with them, as long as the cups had lids. He didn't want to be cleaning up coffee spills when his shift was over.

Fair enough. Cleaning up other people's messes wasn't Shelly's idea of a good time, either, though if she thought about it for more than a couple of minutes — and she had plenty of time to think, sitting here on a Greyhound heading south — she had to admit that she herself had been stuck with a doozy of a mess. She didn't need to be cleaning up after anybody else.

"Next stop, Willing," the driver called. A couple of passengers lifted their heads and muttered to themselves. The bus was almost empty. A couple of senior citizens heading home from the casino — they kept talking about good luck and recounting their money — a young mother with the quietest little kid Shelly had ever seen, three sleepy college kids who looked like they'd had a pretty fun weekend and one older man whose weathered face gave him away as a rancher, Shelly guessed. He was dressed all in denim and he'd tipped his hat when he'd passed her as he'd walked down the aisle to take a seat in the back. He seemed fatherly, too, giving her a compassionate look as he'd noticed her bump. Or maybe he just thought she looked too thin or too pale or too tired. Maybe her pregnancy didn't show when she was sitting down.

Yeah, right. She'd picked up some big shirts at the Goodwill, shirts big enough to cover her unzipped jeans and the belt that held them up over her bump. *Bump.* That's what they called it in the gossip magazines when Britney and Angelina were showing off their pregnant bodies. Well, here in the real world there wasn't much to show off. This particular bump rested on her bladder, meaning every time the bus hit a real bump — which, thank God, wasn't often — Shelly worried that she was going to wet her only pair of jeans.

She'd watched the sun come up after napping off and on through the night. She'd dozed off after an early-morning stop in some windy, gray town. She planned to brush her teeth and clean up a little at the next stop. With any luck the restaurant wouldn't be too expensive and she could get something filling. She reached for her bag, hoping that when she counted her money again there would be more than she remembered from the last time she'd looked.

"Willing comin' up," the bus driver called

several minutes later. "Remember, you've got about fifteen minutes, so eat fast. They'll serve you quick if you tell 'em you're from the bus."

He shifted down, turned off the highway and onto a local road. It wasn't much longer before he eased the bus into a busy parking lot and stopped beside a one-story building Shelly assumed was their destination. She gathered her belongings and was the first one ready to get off the bus. The other passengers were trying to wake up and the old guy was polite enough to let her go first. He'd even tipped his hat again, which made her blink in surprise.

The driver half stood, but he looked annoyed at the stragglers and then glanced pointedly at his watch. "You get right up to the counter and get yourself a hot meal," he told Shelly. "But we're back on the road in fifteen minutes."

"Thanks." She turned toward the steps and rolled her eyes. God. She didn't need any reminders.

"Watch your step," he called. "Come on, folks, get a move on!"

She hadn't known how hungry she was until she went through the glass door and inhaled the smells of coffee and bacon. Of course, she could do without the coffee smell, but she'd always loved bacon. It made her think of Christmas mornings. She made her way to the bathroom before hurrying to the long counter on the other side of the room, but there were no empty stools. The place was overly bright and had a battered, worn appearance. In a nice way, though. It was also noisy, conversation mixing with clattering dishes and country music coming from unseen speakers.

She sank into a small blue booth, plopped her two big tote bags next to her and grabbed the menu stuck behind the napkin dispenser. Pancakes were filling and usually cheap. Today's special was an omelet that came with four pieces of bacon, three pancakes and hash browns. A meal like that would blow her food budget for the whole day.

A dark-haired waitress appeared at the booth, a pot of coffee in her hand. She set a white mug down on the table and smiled. "Hi. Coffee or tea?"

"Uh, no, thanks. Just water."

"Milk?"

"I don't —"

"Bus?"

"What?"

"Sorry. You're from the bus, right?" At Shelly's nod, she continued, "Then don't

64

order anything complicated or Kermit —
the driver — will have a stroke. He keeps to
a schedule, no matter what, like the world
will end if he's three minutes late."

"Yeah, I noticed. What about pancakes?
Do they take too long?"

The waitress had kind eyes and a sweet
smile. "That depends how many orders are
ahead of you. Scrambled eggs are a better
bet. Or oatmeal. We've got that in the slow
cooker, all made up. I can put some raisins
in it. With some brown sugar sprinkled on
top?"

Shelly shuddered. "I'll risk the pancakes."

"Suit yourself. I'll put a rush on it. Would
you like bacon or sausage with that?"

Of course she did. But a side order of
either one, enough to get the taste of
chocolate candy out of her mouth, would
add too many dollars onto the check. "No,
thanks."

"I'll be right back." Shelly watched her
stop at the next table and refill their coffee
cups before she slipped behind the counter
and stuck the order near the grill. Maybe
she could get a job waiting tables until the
baby was born. It didn't look hard. Just like
putting supper on the table at home, only
with folks who said "please" and "thank
you" and left tips. She pulled the worn map

out of her bag and unfolded it to study the vast space that was Montana. Her money wasn't going to last much longer.

The waitress returned with a glass of milk and a glass of water. "It's on the house," she said, her gaze sliding to Shelly's abdomen. "For the baby."

"Thanks." She didn't know what else to say, because she was cold and tired and smelled like the stale belly of a bus. The last thing she intended to do was cry all over a stranger.

"So where are you headed this morning?"

"South, I guess."

"You guess?" The waitress looked over her shoulder toward three of her fellow bus passengers at the register buying drinks and cinnamon rolls from a guy with a white apron and chef's hat. The bus driver had disappeared into the rest room and the older rancher-type guy was drinking coffee at the counter. "I'll be back in a minute," the woman promised.

Shelly wished she'd hurry with the pancakes, because she was starting to get queasy again. She moved the syrup container closer, tugged a couple of paper napkins out of the holder and lined up her silverware. According to the menu, she was in Willing. And Willing didn't look like

66

much, at least not what she could see from the parking lot when she'd walked in. But this restaurant seemed pretty busy for a cold morning. Folks were smiling, talking, acting like everyone knew one another. Weird.

"Here you go." The waitress set a plate stacked with three pancakes and topped with a scoop of butter in front of her. There was bacon, too, crispy and fragrant.

"I didn't order —"

"It was a mistake," the woman said, as if Shelly was doing her a favor by eating it. "It would have been thrown out otherwise."

"Thanks." She picked up one piece and chewed, willed her stomach to settle down. Just the thought of getting back on the bus made her belly churn. "What's it like here?"

"Here in the restaurant or here in town?"

"Well, both, I guess."

"It's home," was the woman's simple answer. She slid into the booth across from Shelly and folded her hands on the table. "I'm Meg."

"Shelly."

"Nice to meet you. Believe it or not, I usually mind my own business. Does your family know where you are?"

"I'm not a runaway, if that's what you're thinking."

"That's exactly what I'm thinking."

"I'm nineteen. I can go wherever I want." Shelly poured a fountain of maple syrup over the pancakes and dug in. She felt bad about lying to someone who had given her free bacon and milk, but then again, since when had trusting total strangers improved her life?

"You may or may not be nineteen, but you don't have any money —"

"Not true," Shelly said over a mouthful of pancake.

The woman continued, "You're a little vague about where you're headed." She smiled, which made her look younger. About thirty, Shelly thought. No rings. She looked harmless enough, so Shelly decided a simple version of the truth would work just as well as a whopper of a fib about meeting her soldier boyfriend in Fort Hood.

"I'm on the road, uh, looking for a guy."

"Well, then," Meg drawled. "You've come to the right town. According to the mayor's latest calculations, we have forty-eight single men from the age of twenty-one to forty-five. You can take your pick."

Shelly drank half the glass of milk. "They *count* them here?"

The waitress looked amused. "Yes, they do, actually."

"Weird."

"Definitely. So who are you looking for? I'm guessing . . . the baby's father?"

"Yeah." She chewed another large piece of pancake and washed it down with milk before picking up another slice of bacon. The year before she'd gotten pregnant she'd called herself a vegetarian, but the baby had changed all that. Now any kind of pork product made her mouth water as if she was a little kid at the state fair.

"Do you know where he is?"

"Not exactly."

"Is he from around here?"

"Maybe." He'd mentioned Willing once, but as hard as she tried, Shelly couldn't remember what he'd said about it. He'd talked of other Montana towns, too. She wished she'd paid more attention to their conversations when they'd been together.

"What's his name? Maybe I can help you contact him. You shouldn't be traveling alone like this."

Shelly shook her head. The less said the better, and she didn't want this snoopy woman calling the cops or social services. Been there, done that. Instead she pulled her cell phone out of her bag and skimmed through the menu until she found what she wanted. She passed the phone, with its fuzzy photo of a smiling young man, to Meg. "Here."

"It's hard to see his face under that hat."

"Trust me, he's cute."

"Yes, but —"

"He's tall, too. And funny."

"I don't —"

"Miss!" The bus driver waved at her. He was heading toward the door, the other passengers following him. "Three minutes!"

Shelly looked down at her empty plate and her stomach heaved. She'd eaten too fast and she was going to throw up now, she really was. "I should have hitchhiked."

"That's never a good idea, sweetie," Meg the waitress said, her voice gentle. She handed her back the phone. "You look a little pale. Are you sure you're okay?"

She thought about the bus fumes, the jouncing, the endless miles to a place with no guarantees.

Shelly was suddenly very, very tired. The busy room seemed smaller, the noise quieted and everything swirled into black.

CHAPTER FOUR

Kermit wasn't known for his compassion, and because his punctuality was the stuff of legends, no one was surprised when the bus headed south without its pregnant passenger.

Meg and her customers managed to move Shelly to the floor, put a makeshift ice bag on her forehead and call the clinic before the girl came to and started to protest.

"Stay quiet," Meg told her. "You fainted."

"I'm okay, I'm gonna miss —"

"There will be another bus." *Just not for three days,* Meg added silently. "You have to stay right where you are."

"Am I on the *floor*?"

"You sure are. Are you having any pain?"

"No." The girl closed her eyes again, probably because the sight of four elderly men staring at her was more than a little frightening. She moved her hands over her belly. "I'm fine."

"Not exactly," Meg said. "Something happened and you passed out."

Shelly kept her eyes shut.

"Remember the time Hank Richards had a heart attack, right in that same booth?"

"No, actually, I don't." She shot George a look that said *be quiet.*

"Uh, he was fine," the old man mumbled. "After the triple bypass."

"My Debbie used to get wobbly and sick like that when she was expecting the twins." Martin peered down at the girl. "Are you expecting twins, young lady?"

"I — I hope not."

Jerry, who'd been the first to grab his cell phone and call for help, leaned toward Meg and whispered, "This could be our lucky day. A new resident *and* a population explosion."

"That's so not funny."

He shrugged. "Hey, we need all the help we can get. In the meantime, what are we going to do with her?"

"We?"

"It takes a village . . ."

"It takes an obstetrician," Meg pointed out, having helped Lucia through her last pregnancy. "And he's sixty miles away."

"Oh, good," Jerry said, looking up as the

72

door opened. "Hip's here. I sure hope he's sober."

Horatio Ignatius Porterman, the local EMT, was otherwise known by his initials. Everyone loved him, everyone owed him a favor and no one questioned why his best friend was Jack Daniel's. That was his own business: a man was entitled to his demons, and, to Hip's credit, he didn't drive. He and his cousin shared a house in town and Theo, a car collector, was always ready to drive his cousin wherever he was needed.

Luckily, Hip's services weren't in great demand. He carved animals from tree trunks in the large shed behind the house when he wasn't administering first aid. In the summer the lawn sprouted bears, moose, elk, prairie dogs and sale signs. Once in a while one of them went home with a passing tourist.

Jerry hoped he'd upgrade to an art studio once the cameras started rolling. Hip wasn't bachelor material, but as an artist he'd give the town another dimension and attract other creative types. Jerry was already thinking how to give artists tax breaks, but first things first. Save the town, bring in the artists, attract the tourists.

"Hey," Jerry said, making way for his city

rescue volunteer. Owen MacGregor, a grim expression on his face, followed Hip across the room. The rancher's frown eased when he saw Meg, but he didn't look exactly cheerful as he stared at the girl on the floor.

Jerry wasn't sure what Hip could do, aside from taking the girl's blood pressure and pulse. Theo would most likely end up driving her to Lewistown, since he owned the ambulance.

"She's looking better," Jerry said. "Not so green."

Meg nodded. "I don't think she's been eating well. You should have seen her shovel in the pancakes."

Owen stepped closer. "Where's she from?"

Hip, crouched over the girl like a paternal crane, asked the same question. He didn't get an answer, but she did open her eyes. She was a pretty thing, but Owen thought she seemed way too young to be pregnant.

Owen tried again. "Anyone know who she is?"

"Her name is Shelly," Meg said. "She was on the bus heading south."

"Alone?"

"Yes."

"You know her?" Owen hoped there was help on the way. Like the girl's mother, who would be wearing a nurse's uniform and pushing a gurney.

"No. We were talking when she slid side-ways."

"Huh." This was from Hip, a rescuer of few words. He removed the blood-pressure cuff from the girl's arm. "Seems fine now. Should rest for a while, though."

The patient frowned. "Can I sit up? You're all kind of freakin' me out."

"That goes both ways," Meg pointed out, and the girl had the decency to look embarrassed as Jerry and Hip helped her sit up.

"Oh. Sorry."

"That's okay. You've had a pretty tough morning, I think."

Owen thought that might be an under-statement, but he kept quiet while Hip asked Shelly — if that was her real name — if she felt dizzy.

"I'm fine. I just have to get out of here. The bus —"

"Is long gone," Hip said. "Sit still. I'm gonna check your pulse again."

Owen watched as three of the older men drifted back to their self-assigned stools, though he noticed they swiveled to face the action in the room as if they were watching television. He thought two of them looked familiar. The burly cook came out of the kitchen to pour fresh coffee and keep an eye on the register. Jerry planted himself in a chair and gave Owen a curious look. As did Meg.

"You weren't gone long. Did you forget something?" she asked in a very polite voice.

"I was talking to Hip when the call came in." *Someone's unconscious at The Shame. Hurry. Might need an ambulance.* He wasn't about to admit to his brief attack of social conscience about the damaged pedestal of the grizzly, which was what had brought him to the Dahl, where he'd found Hip, in the first place. "I thought he might need help, so I followed him over here."

Meg didn't look at him. "That was nice of you."

He shrugged, uncomfortable. It was one thing to order breakfast, but standing next to her like this was odd. Come to think about it, everything about being back in Banner County was odd, including finding his old friend drinking at the Dahl at eleven in the morning.

"I'm okay now," Shelly insisted.

Owen thought that was a stretch. From the looks of the skinny teenager, okay might not happen until the next decade.

"Tomorrow's the doc's day in town," Hip informed them, still crouching by the girl's side.

"She shouldn't go to a hospital?" This was from Meg, who still appeared flustered.

"I can't go to a hospital." The kid stroked her little belly bump and looked defiant. Exactly how old was she? Fifteen? Sixteen? Someone needed to call child services. He exchanged a worried look with Meg, who gestured toward a booth where a battered leather purse and a faded blue duffel bag sat on the vinyl seat. Owen walked over to check it out. Shelly was traveling light, but he assumed she'd have some kind of identification.

"It might be a good idea to stay in town overnight and see the doctor tomorrow," Meg fussed. "Just to make sure everything's okay with the baby and you're approved to travel."

Hip grunted something in agreement, but Owen didn't listen too carefully. He dug around in the purse until he found a cheap cloth wallet. Sure enough, there was a driver's license inside, along with seventy-three dollars in cash. Shelly Smith. *Smith? How convenient for a pregnant runaway,* he mused, studying the Idaho license with a Boise address. According to the state of Idaho, Shelly Ann Smith turned eighteen on August 3 and lived at 3702 Broad Street.

Well, that was a start.

He didn't examine the rest of her things, though he noticed a half-empty bag of candy, a thick packet of chewing gum and a pair of gray wool socks stuffed inside the purse. A small vial of pepper spray hung from a keychain clipped to a set of keys, so at least the girl had the sense to keep her feet warm and protect herself.

On the other hand, she was pregnant, practically broke and half starved. So much for sense.

"Where are you headed?" Owen asked, returning to stand where the girl could see him. "Maybe we can give you a ride."

She shook her head and struggled to sit up. Hip helped her and she brushed her hair away from her face.

"She's looking for her boyfriend," Meg informed them.

Owen crouched next to Hip. "Tell us where he is and we'll get him."

"I, uh, don't know."

Owen looked at Meg, who shrugged. "That's what she told me, too."

"Son of a —" Hip clamped his mouth shut.

Ben Fargus decided to comment. "How the heck can you find someone if you don't know where to look? I don't get it."

Shelly's eyes filled with tears, but she

blinked them back. "I know it sounds dumb."

"You don't know where he is right this minute?" Owen asked. "Or you don't know where he is *period*?"

The girl's silence answered the question.

"His name, then."

"Sonny."

"Sonny what?" Owen was suddenly very glad he'd never had daughters. His patience with teenage girls wouldn't have lasted more than a month. Shelly began to cry and Owen watched Meg lean over and pat her back. He tried again. Surely the kid needed help with this, because Sonny wasn't exactly an unusual nickname. "Sonny *what*?"

"Don't yell at her." This was from Meg, who glared at him with cool brown eyes. Yes, he recognized that expression.

"I'm not yelling."

She didn't look the least bit convinced. "Keep your voice down. You're scaring her."

He looked down at the kid blowing her nose into a paper napkin. "She's got a lot to be scared about," he pointed out. "You'd better call the sheriff or social services or someone who can get her some help."

The girl squealed. "The *sheriff*?"

"No, sweetheart. We're not calling the sheriff. You haven't done anything wrong."

Meg turned to Owen and lifted her chin. When he was young and foolish, that stubborn chin had melted him right to his bones. Good thing he was older and immune.

"I'm out of here," Shelly declared. She struggled to her feet. "Where's my stuff?"

Hip stood, towering over her. "Whoa."

"Got something to hide?" Owen asked.

"Got something to do," was the snippy reply. "*Lots* to do."

"Well," Owen drawled, conscious of Meg's protective attitude toward the kid. God forbid he interject some common sense into this situation. "So do I."

He looked at Meg until she met his gaze. "Her last name is Smith and she's from Boise. She's eighteen years old and she has seventy bucks in her wallet. No credit cards, no checkbook."

"You looked in my *bag*?"

Owen ignored the girl's question and looked at Hip. "Call me about the bear."

Hip nodded. "I can fix it there if Aurora says it's okay."

"Who's Aurora?"

"She bought the place a few years ago," Hip said.

"What happened to Mick?"

"A woman in Santa Fe."

80

Well, that made sense. Mick and his father had been good friends, but the bar owner wasn't the devoted family man Owen's father had been. "Keep me posted, then."

"Will do," Hip promised, packing up his equipment.

And that, Owen decided, striding across the room to the door, just about maxed out his civic responsibilities for one day. He wouldn't be coming back to town again anytime soon.

Nothing had changed, Meg realized, no matter how the man pretended to be pleasant. It had always been easy for Owen Mac-Gregor to walk away. She certainly wasn't surprised. He was as predictable as the bus driver who figured his schedule came first.

Why he had returned with Hip was a mystery, but Meg supposed he'd been curious about the emergency phone call. Not that he'd been interested in anything to do with Willing for fourteen years. So why now?

Meg knew she'd hear about it eventually. Secrets were hard to keep in this little part of Montana. And secrets there were this morning. She watched Hip guide the girl into a chair and say something to make her smile and shake her head. Jerry moved to stand beside her. "Looks like the crisis is over?"

"For now," she told Jerry, whose gaze was also on the girl.

"I'll give her a ride to Lewistown," he said. "And I'll personally take her to the clinic."

"That's nice of you, but then what?"

"What do you mean?"

"I don't think she has any family or any place to go. And obviously not very much money, either."

"I'll talk to social services then, see what they can do for her."

"She could end up on the streets," she worried. Meg didn't think the girl would go along with that plan. She was a runaway, Meg guessed. In trouble because she was pregnant, possibly, and searching for the man she thought would be the answer to her prayers. That was the part that Meg hated to think about: a pregnant teenager putting all her faith in someone who didn't tell her his last name or where he lived. "I think she has other ideas, Jer."

"She certainly didn't want us to call the sheriff. She doesn't look like a criminal," he mused, "but you might want to keep an eye on the cash register."

"Al has that covered." The old grump stood with his arms folded across his massive body, as if daring anyone to order anything from the kitchen. "He doesn't like anything that upsets the routine. And he particularly hates Kermit. The bus passengers are always rushed, which means Al can't get the food out fast enough."

"And Al doesn't like to be rushed?"

"About as much as he likes surprises. Can you keep an eye on the little mother for a few minutes?"

"Sure. And unless I'm going down to Lewistown, I'm going to get posters printed up for the town meeting."

"You're not wasting any time."

"No, ma'am," he said, imitating a Western drawl. "Y'all have to strike while the iron is hot."

"Oh, for heaven's sake." She laughed. With one last glance at Shelly, who looked less pale and sipped water under Hip's watchful eyes, Meg retreated to the relative privacy of the kitchen and its ancient wall phone.

If anyone knew about being pregnant, it was Lucia. The woman had given birth to three boys in six years and still had a sense of humor. Right now Meg needed an expert opinion.

"Hi, Meg," Lucia said, answering the call.

"Hi. Can you come over here?"

"Right now?"

"Yes."

"What's wrong? Are you sick? Is it Al? Did he quit again?"

"No. I need some advice. About being pregnant and —"

"What? Pregnant? You don't even date!"

"Lu," she tried to explain, "I'm not talking about —"

"You called *me*. What do you mean, you're not *talking* about it?"

Meg started to laugh. "Luce, I'm not pregnant. But I have a kid here who is, and she fainted and then the bus left and Jerry called Hip and now I need help."

"Hip? What would he know about pregnant women?" Meg heard the sound of pleading from Lucia's youngest. "In a minute. Find your boots — the red ones — and get your backpack. Sorry about that, Meg. We're getting ready to go to Mama's for lunch."

"Lasagna or chicken parm?"

"Chicken parm."

"Nice." That was an understatement. Lucia had lucked out when she'd married Mama's only son. "That's okay, I won't keep you long. I just needed advice."

"You're not going to get a whole lot from Hip."

Meg agreed. "That's the point. And I don't know what to do with her. She's stranded. And she won't let anyone drive her to the hospital or the clinic."

"You said *kid.* How old is she?"

"Eighteen, but she looks younger than that."

"How pregnant?"

"Enough to look pregnant, but awfully thin."

There was silence as Lucia thought this over. "I'll just bet she hasn't had any prenatal care. Where's she going?"

"She's looking for her boyfriend. Except she doesn't know where he is or what his last name is . . . so I'm not thinking she has a great chance of finding him. Montana's a pretty big place to begin looking for a guy named Sonny."

"Oh, my."

"Exactly."

"Can you talk her into staying and seeing the doctor tomorrow? She's going to need vitamins and blood tests and an ultrasound. Unless you can get her a lift to Lewistown. She could pick up the bus again there, but she'd be better off seeing a doctor first. And anyway, if she doesn't know where to look for him, where does she plan to get to on the bus? This is as good a place to search as any."

Meg peered around the corner to see snow starting to fall outside the windows. "I'll try to convince her, but you might have better luck with that."

"I'll come by after lunch."

"I hoped you would. Thanks."

"You sound a little stressed," her friend said. "Is something else going on?"

"Oh, yeah. I'll tell you about later. Say hi to Mama for me."

"Would someone tell me why MacGregor is back?"

Meg refilled coffee cups as the conversation whirled around her. Those who'd stuck around after Hip left were only to happy to update the men who'd arrived for lunch and missed all the action. Fortunately the customers trickled in slowly and Meg could keep up with the orders.

"I don't think he's back, you know, permanently."

"Ed died in that storm last March."

"You're way behind the times. He's been at the big place for weeks now. Hasn't hired anybody new, though, not that I heard."

"You think he's gonna move that grizzly?"

"Hip said he asked about carving a new

base for it. Old one's been cracked for years, since the kids moved it."

"His old man just about had a cow over that."

"Mick wasn't real happy, either."

"Can I get a cheeseburger?"

"What's the soup today? It's not up on the board yet."

"Man, oh, man, it was a big one. Yeah, sure, more coffee, thanks."

"They didn't find Ed's body for three days."

"This sure is a noisy place." Shelly Smith, perched on a stool at the counter, sipped a cup of tea and waited for Al to grill a toasted cheese sandwich.

Meg couldn't argue with that. She set another glass of milk in front of the teenager. "It's been an exciting morning here in town. I guess there's lots to talk about."

"Like *me*?" She looked scared, which made Meg wonder what else the girl was hiding.

"Probably not, with you sitting right here." She smiled, to show she was teasing. "Missing the bus isn't exactly big news. And you seem to be feeling a lot better, so they've gone on to other topics of conversation."

"I'm not sick," the girl insisted. "I feel

pretty stupid."

"About what?"

She shrugged. "Is this a motel, too?"

"It was, but not anymore."

"Oh."

Meg could read the problem on the young woman's face as clearly as if she was reading a book: How was she supposed to survive on the few dollars she had in her purse? She had nowhere to stay, very little money and the snow had started to stick on the roads. If anyone could be called a "lost soul," it was this young woman. Meg hesitated, but only for a moment, before offering a solution. She couldn't let a pregnant stranger wander off into the snow, and she couldn't spend the night sleeping in a booth in the restaurant. "You can spend the night in my mother's cabin. She's in Arizona."

Shelly stared at her, blue eyes wide with hope and relief. "Seriously?"

"You have another plan?"

She shook her head. "I'm totally out of plans." She thought for a second. "Your mom won't care? You'd do that?"

"If you promise not to run off before you see the doctor tomorrow. He's here every Tuesday."

"MacGregor —" George raised his voice to be heard over the clatter of lunch dishes

"— must have something on his mind, something goin' on, to come into town on a Monday morning and order breakfast as if he was in here every single day."

Meg silently agreed. From the little she'd heard, Owen had come to the ranch after his uncle died, but no one knew exactly why. His real life, according to an occasional newspaper article, was in Washington, DC.

Into the sudden silence, Shelly leaned forward. "Mr. MacGregor is the guy who went through my bag?"

"Because I asked him to."

She rolled her eyes. "He'd better not have taken anything."

"I'm sure he didn't."

"You must get a lot of people passing through here."

Meg took two hamburger plates from the pass and delivered them to customers at the other end of the counter before returning to Shelly. "Mostly in the summer. Fall and winter it quiets right down. The slow season starts now."

"Are there jobs?"

"Why? Are you thinking about staying here for a while?"

Shelly shrugged. "Maybe. Do you need a waitress? I worked at a Dairy Queen in Boise."

"Maybe," Meg said, seeing a way to keep an eye on the girl until she could find out more about what was going on with her. "You'd have to see the doctor. Get checked out, do what he says, get some vitamins. You know, so you wouldn't faint again while you were working."

Shelly seemed to be thinking that over, so Meg delivered the pot roast special to the four tourists in the booth by the door, then wiped down three of the back tables and closed off that part of the dining area.

"I heard there's a TV show coming."

"It's possible," Meg said. "A producer is coming to look at the town and see if it would work for a dating show."

"A dating show? Here?" She looked around the restaurant. "What, for old people?"

Meg couldn't help laughing. "Not exactly. But I guess you never know what us old folks are up to."

"You're not old. Well, not *old* old," she explained, blushing.

"Thanks."

"Who's going to be on TV, then?"

"That's a good question. Our mayor, you met him. Jerry? Red-haired guy with the cell phone?"

"Yeah."

"He's from Hollywood or somewhere around there. One of his friends had the idea of bringing women to Willing and pairing them up with some of the men who live here."

"Why?"

"Another good question." She smiled. "We seem to have an abundance of single men."

"Oh, yeah. Forty-eight, right?"

"That's right."

"Bizarre."

Meg hadn't thought of it as bizarre, or a problem that needed to be solved. But then again, the single women in Willing — not that there were many of them — didn't seem inclined to marry, settle down and raise children in this very small town. What if Jerry was right, and the town's best days were over?

She worried about the empty storefronts, the lack of jobs and the long winters without much income. Each winter she struggled harder to stay profitable, but she was one of the lucky ones who didn't have a mortgage. She also had a career to fall back on; her training in restaurant management, along with her chef credentials, guaranteed jobs if she was willing to relocate.

Not that she wanted to leave Willing.

"What's wrong with the women around here?"

"Not a thing," Meg said through her teeth. "Does something have to be wrong if you don't want to get married or haven't found the right man or want to run your own life your own way?"

"Oops, sore spot, huh?" Shelly dug her spoon into the bowl of chocolate pudding Al had presented to her. "So I guess I should be asking what's wrong with the men."

Out of the mouths of babes, Meg mused, unable to keep a straight face as she reached for the coffeepot one more time. She couldn't wait to tell Lucia. With any luck she hadn't heard about Jerry's plans and Meg would be there to see her reaction when Lucia heard that busloads of women might be coming to town to discover true love.

CHAPTER FIVE

For better or worse, he was home. Owen opened the door of the truck and watched Boo hop out, stretch and then run barking across the wide dirt driveway that fronted the two-car garage and old equipment shed. The dog greeted the feral gray cat that had slunk from its latest shelter, a root cellar that had seen better days. For some reason, Boo and the cat had bonded. The cat tolerated the barking as long as the dog didn't get too close to her.

"Boo," Owen called, as much to stop the noise as to direct the dog toward the house. "Leave her alone."

The dog gave the cat one last yip and trotted obediently toward the big house, as it had been called for more than one hundred years. Owen studied the homestead, wondering what strangers would think of the place. When his father had been young, his grandparents had welcomed visitors to their home, tourists with an interest in Western history or students from the college writing theses with topics such as Scottish Emigration in 1850 and Early Settlers of the American West. Some had been published, and copies proudly lined the bookshelves in the living room.

From the outside, Owen supposed it looked the same as it ever had. The big house, a white-painted two-story frame Victorian, sat in the midst of a large patch of brown grass surrounded on three sides by windbreaker pines. Off to the west were the outbuildings: the garage and other sheds that housed both necessary and long-forgotten equipment. To the east were Owen's favorite structures: the original log buildings built by the Scot whose vision had led to owning one of the largest ranches in the state. The log house, with its low roof and small windows, had been carefully preserved, along with the attached log barn.

The outhouse had long been torn down, as had the first corral. Over the rise were the modern barns, corrals, storage buildings and tin-roofed cattle sheds.

Owen headed toward the side of the house, where Boo waited on the cracked concrete pad outside the back door. Owen hadn't bothered to lock up the place. Connected by a wide passageway to the back of the house, just to the right of the door, was the summer kitchen. Originally used as its name implied, the massive one-story room had been modernized over the years. Yet its worn picnic tables were original, as was the cook stove tucked into the corner. On that same distant wall sat an avocado-green gas stove, two deep porcelain sinks and a worn gold-flecked Formica counter. Mismatched cabinets and cupboards had been cobbled together over the years from leftovers of other projects, other ranch houses. Two old round-shouldered refrigerators filled in the other end of the wall. He supposed they'd be considered vintage now, but he didn't doubt they'd still work when plugged in.

The days of feeding dozens of men in here were long gone, yet Owen couldn't think about getting rid of anything, not even the peeling green-painted benches stacked against the near wall.

He'd first seen Meg right here. She'd turned from the refrigerator, a sweating gallon jar of lemonade in her arms, and he'd hurried over to help her.

"I've got it," she'd protested, but her cheeks were flushed from the surprising early June heat. She'd let him take the slippery jar and set it on the closest table.

"You're new," he'd said. That was when summers meant extra hands to feed and Irene MacGregor hired a kitchen crew to make sure no one who worked on the ranch ever went hungry.

"Yes. Today's my first day." She'd blushed again and looked away. Her dark hair had been tied back in a long ponytail; she'd worn denim shorts and one of Mrs. Hancock's red-checked aprons over a blue T-shirt. A strip of blue beads had dangled from each earlobe, but she'd worn no makeup. She had seemed tiny, he realized. Or maybe she'd made him feel eight feet tall.

"Do you like it so far?" He'd sounded twelve when he'd said that, he remembered, not twenty and two months away from being a junior in college. Too eager.

"Oh, yes," she'd said, and her brown eyes had lit up. "I like to cook."

"Margaret, Margie, Peg, whatever your name is," Mrs. Hancock had called, interrupting that long-ago moment with laughter in her voice. "Don't let the ranch hands turn your head, now. They're awful flirts!"

Owen turned away from the memories and shoved open the back door. He eyed the heaps of junk-stuffed boxes that stretched from one wall to another and beyond, in rooms that weren't visible from the crowded mudroom. He smelled leather and dust, old coffee and dog.

If there was anything to jolt him out of the past and into the present, it was looking at the mess his life had become. The real-estate agent he'd met with last week had suggested tearing down the buildings.

"It's all about the land," the man had said.

As if it was that simple.

Lucia smoothed her black hair over her shoulders after she'd listened to Meg's concerns about the stranded bus passenger. "You want me to talk to her? Explain the ins and outs of pregnancy?"

"Ins and outs," Mama Marie snorted. "A little late for that."

"Mama!" Lucia hid her smile. "Be kind. We don't know her circumstances, or where her family is or what she's going through."

"No family," Mama muttered. Tony, Lucia's youngest, cuddled in his grandmother's ample lap, his head resting on her shoulder. He'd given up trying to wriggle away and had decided to close his eyes. "A girl with no family — I don't understand this at all."

"Mama, you've seen unwed pregnant girls before," Lucia pointed out. "They're everywhere."

She pulled out her rosary. "That doesn't make it right."

"No, but —"

"A girl with no family needs our prayers."

Meg silently agreed with her. "Mama," she said, because everyone in town who knew Mrs. Swallow called her Mama, "I think she's a runaway."

"She certainly doesn't look eighteen," Lucia said. Shelly sat in a corner booth, where she nursed a cup of tea and played with her cell phone. "If you can't keep her here at least overnight, then she might run away again before she sees a doctor."

"Run away?" Mama snorted. "Where's she gonna go? And how's she gonna get there?"

"I told her she could stay in my mother's cabin tonight so she can get checked out at the clinic tomorrow."

The statement was met with silence from the Swallow women.

"That's awfully nice of you," Lucia said finally. "Considering you don't know her."

"It's not as if there's anything worth stealing," Meg said. "Unless you count Loralee's T-shirt collection."

Lucia gave her a "what's really going on here?" look, but after a quick glance at her curious mother-in-law, simply asked, "And then what? She gets back on a bus? That doesn't seem like a healthy thing to do in her condition."

"These girls today," Mama muttered, "they don't think."

"Maybe she doesn't have any choice," Meg pointed out. "She asked me about waitressing, if she stayed here."

"Is there enough business?"

"There could be. And I could use a few hours off to start working on the cabins, at least do some painting inside on the ones that aren't in bad shape. I might be able to rent them before the end of hunting season." She lowered her voice, as Mama had begun praying rather loudly. "And there could be more business, lots of it, at least for a little while. There was a town council meeting here this morning."

"And that's interesting because?"

"Jerry has a Hollywood connection . . ."

"Tracy," Lucia prompted.

"Yes. How'd you know her name?"

"She's all he talks about. I taught that bread-baking class last winter, remember? He flunked."

"He did?"

"He had no sense of dough," Lucia stated, eyeing her napping child. "They're so sweet when they're asleep. He woke me at four

99

o'clock this morning to ask if there were cookies in heaven."

"No sense of dough?" Meg stared at her friend. "What does that mean?"

Lucia turned her attention back to Meg. "I think he was afraid of it."

Afraid of dough. Meg considered that for a few seconds. "Like a horror movie." She continued on with her news. "Tracy has an idea for a reality TV show, for here, in Willing. And Jerry thinks we could use the publicity. As a way to attract new people to town."

"What kind of reality show? Like *Survivor,* only in the winter?"

"Uh-uh. Like *The Dating Game,* only with city girls and country guys."

Lucia's brow furrowed. "I don't get it."

"They'd use local men," Meg explained. "Our bachelors, from around here. The idea is to bring city women to date, well, Western men. You know, like the Marlboro Man from a zillion years ago. Clint Eastwood, only lots younger."

"The guys around here aren't exactly movie stars."

"No."

They both giggled.

"Stop that." Mama broke into their conversation. "We could use some movie stars, some people other than the ones we already know. I'm thinking I'd like to open up a pizza shop. Everyone likes pizza, especially movie stars."

Meg couldn't help smiling. "You're going to give me some competition in the restaurant business?"

"You don't sell pizza," Mama said. "But I'll always make your meatballs for you, don't worry."

"That's a load off my mind," Meg answered, still smiling. "But there won't be any real movie stars coming here, just normal people who want to be on television."

"Normal people," Lucia said, reaching for her coffee, "don't *want* to be on television."

"Normal people come to Montana," Meg pointed out. "You did."

Lucia smiled. "I did, all the way from Wyoming. And so did you."

"When I was sixteen," she reminded her. "Because my mother fell in love with a man in Billings who ended up inheriting this place."

"Husband number two?"

"Five."

"That," Mama said, frowning at them, "is too many husbands. Your mother was a very busy lady."

"And very optimistic."

Mama looked across the room at Shelly. "Maybe I can find a job for her. In my pizza business."

"If she sticks around," Lucia said. "I thought you said she was looking for her boyfriend."

"That's what she said. She seems to think she'll find him and live happily ever after."

"And where is he, this boyfriend?" Mama wanted to know. "And what kind of a boyfriend is this, who gets a girl pregnant and can't be found? Who would want a boyfriend like that?"

"Mama, shh. She'll hear you."

They were an odd pair, the two Mrs. Swallows. Both women were short and dark haired, but there the resemblance ended. Lucia, one-quarter Lakota Sioux, was fine-boned with delicate features and hazel eyes. She looked younger than her thirty-four years, and too slim to have had three children. Quiet, kind and dependable, Lucia hid the pain of widowhood and buried her heartache under the enormous love she had for her sons.

Mama was the last person anyone would expect to move from her Italian neighborhood in Rhode Island and settle in a remote Montana town, but the death of her son and her daughter-in-law's third pregnancy had meant Mama was needed. And Mama went where she was needed. She'd stayed, so here she was almost five years later. In her own little home one block around the corner from Lucia and the boys, she cooked and babysat and watched over her son's family.

"I hope hundreds of women come here," Lucia said. She leaned over and lifted her sleepy son from his grandmother's lap.

"Why?" Meg and Mama asked at the same time.

"Because I don't want to date. I don't want to marry. And I'm tired of saying that, over and over again. I mean," she said to Meg, "if you or I were going to fall in love with someone in Willing, it would have happened by now, wouldn't it?"

"So, Lucia's like your best friend, huh?"

"Yes."

"She's nice."

"Yes, she is."

Shelly didn't add that she thought Lucia's mother-in-law, that Mama person, was scarier than Judge Czercic, who had sent her to foster care when she was thirteen. She was sure — pretty sure — Sonny's mother would be really nice. But then again, she guessed that in-laws were a "you get what you get" deal. His family would be her family, the baby's family. It would all work out. She'd make it work out.

Shelly, her bags in hand, followed Meg across the parking lot to the L-shaped group of cabins. "Did you ever think about putting in a pool?"

"A pool?" Meg was fumbling with keys.

"Yeah, don't all these old motels have pools in the middle?"

"Not here," Meg said, stopping in front of the end unit with rose flowered curtains in the window. "We go for the rustic-parking-lot look."

Shelly wondered if that was a joke, but Meg was fiddling with the doorknob and Shelly couldn't tell. This one looked larger than the other five buildings.

"This is my mother's," she said once again, finally opening the door. "She's out of town, so it's going to be a little dusty."

Shelly didn't care about dust. What she cared about was sleeping in a real bed. She worried that Meg would call the sheriff. She was scared she'd lose the baby and she'd never find Sonny. She might have nightmares about that strange old woman who glared at her from across the café, but she *didn't* care about dust.

Meg switched on a set of lights to the left

of the door, revealing a pine-paneled room that held a small combination kitchen and living area. A square table butted against the wall with two white chairs on either side. Across the room sat a rose velvet sofa, a tall lamp, a coffee table and a surprisingly new flat-screen television.

"Wow," Shelly said. "It's really pink."

"My mother's favorite color. After she divorced her last husband, she bought as much pink stuff as she could fit in here."

"Why?"

"To remind herself to stay single."

"Really?" The pink was a little weird, but Shelly had lived in some pretty ugly places in the past years, and this cabin was nothing to complain about.

"Really. There's a bathroom in there." Meg pointed toward the other side of the room where two doors were closed. "And a bedroom. I'll find sheets and get you fixed up."

"I can do that," she said. "You don't have to go to any more trouble. . . . Where is she?"

"Who?" Meg had rounded a corner and opened a closet.

"Your mother."

"Visiting her sister."

"She's not going to be mad if I stay here?"

"Not at all." She handed Shelly a stack of

sheets with pink daisies scattered on them. "How are you feeling? Tell the truth."

Shelly gulped. "I'm okay. Just really tired. Lucia said it was normal to be tired like this."

"You're not feeling sick again, are you?" Meg led her into a small bedroom, most of the space taken up by a double bed — with a pink comforter, of course — and a long narrow dresser painted white. The carpet was also white, and the one window was covered in long panels of white lace. Shelly thought it was the prettiest room she'd ever seen, but she tried not to look impressed.

"No." Not that she'd admit feeling sick even if she was, having caused a big scene this morning with everyone staring at her as if she was a corpse on *CSI*.

"I have to get back to the café, but Mondays are slow. Come over later if you want a burger or something." Meg frowned at the bed. "Are you sure you don't want help with the sheets?"

"It's okay, honest." She set them carefully on the fluffy comforter. "How late do you work?"

"Oh, maybe eight o'clock. Now that it's getting dark so early, I think we'll close early. Especially if it starts to snow. But I'll check on you before I go home."

"You live here, too?"

"In the cabin closest to the café, on the other end." She smiled. "And there isn't one pink thing in it."

"I like pink," was the only thing Shelly could think to say. She didn't understand why this stranger was being so nice. Why she'd given her a place to sleep tonight and free milk and bacon this morning. It was because she was pregnant, Shelly decided. Everything had been different since she got pregnant.

"Are you going to be okay here by yourself? It's pretty quiet, but you'll probably hear cars coming and going. Turn up the heat, use the television and make yourself at home. Help yourself to anything in the kitchen."

"Thanks." Shelly didn't know what else to say. For the first time in months, she felt as if everything was going to be okay. At least for a little while.

He had done it.

In fact, he'd accomplished a heck of a lot more this morning than he'd ever dreamed of. *Momentum,* Jerry realized. He was now experiencing the momentum of a good idea turning into a great undertaking. And Owen MacGregor, of all people, had sat right there in the café, eaten his breakfast and studied Jerry's information as if he was interested, just as if he spent every Monday morning catching up with town business.

He couldn't wait to call Tracy. She'd eat up the whole "historic ranch" angle. She'd hinted about cowboys and horseback riding all along. And if anyone could come up with a ranch to impress the producers, it would be a MacGregor, descendant of the first cattle rancher in the county, old Angus, who'd come from Scotland with a plan. Jerry had done his research into town history when he'd first decided to run for mayor, and his own plans for a prosperous town — and luring Tracy back into his life — would have made Angus proud. Jerry had never been out there to the Triple M, but he intended to wrangle an invitation from Owen very soon. He'd take pictures so Tracy wouldn't waste any time getting out here.

Getting out to MacGregor's had been on his list for weeks, but he'd been told the uncle was unfriendly, remote and rarely concerned himself with county business, never mind small-town concerns. But then along came Owen, and he'd been open to hearing the issues; he'd listened to the ideas and joined in the conversation.

Jerry leaned back in his office chair and admired the big glass windows that showcased Main Street. Owen MacGregor had been polite, agreeable and friendly. Sure, he hadn't completely agreed to serve on the location committee, but Tracy wouldn't let a setting like that go to waste, not when she wanted atmosphere. Montana atmosphere.

She'd get it, and more.

To top it all off, Meg Ripley, as outspoken and stubborn as she was, had sensibly agreed to back a project that would mean money in her bank account. At first she might have thought the idea of a dating show was amusing, but she'd recognized the importance of good publicity and an influx of people into town. The numbers didn't lie; all those visitors would need food. And when the other people in town saw Meg supporting this, there wouldn't be many who would argue with the formidable café owner. He had no doubt she was scribbling down menus and fancy catering ideas right this minute.

His illustrious town council had voted yes to presenting this at the town meeting. Unanimously . . . if reluctantly. The posters were being printed, the announcement of a special emergency meeting would be in the paper Wednesday morning and at seven o'clock Thursday night he would explain to his constituents his plan to keep Willing from sliding into oblivion.

Jerry could almost hear the applause now.

Heady stuff, this momentum.

CHAPTER SIX

"I've been thinking about what your grandfather would say about this," Ben Fargus drawled. "I'm not sure he would have liked all of this hoopla. The old man wasn't much for crowds, if you know what I mean."

"Well —" Owen began to say into the phone.

"He preferred horses. Always did, right up until the accident."

"Yes, but —"

"Your father, on the other hand, was a more social type. He believed in community involvement, I will say that."

"Yes, he did," Owen said, giving up trying to get a word in. He promised himself to never answer the ranch's phone again.

"A finer man never was born, least not in Montana. The town still misses him. Shame him going so young." The elderly man, whom Owen remembered as one of his father's acquaintances, sighed. "Now, Jerry has some interestin' ideas, which you heard all about the other morning, over breakfast, he said, and he says you're on board. He's told you about all this publicity stuff, right?"

"Yes, but —" Before he could explain, once again, that he'd only *listened* to the mayor and hadn't committed his money, ranch or hot tub to the cause, Mr. Fargus interrupted with a monologue on the hardships of marriage.

"I can't claim to know everything about women, but after living with the same one for more than sixty years . . ."

Owen stopped listening. He stared at the thick plastic phone stuck to the wall, its once-white coiled cord stretched from years of use at its station to the right of the stove. Uncle Ed hadn't been much for renovations or updates, as the interior of the house illustrated. Uncle Ed had kept to himself, spent more time outdoors than inside and, as Mr. Fargus had said, had liked horses more than people. Owen guessed it ran in the family, which explained his own solitary lifestyle.

Ed hadn't spent much time talking on the telephone, either. As far as Owen knew, Ed had visited a cousin in Missoula whenever he'd felt like socializing, and he only called his nephew when there was business to discuss. The silent rancher hadn't believed in wasting time with "chitchat nonsense," which explained his hermit-like behavior.

Or caused it.

"Your father would sure be pleased," the old man on the other end of the phone was saying.

"Yes," was all Owen could manage to say. He wasn't sure what Mr. Fargus meant.

"This town needs a MacGregor, sure enough. Hello? Hello? Are you there, Owen? These cell phones, always cutting out." With that, the connection ended and Owen listened to the blissful sound of a dial tone. In the past seventy-two hours, he'd been contacted by various town residents — all male, of course — and all six members of the town council. Their conversations had ranged from stressed to enthusiastic, depending on their ages and opinions about blind dates, California women and bachelorhood. Each one had wanted to know if, how and why Owen was getting involved.

No, he'd said. *I'm not on the location committee.*

No, I'm not on the welcoming committee, either.

No, the hot tub isn't functional. Really, it's not. Hasn't been used in years.

No, the ranch is not about to become a golf course.

And no, I am not attending the town meeting.

Jerry Thompson, who had called three times, never accepted the "not attending the town meeting" statement. He refused to believe that Owen could ignore the opportunity to solve the town's financial problems.

"You've seen the figures with your own eyes," he'd cried. "Your great-great-great-whatever grandfather founded this town!"

"Not exactly." Owen had tried to explain that his famous ancestor had founded a cattle business, not a town. He didn't go into detail about the family's rumored connection to the first brothel or the legendary train robber in Kansas who might or might not have been the black sheep of the family. The original Angus MacGregor had been a decent man with a dream, and he'd proudly seen it come true.

"We need you. You're supposed to be on the location committee, remember?"

"Sorry, but —"

"You have a historic ranch, Owen. I heard your folks used to open it in the summer and let tourists see the place. I saw some great old postcards framed at the library.

114

When we *had* a library."

"What happened to the library?" He was afraid to hear the answer.

"We couldn't keep it up. Now we get the bookmobile on Thursdays."

"Look, Jerry, the ranch used to be a showplace, but that was a long time ago. The house — the entire place — is old. It needs work." He didn't add what the real-estate agent had said about a bulldozer. "My uncle didn't —"

"I'm sure it has atmosphere," the mayor insisted. "Tracy will be able to get some great shots of the ranch exteriors and views of the cattle. They call it B-roll, you know."

"There are no cattle right now," Owen said. "We've leased out —"

"We'll get some. What about horses? If you don't have any, we'll get those, too."

Mayor Thompson, Owen decided, was a real pain in the butt. And if one more person called to ask his opinion about the emergency town meeting and the "mayor's dating show," Owen thought he might just move out to the barn. God knew he'd spent enough weeks cleaning it out.

Getting caller ID would help, once he bought a phone that displayed the numbers. He could buy a new cell phone to replace the one that had died shortly after he moved back here. Voice mail might be less annoying than he remembered, too. But he would need to go somewhere other than town to buy these necessities, or order them online and have them delivered here to the ranch. Fortunately the internet connection was more or less reliable.

He didn't want to go to Willing. Meg was there. He could avoid the café easily, but he had no doubt that if he set foot into the grocery/liquor/hardware store — or anywhere else, for that matter — he'd have the bad luck to run into her and she'd smile politely and act as if they hardly knew each other. Again.

She'd broken his heart all those years ago, when he was twenty and in love and desperate to be with her for the rest of their lives. And now there'd been the revelation that eighteen other men had proposed marriage to her. While he could understand a few drunken pleas on Valentine's Day, eighteen seemed a little . . . excessive. Had shy Margaret Ripley taken after her mother after all?

He didn't know why that thought rankled him so much.

He sure as heck didn't intend to dwell on that time, on the shock of losing his father and everything he'd thought would always be there.

A broken heart had been the least of it that year.

"Oh, my goodness, that is one handsome man."

"Who?" As Meg turned to look in the same direction as Lucia, she had a sinking feeling she knew exactly who her friend had described. And yes, there he was making his way along the edge of the crowd by the far wall of the community center. He paused, shook hands with Pete Lyons and unzipped his waterproof jacket. A white button-down shirt was tucked neatly into his jeans, of course, because a MacGregor took pride in his or her appearance. Still, Meg thought he needed a haircut.

"Owen MacGregor."

"That's him, huh? Wow. I don't think I've ever seen him this close up before. He's really tall."

"Yes, he is. What, are you interested?"

"And you're not?"

"Uh, no. No. And *no.* But feel free to introduce yourself. I see Iris and Patsy heading over to him now. I hope they don't trip on their tongues."

"He looks immune," Lucia said. "Aloof." Almost as an afterthought she muttered, "I can't believe that after three kids I can still remember the word *aloof.*"

"It was probably on Davey's spelling test."

"Thanks a lot."

From their seats near the far end of the third row, they watched as members of the town council chatted with other attendees. The meeting was taking place at the center instead of the café or the clinic's meeting room because of the crowd Jerry expected. Meg deliberately studied the arrangement of autumn leaves and gourds that decorated the folding table set up in the front of the room. She certainly wasn't interested in whom Owen spoke to or whether Patsy Parrish flirted with him. Patsy flirted with everyone, and had since Meg had met her in eleventh grade.

"My, my," Lucia murmured again. "The handsome rancher is attracting quite a crowd. You know him, don't you?"

"Yes, from a long time ago."

"Didn't you work at the ranch?" Lucia shrugged off her denim jacket and folded it in her lap. She wore one of her signature multicolored skirts, its wide ruffles grazing the calves of her suede boots. A black sweater, a cluster of silver necklaces and beaded earrings completed an outfit that made her look like a fashion model.

"How do you do it?"

"Do what?" She smoothed her black hair behind her ears.

"Look so gorgeous." Meg wished she'd worn something less practical than jeans, hiking boots and a four-year-old black turtleneck. At least she'd remembered to slap on some makeup and lipstick before going out. Loralee had ingrained in her the importance of mascara.

"Thrift shop in Billings," she replied. "This skirt was on the two-dollar rack. So, back to the question, Aunt Miggy," she said, using her sons' pet name for her friend. "You knew him, right?"

"Yes. When I was a kid." She'd been seventeen. Then eighteen. He'd brought her flowers. She'd thought she was all grown up and knew it all. "He was in college."

"I wonder what he's doing here. I heard he hasn't been seen in town five times in the past fifteen years or so. Mama and Aurora think he wants to be on television."

"No, that wouldn't be it." *I'd rather sit naked in a pit of rattlesnakes,* he'd told the mayor. Leave it to Owen to say exactly what he was thinking.

"Are you sure?" She craned her neck for another peek at him. "He looks like every woman's fantasy of the Western male."

"He already said no." At Lucia's questioning look, she added, "Monday. At the meeting. Besides, I'm sure he gets all the women he wants without having to go on television."

"I sense some animosity on your part. See? Another big word. I'm *so* proud of myself."

Meg riffled through her purse to find a pen. "You go, girl."

"A-n-i-m-o-s-i-t-y."

"Now you're just showing off." She wished the meeting would begin. It was already ten minutes past seven.

"Don't look now, but he's staring at you."

"What is this, fifth grade?"

"Sorry, just teasing." Lucia chuckled. "Hey, I'm happy to be out of the house and away from the boys for an hour or so. We're going to the Dahl after this, right?"

"Right. You can torture Joe Peckham with your beauty. He wants to get you a dog, by the way."

"I wish he'd crush on someone his own age," Lucia said. "Mind you, I'd rather have a dog than a boyfriend any day."

"Amen, sister." Meg took the edge of her pen and scraped some hardened frosting off her jeans. She'd never told her best friend about her first love. Oh, she'd implied she'd had her tender little teenage heart broken — hadn't everyone? — but she'd never given the name of the person who'd caused the pain. She'd never told anyone the whole story, how she'd almost married the son of the richest man in the county.

Now he'd walked back into her life. She'd thought his appearance Monday morning was a fluke and had assumed she wouldn't see him again for another five or six or ten years. In fact, when she'd thought about seeing him again, she'd deliberately put it out of her mind. Self-preservation was a wonderful thing.

Owen had appeared so relieved to escape the café Monday. He'd seemed to have little sympathy for Shelly, who had been surprisingly cooperative on Tuesday after a good night's sleep and a list of dos and don'ts from Dr. Jenks. The girl already looked healthier, and Al hadn't minded the extra help in the kitchen. Shelly had stubbornly insisted on paying her own way by working at the restaurant a few hours a day. Owen would be surprised to learn she hadn't run off with the bank deposits.

What was he doing here? She hadn't thought he was that impressed with the mayor's new project. Meg had assumed he'd been amusing himself over breakfast.

Or bored. Then again, Jerry would have hounded him unmercifully.

Meg glanced past Lucia to see if Owen still stood near the wall. He would be the center of attention anywhere he went, of course, but this time she didn't see him. She supposed he'd be hovering near the back so he could make his escape without being noticed. Maybe he was here to object to the whole thing.

That didn't seem fair. Why would he deny other people a chance to make a living? A chance to make some money in the otherwise bleak months before tourist season returned? And why would he care what went on around here? Sure, she'd heard he was doing some work on the old ranch, but he had a life back east. Ran some kind of successful agriculture business, was taking time off to get the homestead ready to sell. Was engaged to a woman from Dallas and had leased the ranch to an artist, a conglomerate and the government.

Rumors were clearly running rampant, especially in the café, where there seemed to be plenty of time and people to spread them.

"Attention, attention!" Jerry climbed to the podium and banged his gavel three times. "Would everyone please find a seat so we can start the meeting?"

No one paid the least attention. The noisy crowd continued to talk as if not one of them had seen other human beings in years. Jerry banged his gavel again, but those standing around the perimeter of the room didn't stop talking and didn't sit down.

"That man's a born leader," Meg said, which made Lucia laugh and shush her. They watched as Hip connected a cable to a sound system and handed Jerry a microphone.

"Welcome," he said as an earsplitting shriek emanated from the speaker. Those still standing stopped talking and hustled to find seats.

"While you're all getting settled, I'll remind you . . . uh . . ." Jerry studied the piece of paper he held. "The Banner County Quilters quilt show is being held here from nine to five on Saturday and noon to four on Sunday. There will be door prizes," he read, "as well as coffee and assorted cakes and cookies for sale, plus an auction to raise money for the Thanksgiving food drive. There is also a quilt raffle, so please buy tickets and support the food drive."

Several people applauded.

"Oh, and raffle tickets can be purchased at the café, the Dahl and Thompson's market until mid-November. The quilt will be on display here during the show, and there will be posters of it around town, so you can see the amount of work and time put into this by the talented women in this community."

"Excuse me," Meg heard a deep male voice murmur behind her. A familiar male voice. "Is this seat taken?"

"Help yourself," someone said, and metal chairs scraped the floor.

"Thanks." Something brushed against her hair. Familiar aftershave and the scent of leather hinted that the deep male voice belonged to the man she'd hoped to avoid. Not that she had any reason to, she reassured herself. She made her shoulders relax as Lucia turned to see who took the empty seat behind Meg, then thankfully pretended she had no interest. Her attention returned to the mayor, who called the special meeting to order and unnecessarily introduced the six members of the town council scattered among the crowd.

For the next twenty minutes, Meg listened to a more formal version of Monday morning's meeting, complete with financial information and future forecasts. Jerry explained what attracting a television show could mean to the town's bottom line and why the town council had voted to pursue it.

"We have a producer and small crew arriving in a couple of weeks. We'll be showing them around, giving them a chance to meet you, scouting the area for places to shoot and things to do. We're going to need your support, ideas and cooperation. And you single men out there?" Jerry paused long enough for the burst of conversation to die down. "We need you on the show."

"This," Lucia whispered, "is nothing short of bizarre."

"I know, but bizarre or not, I get to cater it," Meg reminded her. "Meaning we both make money. *Bizarre* amounts of money."

"What if the Californians don't eat pie? Or cinnamon rolls? Or sugar cookies?"

"Who doesn't eat pie?"

"Women on diets," Lucia said. "And they'll all be on diets."

"Could you be more optimistic, please?"

Lucia laughed.

When Jerry opened the meeting for questions, Meg twisted in her seat to see that at least ten pairs of hands had flown into the air. And all of those hands belonged to women.

"Where are these folks going to stay? I can take eight, max, but even that's a stretch," Iris, who owned the town's only B and B, wanted to know. "I'd hate to see Lewistown or Great Falls or Billings get our business just because we don't have enough beds."

"I'm working on that," the mayor assured her. "I have a couple of empty buildings I might be able to turn into temporary living quarters. Meg Ripley has the cabins."

"Uh-oh. They haven't been rented in years," Meg said, but Jerry was too far away to hear. "I'd love to rent them, but —"

"I'll help," Lucia whispered. "A little paint —"

"A lot of *plumbing,*" Meg pointed out. Renovating the four empty cabins had been a pipe dream. Until now. "It can be done," she added, hoping as her excitement grew that she'd be able to sleep tonight.

Jerry was still talking. "I'd even considered the Triple M —"

"The MacGregor place?" someone asked. "No kidding!"

Meg heard Owen swear softly, heard his seat creak as he shifted. It was actually a great idea, considering the beauty of the old ranch house. She desperately wanted to turn around and see the expression on his face, but she restrained herself.

"Every idea is welcome," Jerry said. "But

first we have to show Tracy — the producer — what a great town we have, and what the possibilities are if she chooses Willing for the show."

The questions continued from the female residents of the town. As did the jokes. While the town's single men fidgeted in their seats and looked longingly at the door, there was no doubt that the idea was being met with enthusiasm. Just about everyone stood to benefit from an influx of out-of-state dollars and an increase in population — temporary or otherwise — not to mention the excitement of seeing new faces in town. The volume of chatter increased, but now Jerry kept his hand off the gavel. He was obviously thrilled with the response of the voters.

"Now," he said, his voice booming into the microphone, "we need bachelors! Les, Pete, Jack? Stand up! Even the town council members are getting involved. Let's give them a round of applause."

The crowd cheered. Meg applauded and Lucia did a fist pump.

Meg heard Owen chuckle, then call, "Way to go!"

"This is for a good cause, after all. And it should be a lot of fun, too. Who knows? You might get to go to Hollywood, get your picture in *People* magazine. At the very least, you'll meet some nice ladies and show the rest of the country what living in Montana is like. So who else wants to join in the fun?"

No one moved. There was a rustle of clothing, low murmurs, nervous laughter. Jerry waited for a moment, then continued on as if everything was going to be just fine.

"It's come to my attention that some of us need a refresher course on dating," the mayor stated with a great deal of diplomacy.

"Understatement," Lucia muttered. "*Giant* understatement."

"Fortunately for us guys, Meg Ripley, from the Willing Café, has volunteered to help with that. I've asked her what women expect from a man, how to treat a lady and, ultimately, what makes a good husband." He grinned at the crowd. "And I'm sure you ladies out there have suggestions of your own, so talk to Meg and she'll set up some workshops before Tracy — the producer — arrives."

There was more applause and a lot of female cheering.

Someone yelled, "Get 'em all married, Meg!"

"I didn't volunteer," she sputtered, but no

one was listening except Lucia, who looked hurt.

"Seriously?" Lucia asked. "And you didn't tell me? I could have come up with a *list.*"

"I didn't volunteer," she repeated, much louder than the first time. She waved her hand in the air. "Jerry! Mistake here!"

The mayor ignored her, because he had brains and a strong sense of self-preservation, Meg figured.

"I want to help," Lucia said. "I can't believe you didn't ask me to *help.*"

She felt a tap on her shoulder and reluctantly turned around. Sure enough, Owen MacGregor was leaning toward her. He looked amused. "What?"

"Congratulations," he said. "I didn't know you were an expert on marriage."

She glared at him. "I'm not," she said. "And you know it."

He shrugged. "A woman who's been proposed to eighteen times —"

"Nineteen, actually," she said, daring him to remember.

"Nineteen times," he amended smoothly. "A woman who's been proposed to *nineteen times* must know a lot about men."

Meg pretended to think about that for a moment. "I'm sure you're right," she said. "It's a gift."

She ignored Lucia's snort of laughter and kept her gaze on Owen. She liked the little age lines around his eyes and the way they crinkled — oh, for heaven's sake. She needed to get a grip, so she attempted a serious expression. "And what about you?"

"What *about* me?"

"You're single. Are you planning to try to get a date while you're here? Or are you on your way back to — where have you been all these years?" Meg deliberately furrowed her brow.

"Washington, D.C. But I'm here, at least for a while," he said, as if the past fifteen years didn't matter, as if she hadn't cried into her battered ladybug pillow for three months after he'd been sent back to college in Bozeman.

"For a while," she repeated. "That's too bad. We could use your help."

She turned back around in her seat and pretended to be enthralled with the sight of Jerry writing down names and handing out information sheets.

And then Owen MacGregor cleared his throat and stood. His hand brushed Meg's shoulder, but she was too old for shivers. Although it was cold in here. October. Montana. Goose bumps were expected until July.

"Jerry," he called. "I'll take one of those, if you don't mind."

The mayor's face lit up. "Really? Cool!"

"Yeah," she heard Owen reply. "Why not?"

More hands went up and good-natured ribbing followed as Jerry passed out information sheets to those who volunteered. From Meg's point of view, it looked as if every single man in the county was now anxious to go on a date.

"I don't believe this," Meg whispered to Lucia. "Some of these guys are at least seventy."

"Use it or lose it," her friend replied. "And it looks like your rancher friend saved the day."

Ideas were all she had. And when a person had nothing — no money or home or family — then ideas could grow bigger and bigger. Or at least seem like really good ideas, even when they're not.

Tonight was one of those ideas gone wrong. Shelly stood on a patch of sandy dirt at the end of the sidewalk in front of the community center and watched the last of the people leave the building. She shivered, but more from disappointment than cold. She'd borrowed Meg's mother's coat, an ivory fake fur that had seen better days. It fell to just above her ankles and hung off her shoulders, but it was so cozy and warm that Shelly could have used it as a blanket if she was still on the bus.

She hadn't wanted to borrow the fancy black leather blazer or the down ski jacket. No, something old was just fine with her. She didn't think her boss would mind, but Meg wouldn't approve of her standing alone in the dark watching people head to their parked cars or across the street to the bar. In fact, now that the mayor — he'd said to call him Jerry — was locking the front door to the center, the bar was the only storefront with lights on.

Meg and Mrs. Swallow had been some of the first people to leave the meeting. They'd left through a side door that Shelly was glad to know about. After all, she'd had the brilliant idea to watch to see if Sonny came to town.

On one hand, she wanted to find him more than anything she'd ever wanted in the entire world. She'd imagined the smile on his face when he saw her, his disbelief that she was really in front of him, his happiness about the baby. *Sweet Shelly,* he'd say. *I've been looking everywhere for you. I thought you'd disappeared forever.*

Or, *Come on, girl! Git over here and give*

me a kiss!

On the other hand, if Sonny had gone to the meeting, would that have meant he was looking to meet a woman from California?

Shelly told herself it was a darn good thing that he hadn't been in Willing tonight.

CHAPTER SEVEN

"What just happened?" Meg slid onto an empty stool at the bar of the Dahl and leaned one elbow on the scarred wooden counter. She didn't really expect Lucia to answer, because she'd asked the same question three times while they had hurried across the street after the meeting concluded. Jerry had still been pumping his fist in triumph as they'd slipped out the side door and into the cold.

"You need a drink. How about a glass of wine?" Lucia stood next to her and waved to Aurora, who wore a black T-shirt decorated with orange pumpkins. She was opening bottles of Moose Drool, the week's special, according to the sign on the counter.

"Now there's someone who would be good at this whole thing," Meg grumbled. "I'll bet she knows these guys' issues better than I do."

"That I doubt. And besides, she and Jerry

don't get along."

"But . . . what just happened?"

"Among other things," Lucia announced, looking positively thrilled, "Owen Mac-Gregor was flirting with you."

Meg shook her head. "You know well enough that's not what I'm talking about."

"It should be. I have a few questions about that, but I have a feeling we're going to need privacy." She assessed Meg. "Are you okay? You look a little flushed."

"I could be going into shock," she muttered, touching her hot cheeks with her fingertips.

"Just back Jerry into a corner and tell him you won't do it," Lucia said. "Though I don't know why you wouldn't want to."

"Hey, ladies." The Dahl's owner and bartender appeared in front of them. "Girls' night out?"

"It is now," Lucia said. "Nice shirt. I suppose you've heard all about the TV show?"

"Only bits and pieces, thank goodness." Aurora was tall, blond and elegant. She had the kind of beauty that landed women in the *Sports Illustrated* swimsuit edition, which was only one of the rumors about her floating around. She didn't date, and Meg's theory was that none of the local men had the nerve to ask her out. Aurora simply didn't seem interested, leaving Meg to wonder if there was a mysterious long-distance relationship somewhere in Aurora's life. "I still can't believe I had to cancel karaoke night because of an idiotic 'special' town meeting."

"A shame about the karaoke," Lucia said, keeping a straight face. "Meg's been practicing."

"She's teasing," Meg said. "I wouldn't do that to you again."

"It wasn't that bad. Everyone should get to sing 'Ring of Fire' on their birthday," Aurora assured her. She looked toward the door, which kept opening to admit thirsty civic-minded men. "The idiot *mayor* —" she rolled her eyes to illustrate what she thought of that title "— just walked in looking like he won the lottery. What can I get you?"

"Just some white wine, I think. Pinot, please."

"You're not going to make me put ice in it, are you?"

"No. Tonight I'm going to drink it straight."

"Thank God."

"You're a wine snob," Meg said, as Lucia grinned and ordered the same thing.

"I don't believe in watering the liquor,"

Aurora countered, smiling. "But yes, I'm a bit of a wine freak. And as soon as I get this crowd served and happy, you're going to tell me why you looked like a trapped rabbit. I'll start a tab for you."

"Trapped rabbit?" she repeated, but the bartender's attention had focused on other customers, and the bar began to fill with loud baritone conversation.

Lucia took both of their wineglasses and headed for a table for two between the bar and the stage. "Hurry up, Miz Meg, before your students take all the seats."

"Miz Meg. For heaven's sake."

"It's not like you to be flustered like this." They slid into the two mismatched wooden chairs tucked into the corner, giving Meg a chance to survey the room. It wasn't a large bar, so even though they were in the back, Meg felt exposed to the many curious men who began to crowd around the tables against the far wall. The Dahl was one of her favorite buildings in town; its hand-hewn logs and the mirrored wall behind the worn bar gave it the character of an old saloon. An enormous stuffed bear stood in a corner near the entrance. Looking a little ragged, it wore a Montana State baseball cap and three strands of Mardi Gras beads. The Dahl had sat empty for almost a year before Aurora arrived in town and bought the place a couple of years ago. Wisely she had changed nothing, except for having the bathrooms updated and the glassware replaced.

"Here's to dating class!" Lucia held up her glass to clink against Meg's. "So you were actually asked what women want? I wish I'd been there."

"It was pretty funny. The men around the table looked overwhelmed and desperate and Jerry was so excited and really, really serious about Willing turning into a ghost town."

"He's right." Lucia took a sip of wine and looked down at her glass. "Things have changed since Tony and I moved here. And that was, what, ten years ago?" She didn't wait for an answer, but her expression had become serious and sad. "Mama's hinted about moving to Lewistown, or Billings, even. The library's closed and most of the stores are gone, except for the ones that sell fishing equipment and stuff for the tourists to buy. I'm driving there now for almost everything. I don't mind, except it's almost an hour and a half round trip, and that's when the roads are decent."

"I know," was all Meg could think to say.

"I want to open my own bakery someday,

but I can't do it here. Not the way things are going. At least in Lewistown I'd be closer to the city."

"You're a brilliant baker. You should be doing fancy wedding cakes instead of huckleberry muffins for me." She sipped her wine and thought about Main Street and how little she shopped in the few stores left. "I'm sorry. I know there's talk of the elementary school closing, but Jerry won't let that happen. And maybe this whole publicity scheme will work."

"I love it here. You know that."

Meg thought for a long moment as the din in the bar increased. "Let's make a big pastry display in the café. Something special, for when the women arrive."

"If the men don't appeal to them, the chocolate will?"

"Something like that." Meg tried not to think of what life in Willing would be like without Lucia and her boys. "And while we're here, let's come up with a list of things for the guys to know."

Lucia brightened. "Good idea."

"I don't want to live in a ghost town, either," she said. "Jerry has officially scared me to death."

"Speaking of scary," Lucia said. "Look who's over there with the town council."

Meg saw Owen, a beer in his hand, listening to Hip talk. The usually silent wood-carver pointed to the oval stand on which the bear, his paws up and ready to take on an imaginary enemy, was mounted. Owen leaned over to see and then nodded. Soon four other men stood staring up at the bear and one of them slapped Owen on the back. General laughter followed. "He certainly looks at home," she said.

"Why wouldn't he?"

"It hasn't been his home for a long time. He went away to college. After his father died, he and his mother left the ranch and never came back."

"I heard he's been home for a few weeks now," Lucia pointed out. "Maybe he'll get the ranch running again, employ a few people."

They were interrupted by Jerry, who strutted over with a handful of papers. "Here they are," he announced. "Your new students!"

"You railroaded me," Meg said as Aurora joined them.

"Sorry about that. These are desperate times," he replied. "A man's gotta do what a man's gotta do."

"Wow," Aurora said. "You have such a way with words."

"Give it a rest, will you? I can't do anything about the parking lot till spring." He turned back to Meg and Lucia. "How about Saturday afternoon? At the café. Put together a buffet for afterward and I'll pay for it."

"Okay." She took the papers, noting they looked like job applications.

"I figure if there's free food, they're bound to show up on time. At least that's what I'm hoping, because we don't have time to waste. I'll go put out the word. Four o'clock?"

"Sure."

He backed away as Aurora glared at him, then turned and hurried over to Owen's crowd by the grizzly. Aurora gestured to a nearby customer and he gave her his chair, which she dragged over to the table. "You realize this will never work."

Meg took another sip of wine. "I've decided it's the chance of a lifetime. I get to shape them, like clay. Like writing on a clean slate."

"Starting from scratch," Lucia chirped.

"A blank canvas."

"Blank, all right." Aurora eyed two young members of the council and the boyfriend Joanie had recently dumped, who stood talking nearby. "Pete Lyons looks like he

141

slept in his clothes, Cam keeps belching and Les — sweet Les — is hiding under his hat."

"You're welcome to get involved," Meg said, pulling a pen out of her purse. She eyed the stack of forms. "There must be thirty, thirty-five hopeful bachelors here."

Lucia drained her glass, set it on the table and took a wad of papers from Meg. She divided them in half and handed a stack to Aurora. "I'll bet every single one of them has asked you out."

"Or is afraid to," Meg added.

"I'm running a business," Aurora said. "Not looking for a boyfriend." She rolled her eyes. "Does anyone use the word 'boyfriend' anymore?"

"You're not looking for a relationship," Lucia stated.

"Not even close." Aurora shuddered.

Meg wondered what Owen had thought of Aurora Jones when he'd walked into the Dahl tonight. With her long legs, tight jeans, intricately stitched Western boots and platinum hair to her waist, Aurora inspired awe. The pumpkin-print T-shirt was definitely out of character, but it made her look deceptively accessible when she was anything but. Meg guessed she was about thirty-five, but her age remained as mysterious as her past.

"I must invent a new drink," the bar owner mused. "How does Lost Cause sound?"

Meg pretended to read through the forms. Owen's wasn't in her batch, but she'd make sure to get them all to take home with her. She dared a glance across the room, but his back was to her. Owen still hadn't looked her way. She told herself she was relieved.

"I feel sorry for these guys," Lucia said. "They must be embarrassed. It's not as if it's their fault they don't have anyone to go out with."

"This lot? Embarrassed?" Aurora looked around the room. "Not that I've ever noticed."

Cam belched again and the others shook their heads and laughed, though Les shot a look at the women to see if they'd heard.

"We'll need to work on table manners." Lucia took Meg's pen and made a note in one of the margins.

"I'll do that Saturday. Are you making a list?"

"Yep. Grooming is another issue. I can help with their clothes, get them looking presentable. I imagine the show is going to want them to look like rugged Montana men, but —"

"Cleaner," Aurora finished for her. "They

tend to stay in their dirty work clothes, no matter what."

Meg took the pen back and scribbled a note to herself. "Good point. I won't do their laundry, but we'll have a step-by-step tutorial at the Laundromat. I'll do a special demonstration on stain removal."

"Yeah," Aurora drawled. "A man with a Tide pen is a real turn-on."

Lucia looked up. "Okay, if you're so smart, you can make a list of the things that turn women on."

"I'd like that," she surprised them by saying. "But I have to get back to work and make some money now. I'll email it to you. Both of you."

"Thanks."

Aurora hesitated after she stood. "I'll get you two more glasses of wine. Are either of you coming to the quilt show?"

"I am," Lucia said.

"Me, too." Meg looked up from her notes. "Why?"

The woman blushed. "I'll have a quilt there. It's my first."

"Congratulations," Lucia managed to say. She seemed taken aback at the thought of glamorous, nondomestic Aurora with a needle and thread in her hand.

"I'm going Saturday," Meg added, "after

the breakfast rush. I can't wait to see it. I didn't know you were a quilter."

"Janet Ferguson talked me into joining last winter. I didn't have anything else to do . . . and then I started learning how to appliqué and I really loved —"

"Aurora! Can we get another round of beer over here?"

"The natives are restless," she muttered before hurrying away. "I'm coming! You're not going to die of thirst, you know!"

"This," Lucia said, draining Meg's half-filled wineglass, "has been a very interesting evening."

Meg felt a little overwhelmed herself. "Yes," she agreed. "We obviously need to get out more."

He used to love teasing her. Her cheeks would pink up and she'd bite her bottom lip and stare up at him until he burst into laughter and wrapped her in his arms. Her muffled giggles against his chest had been the biggest turn-on of his twenty years.

Now he watched as she laughed in the corner with a black-haired woman he'd seen once before corralling three little black-haired boys into an old minivan.

He wanted to talk to her, to ask her about her life. Was she happy, did she ever dream of living anyplace else? Why had she stopped loving him so quickly?

Instead he was stuck listening to old high school football stories and hunting adventures and speculation about the silver-haired owner of the Dahl. She seemed pleasant enough. Cool, classy, high maintenance. Besides, he looked at her and felt no spark, no passion. She'd given him a beer and taken his money. And that was the end of that, fortunately. He hadn't come to town to get involved with anyone.

He refused to make the time for any kind of *relationship,* the word women loved to use these days. Even Meg, the first girl to break his heart, couldn't break it again.

Owen watched her follow her friend through the dwindling crowd and out of the bar. A number of people called good-night to them. And then he said his own good-byes and made his way outside. He told himself he was simply tired of the crowd and the noise and the overheated room. As he stepped onto the sidewalk, he saw Meg and Lucia go in two different directions, to two different vehicles.

Meg unlocked the door of a Toyota High-lander, which happened to be parked in front of his truck.

"Meg."

She turned around without opening the car door, but she didn't say anything.

He shoved his hands in his jacket pockets and walked around her car. "You've taken on a big job," he said, feeling foolish. He hoped she didn't think he was stalking her.

"I suppose you think it's all a big joke."

"I —"

"But it was good of you to volunteer." She didn't seem angry. But with women, who could tell?

"What am I supposed to think is a joke?" He kept his voice soft.

"Everything. The town. People will be moving out. People *have* moved out." She waved her hand as if to indicate the entire street. "It's not the same, and . . . never mind." She turned away and grabbed the door handle.

"I didn't know," was all he could think to say. He put his hand on her shoulder. "Stop, will you? Just for a minute?" She hesitated, and then looked at him again with expressive brown eyes. "You stayed here, in town," he said. "Why?"

"I left," she answered. "But I came back."

That hadn't answered his question.

"What about you?" she continued, before he could ask her why again. "Why did you change your mind?" His confusion must have been obvious, because she clarified the question. "About doing the TV show."

Owen tried to smile, but it felt awkward when she looked at him so seriously. "Okay, that's a fair question." He hesitated for a few seconds as he tried to figure out how to avoid the truth and come up with something she'd believe. "There's a streak," he began, "in my family. Do you remember Ed, my father's older brother?"

"No."

"Exactly. The man kept to himself. My grandfather was the same way, no interest in people, just cattle and horses and dogs and basically anything on four feet. I don't know how or why he ever got married, but she — my grandmother — died young."

Meg waited, listening. He still had his hand on her shoulder, so he slid it down her arm and up again. The material was dark and soft, some kind of sweater that zipped up to her chin and brushed her earlobes. Meg stepped back and Owen dropped his hand to his side. The knot of tension that had tormented his gut all evening expanded.

"So," he continued, "I've been getting a lot of phone calls, folks wanting to know if I'm going to get involved."

"You know how small towns are."

"Yes, I certainly do." He chanced a smile but she didn't return it. "I kept saying no."

"Go on. What does this have to do with the streak?"

"Yeah. The streak. I looked around the house today and saw Ed. Saw my grandfather. I'm not sure you'd call them hermits, but whatever they were was something I didn't want to be. And I could see it happening."

"How?" She took another step back, as if she wanted to remove herself from the conversation.

"I've been living out there. With my dog. The house is, well, the house is the same as it was when I was a kid. And not in a good way."

"And you're afraid you'll turn into Ed."

"It's a real concern," he admitted, embarrassed now for having said of all of this. Maybe he'd come closer to the truth after all. Maybe she'd go home and laugh to herself about Owen MacGregor's fear of becoming a hermit. He tried for levity. "I talked it all over with my dog and we agreed I should get out more."

"I don't —" She stopped. He caught a glimpse of disappointment before she turned away from him, so he didn't say anything else. It wasn't as if there was more to add.

He opened her car door, made sure she was tucked inside and even drove past the café to make sure she'd arrived at her cabin safely. Only four blocks, but it was the polite thing to do.

He had no reason to be less than polite, no reason to be more than that. They had a past together, with memories and pain and sweetness and heartache. Revisiting that summer meant remembering all of it — his father's death, his mother's despair, the explosion of everything Owen thought his life would be — and he didn't want to relive it. He never wanted to go through anything like that again.

Meg and Shelly studied the enormous, intricate quilt hanging in front of them. Stitched entirely of small triangles in shades of blue and white, it formed an impressive star.

The girl leaned closer to frown at the tiny running stitches crisscrossing the fabric. "I thought they only did this, you know, in the old days."

"You mean on the wagon train?"

"Yeah." She darted a quick look at her boss. "No offense. It's nice of you to, uh,

150

take me to see this stuff."

"You're welcome. I'm glad for the company."

"I wonder how long it took to make this."

"Three years." At Shelly's startled look, Meg added, "It's in the program."

"The quilter must be a very patient person."

"Yes, she must." Meg couldn't fathom sewing all those triangles together either, but she loved to look at them. The community center was filled with rows of quilts attached to wooden stands, hanging from walls or pinned to bulletin boards. Each one was different from the rest.

"Sometimes you don't have any choice except patience," Shelly mumbled.

"Is that the way you feel? That you don't have any choice?" Meg asked, remembering how she'd waited to hear from Owen after he'd been sent back to college. She'd poured her heart out in a letter, but he hadn't replied. So much for patience.

The girl shrugged her thin shoulders. She wore an old cotton blouse of Meg's, and Meg knew that under it, Shelly's jeans were unzipped to allow for her expanding belly. Al had donated a belt big enough to get her through the entire pregnancy.

"You have choices." Meg walked over to

the next quilt, a modern red-and-white log cabin. Aurora had outdone herself.

"Wow, this is cool," Shelly said, gazing at the bartender's small quilt.

"You can go home to your family," Meg suggested. "Your mother? She must be worried about you."

"Not likely."

"Is there any family you and the baby could live with, you know, until you get on your feet?"

"I wish there was." The girl sighed. "But that's not gonna happen. I don't want my little guy here to grow up like that."

"Like what, Shelly?" Meg pictured neglect, abuse, divorce, poverty — all sorts of situations in which a child would suffer. But the girl didn't answer, instead moving sideways to another displayed quilt.

"I think it's a boy, you know." She patted her growing bump. "He's gonna need a father."

"Have you thought about adoption, then?"

Shelly's blue eyes widened. "You don't think I'll find Sonny, do you? You don't think he'll want us!"

Several elderly women examining a nearby antique quilt turned to see what the commotion was. Meg put her hand on Shelly's thin back and moved her toward the metal chairs along the side of the room.

"Come on," she said. "Sit."

Shelly sat, but she blinked back tears and hugged the show's program to her chest. "I know I can find him. I just need some luck, that's all."

"Look, honey, you need a lot more than luck." *Such as a loving husband with a job, a man who will be a loving father and provide a home for his little family.* Somehow Meg didn't think Sonny, probably Rodeo King of the One-Night Stands, was likely to turn up or step up. "I'm still not clear why you ended up on a bus in Montana. Where do you think this guy is, precisely?"

"He told me Willing was a cool town."

"But he didn't live in Willing when you met him?"

"No. He'd worked in Lewistown. And Big Timber. And he said he had family in Billings, but I checked on the internet and Facebook and couldn't find his name anywhere."

"And you're sure he told you his real name?"

She nodded. "It was on the program. The rodeo program."

"But why the bus?"

"It seemed like a good idea at the time," the girl sniffed. "I don't have a car."

Meg tried again. "But where were you going on the bus? Your destination?"

"Billings," she said. "And then Denver. Sonny said he always wanted to live in Denver."

"Denver is a long way from Willing," Meg pointed out. This girl was either incredibly naive or totally desperate. Or both.

"Lucia's taking me to Lewistown with her on Tuesday, after she takes the boys to school. There's a library there, with yearbooks. So I can see if Sonny grew up around here."

Meg nodded. "Well, that's a plan."

Shelly wiped her eyes and took a deep breath. "Yeah, well, right now it's the only one I've got."

"Men get in trouble when they have opinions," George confided, taking a sip of the hot coffee Meg just poured for him. "Have you ever noticed that?"

"Yes, I think I have." Meg wanted to laugh, but one look at the old man's expression as he sat on the stool on the other side of her counter told her that he was serious. "There seem to be a lot of opinions around here lately."

The breakfast crowd had been surprisingly small this Monday morning, which gave

Meg more time to browse through building supply websites on her laptop. She'd moved a napkin holder, salt and pepper shakers and a ketchup bottle to make room for her notes. She was trying to come up with a renovation budget, just in case this whole Hollywood thing actually worked out.

"My wife has a few. Got one right here." George handed her a yellow sheet of paper with a daisy border.

Meg picked it up and read:

He should bring his wife coffee in bed.
A mother-in-law should not visit longer than a week.
The man takes out the garbage.
Never go to bed angry.

Meg had received plenty more advice from the women in town. Those who had been married for a long time approved of the attempt to find wives for the local bachelors. Others thought it was a joke and highly humorous. Meg had heard grumbling from a couple of single women who weren't happy with the idea of competition coming to town. But then again, neither one of them planned to settle down anytime soon. And like Meg herself, neither one was in love.

Meg worried about Lucia, whose own

155

husband had been killed in Afghanistan when she was three months pregnant with her third child. All this talk of husbands couldn't be easy for her friend. She'd loved Tony Swallow, of that Meg was certain. Meg could only hope that Lucia was telling the truth when she said she would be relieved to be left alone by her neighbors. She hated hurting anyone's feelings, but dating was out of the question.

The quilters had even held a special meeting at the center Sunday afternoon over coffee and zucchini bread. There was talk of making a wedding quilt for next year's raffle and they'd also put together a pile of suggestions for Meg's class. It seemed that there were more opinions about husbands than there were deer in Montana.

Don't think you're going to change him that much.

Make sure he loves his mother, but not too much. You don't want to marry a mama's boy.

A good husband doesn't say "I told you so."

A good husband calls home if he's going to be late.

Please teach them to pick up their socks. Even though that doesn't sound important, it can get aggravating, especially when you get older and have a bad back.

No gambling, smoking or drinking.

Pick a man who will be a good lover and a good father and a good friend.

Meg liked that one. Janet had pressed that slip of paper into her hand, saying, "I suppose this is advice more for women, but men should know what's expected of them, don't you think?"

The married men were free with their advice, too.

"Don't walk across a clean floor. And don't slice into a cake unless you ask first, in case it's for taking somewhere. That's all I've got," George said. "Shouldn't get me into any trouble with the missus, I don't think."

"They should put signs on them," her customer at the closest table called. "Cakes, I mean."

"There are a lot of ways to get in trouble," Gary Petersen muttered around his grilled cheese. "That's why I've been divorced twice."

"And because you drove truck," the FedEx driver beside George at the counter said, then tipped back his coffee.

"True. I always liked being on the road better 'n being home." He called to Meg, "Make sure you tell the single guys not to get married unless they're gonna stick around!"

"We're concentrating more on dating," she attempted to point out. "Etiquette. Dancing. Things like that."

"And seduction, I'll bet," he said, giving her a little wink.

"Boy, howdy," George moaned. "You can bet there are a lot of rules to that, too!"

CHAPTER EIGHT

"Look at this." Jerry gestured toward the crowd. "We're making history."

"No pressure, then." Meg continued to organize the handouts Jerry had printed for her. She and Lucia had spent hours putting the information together. They'd debated using Aurora's suggestions and decided to eliminate the more suggestive "what women want from men" ideas.

"She might want to teach an advanced class," Lucia had said.

"Maybe it should be an optional hand-out."

"Even better. We don't want to scare them off."

Men were everywhere. They trickled into the café, sauntering in from the parking lot, arriving early for coffee. Some looked resigned or embarrassed, others excited. They were all ages, shapes and sizes. And there were thirty-two of them. Most of them looked as if they were going camping or just returning from three days in the wild.

Meg recognized all of them, knew most of them by name. At least three were older than forty-five, Tracy's age limit, but Meg assumed they hadn't wanted to be left out of the excitement. Or the free buffet.

"We should have had name tags," Jerry muttered.

"Too formal."

"Do you have enough handouts?"

"Absolutely."

"Want me to start passing them out?"

"No. I'm going to give them out at the end of the night, for them to take home."

"But —"

"I want them listening, Jerry, not reading." The mayor was going to drive her crazy before the workshop even began. When he wasn't pacing, he studied the information she'd assembled. When he wasn't reorganizing her papers, he worried about what could go wrong. At the moment he was picking imaginary lint off his sweater and mumbling about aftershave.

"Okay. Whatever you say. How do I look? I wanted to set a good example."

"Navy blue suits you," she said, wishing he'd take his nerves to another side of the room. "A dark forest green would look good on you, too."

"I don't know," he pondered. "With red hair I could look like a carrot. Where's Luce? She's doing clothing tips, right?"

"She'll be here in time for the speed dating session." Against her better judgment, Lucia had agreed to take part, after she'd made Meg promise to keep her away from lovesick Joey.

He scanned the crowd again. "Maybe we should have another class called How Not to Dress Like Paul Bunyan."

"Jerry, there's decaf coffee in the urn over there." She pointed to the rectangular table in the back of the dining room. "Go. Help yourself."

He pulled out his fancy cell phone, read a text message and then quickly texted back. "Tracy," he explained after he finished. "She wants me to send her some pictures."

"When is she coming?"

"That's still up in the air. I'm hoping for Halloween. The town always looks good on Halloween, with the party and all."

"That doesn't give us much time." She looked at her list. Manners, grooming, conversation, dating, dancing, children, romance and the importance of listening. "If anyone can do it, it's you," he said, scanning the crowd. "We've got a good turnout.

161

Hey, there's my star now." He waved to Owen and took off across the room to greet him.

Star? Well, Meg supposed Owen would be. He had a confident way about him that attracted attention without his having to do or say anything. He made her more nervous than she already was.

"Meg?" Shelly, a blue-striped apron tied around her waist, held a tray of sliced sourdough bread, salami and assorted cheeses covered with plastic wrap. "Do you want this on the table now?"

"Not yet. Not until I get to the part about food." Shelly had insisted on working tonight, and Meg could guess why. "Is he here?"

The girl blushed. "No."

"Leave when you get tired, okay? And if anyone named Sonny shows up, I'll come get you."

"Thanks, but I kinda want to ask Les about the rodeo. I heard he was on the circuit." She set the tray down and wiped her hands on her apron. "I met his grandma at the quilt show. She told me."

"You'll have to hurry." Meg glanced at the clock above the door. She'd start in about five minutes. It wasn't going to be easy to create the perfect men in two hours, but

162

she was going to give it her best shot.

In and out. He'd make an appearance because he'd said he would. In the name of doing his civic duty, he'd filled out the dating form.

He'd felt like an idiot, but he'd done it. He didn't want to go out with anyone, didn't want to meet the love of his life while cameras were rolling — if such a thing existed, which he doubted. He didn't intend to add to the population of Willing by getting married and making babies.

Certainly not that.

Owen stepped inside the café and found a seat at an empty table by the door. With luck he would be able to sneak out after half an hour, tops. He looked at his watch. The meeting would start in six minutes. He'd timed it perfectly. He unzipped his jacket and tossed it on the empty chair to his left. The mayor had drawn quite a crowd, but most of them had gathered near the refreshment stand and a platter piled high with buffalo wings. Owen wondered if Chili Dawgs would still be open later. Les, the youngest member of the town council, took the empty seat next to him.

"Wow, hi, Mr. MacGregor." He didn't bother to hide his surprise.

"Owen, please." He shook the young man's hand. "Big crowd tonight."

"Yeah." Les looked around the room and drummed his fingers on the table. "Have you seen Shelly?"

Ah. Owen tried not to wince. "No, I haven't."

"Huh." The kid continued to scan the crowd, and Owen leaned back in his chair and decided to mind his own business. *Kid,* he wanted to say, *she's too young, too pregnant and too eager to find her boyfriend.*

Which made entirely too much sense and of course would not matter in the slightest. Owen felt a hundred years old and thought about leaving right then and there. Unfortunately Jerry chose that moment to step up to the microphone.

"If you'd all find seats," he began. "We'll go over some basic dating information and then, while we're enjoying Meg's famous pot roast, I'll outline the rest of the agenda. Any questions before we —"

"When are these Hollywood people coming?"

"How many?"

"How old?"

"How young?"

"How do we get on television? Do we get paid?"

"Do we get to pick who we go out with?"

"What are we going to do on these dates?"

The questions kept coming, with Jerry responding to all of them the same way: "That will be decided by the producer and her staff." He finally turned to Meg, who stood next to him with her list in her hand.

"First things first," Jerry said. "Let's learn how to impress our future guests. Meg, want to start?"

Meg looked up at the audience. "Have you ever wondered why a woman you liked wouldn't go out with you a second time?"

No one said a word.

Then one hand rose in the air. Pete Lyons, the school bus driver, asked, "What about if she won't go out with me the *first* time?"

"We'll get to that," she promised. "We'll talk about flirting and making conversation and making a woman feel comfortable around you, but for now, let's go over how to make a good impression when you're on that first date, presumably with the women from the show, all right?"

"Sure."

"Okay. Here are some of the suggestions women have given me." She took a deep breath. "Don't talk about your ex-girlfriend or your ex-wife. Don't pick food out of your teeth with your fingernails. Don't belch, or

165

do it quietly and say 'excuse me.' Open the car door for her. Open *doors* for her. Don't stare at her chest. Make sure your clothes are clean, you wear deodorant, you've brushed your teeth and you have not poured on aftershave lotion by the tablespoon. Do not talk badly about your mother. Do not talk badly about her mother, if you happen to know her mother."

Owen assumed Meg had contributed that one herself. He'd personally heard enough rumors about Loralee to fill a tabloid.

Meg took a sip of water while the men sat in silence. Someone whined, "Are we dating the queen or what?"

She looked up from the list. "Are you dating *anyone*?"

Silence greeted the question. Several men began to sidle toward the door, so Owen stood up and placed his back to it. They'd have to get through him first.

"Sure seems like we don't do anything right," someone else muttered.

"I need a drink."

"When do we eat?"

"Cripe, how many rules are there?"

"No kidding. I could use a beer right about now."

Les turned to Owen. "My grandmother taught me a lot of this. But it's hard to remember sometimes, especially if a guy doesn't have a steady girlfriend."

Owen agreed. "Takes practice. My mother was a stickler for good manners."

The chorus of protests continued. "I thought we'd just get a drink or somethin'."

"Can I take her to the movies instead?"

"If she has blue eyes, I don't care if she's a vegetarian."

"This is getting pretty serious all of a sudden. They're gonna ask us this stuff on television?"

"Why? Can't we just have fun?" This question came from a young man with a cast on his arm.

"Sure," Meg said. "Dating should be fun."

"Sounds serious to me," he said. "I'm only twenty-four, too young to settle down and talk about politics."

"You're right." His glasses were broken and taped at the temples. He looked as if he'd been in a fight and lost.

"So Patsy, Lucia, Iris, Joanie and Aurora are joining us for dinner," Meg announced. "But before we eat, we'll do some informal speed dating."

That announcement got a mixed response.

"Okay, okay," Jerry said. "We won't call it speed dating. You have a number — remember the number you were given when you arrived? There's a letter on it, too."

Owen glanced at the notecard with "P-2" printed on it in black marker. Patsy Parrish sat down at a table for four and fluffed her golden hair around her shoulders.

"P is for Patsy, L for Lucia, I for Iris, A for Aurora, J for Joanie. Simple, right?" The mayor paused while the men found their cards. Owen folded his in half and slipped it into the pocket of his jeans as the mayor continued.

"Try to keep your conversations to ten minutes. The ladies will help you come up with things to talk about if you're unsure. Just relax and have fun. Just be yourselves," he added. "Smile, even."

No one smiled. Les looked sick. Owen eyed the four women who'd come in the side door and watched Jerry move to block the second obvious exit. Bribed by the promise of a home-cooked meal and distracted by the female volunteers who took their places at five empty tables, the bachelors of Willing did as they were told. They took numbers, they lined up, four deep in front of the ladies' tables according to Jerry's directions. They seemed determined to do their best to be social.

Jerry was in charge of the timer. "I'll tell you when your time is up. Then you move

168

to the end of the line at the next table over. After dinner we'll have the ladies share what they enjoyed most about the conversations. Everybody cool with that?"

A couple of men replied positively, Jerry said, "Go!" and Meg fled to a booth in order to go over her notes. She didn't think she'd done a very good job so far, but she wasn't sure how to fix things.

And she didn't expect Owen to follow her.

"Do you mind?" He didn't wait for answer before settling into the booth across from her.

"Aren't you supposed to be speed dating?"

"I'm avoiding it."

"Nervous around women, are you?" Meg ignored him and looked back at her lists. Over the next few weeks they'd have to cover a lot of subjects. The bachelors she'd seen on dating shows had been charming, smooth and confident. Like Owen. If he was still around when Hollywood came calling.

"Why aren't you talking to the men?"

Meg didn't look up. "I'm avoiding it," she echoed. "And I'm terrible at small talk."

"Try," he urged. "Or do we pretend we've never met?"

"Of course not." What a ridiculous question. He folded his hands on the table. "You could tell me why you're here, though."

"I thought I did." His smile was brief.

"Uncle Ed," she said. "Hermit streak. Sorry, I'm not buying the hermit phobia as the reason you're getting involved in this whole thing."

"Okay, that's only part of it."

She waited.

"I was reminded," he said eventually, "of my father."

Meg resisted the urge to touch his hand. "He was a very special man."

"And he would have expected more of me, I'm sure," was Owen's answer. He looked around the room, at the other men chatting with the volunteers or waiting patiently in line for their turn to practice their attempts to charm. Jerry drank from a plastic water bottle and kept an eye on his stopwatch. Lucia looked sympathetic, while Patsy flirted and smiled. He couldn't see the faces of the other women, but he'd guess that Aurora would appear intimidating to most men. Someone laughed.

And then Owen's gaze returned to Meg. "My father wouldn't have been pleased to see the town fighting for its life without a MacGregor leading the charge."

"I'm sorry," she said. "I didn't get to talk to you at the house, after the funeral."

"I hid in the horse barn," he admitted.

"I looked there," Meg said.

"You were the last person I wanted to see."

"I would have told you I was sorry. About everything."

"It wouldn't have helped," he snapped. "That's not what I wanted from you and you know it."

That certainly put her in her place. There was a brief silence as Meg wondered what to say and decided to say nothing. He'd hurt her, as he'd meant to.

"Time's up," Jerry called. "Everyone move up one, number twos take your place at the table and those who just practiced move to the end of the line at another table!" He looked around the room until he found Owen.

"Come on," he said, waving him over. "Owen, what's your number?"

Owen held up two fingers.

"You're up, then."

Meg examined her notes once again. She didn't want to watch him leave the booth, didn't want to see which woman he was going to talk to. She was sure he would be charming and polite, attentive and maybe even a little self-deprecating.

He could teach the class himself, and maybe he should.

"How's it going?" This time it was Jerry joining her. "What do you think?"

They both turned to watch the speed dating tables. "I made sure Joey got Aurora first," Meg said.

"So he wouldn't drool all over Lucia?"

"Exactly."

"And now he's talking with Iris," Jerry observed. "And she's drooling all over him."

"Ah, romance. . . ."

They both laughed. The men who were not at the tables helped themselves to pretzels and beer, cheese and crackers, water and smoked sausage. The noise level ratcheted up a few notches during the final minutes of session two.

"Time!" Jerry hustled out of the booth and issued more directions. Meg left her notes and went to the refreshment table for water. She intended to circulate among the bachelors to see if anyone had questions, but Owen reached past her for a glass.

"The summer kitchen still looks the same," he said, pouring water from the pitcher into his glass. "I should paint it, put in a new floor or something."

"Or not," she replied. "I can't picture it modernized."

Silence.

"So," he said, his voice steady and cold.

"You're going to renovate the cabins?"

"I hope so. They've been empty for years. They just need so much work, but I think I can afford to have the bathrooms redone and buy some beds and mattresses. And rugs, maybe."

"They look well built."

"We had the electricity rewired ten years ago when we had big plans to run a motel again, but then Loralee lost interest and I was too busy with the café to do it myself." She noticed Lucia laughing at something Les was saying. The young cowboy seemed more relaxed than she'd expected he would be. "Shouldn't you be making small talk somewhere?"

"No," he said. "I've done my part."

She wished he'd kill time with someone else, but Meg attempted to match his clipped tone. "How did it go with Patsy?"

He shrugged. "She wanted to know why I never asked her out when we were in high school."

"Seriously?"

"No. She was just giving me a hard time."

Meg took a sip of water. "I'd better circulate," she said. "See how the guys are doing."

"Time!" Jerry again, on top of things with his stopwatch and his enthusiasm. The men did as they were told. Jack Dugan brought Iris a beer. Aurora fanned herself with a napkin. Someone turned the music up.

"Excuse me." Meg took a step away from Owen, but he wasn't done with the conversation. He'd used up any charm he had with Patsy, she supposed, because he acted like a man who wanted to pick a fight.

"How is your little runaway mom doing? I see she's still in town."

"She's helping me out in exchange for a place to stay." At his raised eyebrow, she explained, "She's living in my mother's cabin."

"And where is the lovely Loralee these days?"

"Golfing in Tucson. She lives there now."

"Ah. Married again."

"No."

Jerry joined them. "One more round, then we'll wrap this up and feed them before we do another set of speed dates, okay?"

Meg picked up her notes while Jerry called for attention and outlined the rest of the evening. While the last session took place, she made sure the buffet was ready. She'd managed to avoid Owen for the rest of the night, and she thought he was avoiding her, too. Which was just fine with her.

Much later, Meg hurried into the warmth

of her tiny home and locked the door behind her before switching on a light. She shrugged off her coat, turned on the heat and walked through the L-shaped kitchen and living area to her bedroom. There, in the back of her cabin, she sat on her quilt-covered bed and untied her practical brown shoes.

The class had gone well, better than she'd expected, though she clearly had to stop telling the men what not to do and instead show examples of how to succeed.

Aurora and Lucia had agreed that the men needed their egos boosted. Patsy and Iris figured it was a lost cause, but they'd had a good time. And Joanie? She wanted Cam kicked out of the class because he wasn't sober. She had a point, and Jerry had agreed to consider it.

But why had Owen really come tonight? Was this some kind of game to him?

She'd refused the chance to marry him so long ago. Oh, she'd gone along with the wonderful, passionate fantasy of running away together and eloping. Against her practical nature and against all of her plans to get out of Willing and educate herself, she'd jumped into Owen's truck to ride off into a very married sunset.

And when his father, that strong, kind

man who had only wanted what was best for both of them, had caught up with them at the Gas 'N' Go, Meg had realized she wasn't ready. She was too young.

They both were.

And obviously Owen had never forgiven her.

"Just tell me one thing," Loralee said immediately after Meg picked up the phone in her cabin the next afternoon. "Tell me I'm wrong, that I didn't hear that the MacGregor boy is back in town."

"Hi, Mom."

"Well?"

"He's no longer a boy. He's a thirty-four-year-old man now."

"I guess that answers my question. And I really don't care how old he is." Loralee sniffed. *"He broke my baby's heart."*

"And I broke his. I was only a teenager. Somebody was bound to break my heart sooner or later. It just happened to be him." Meg was pleased to sound so casual about it.

"You and I both know you had no business getting caught up with that family — Irene wasn't going to let her only son marry the kitchen help."

Meg sighed. Was she ever going to be allowed to forget what an idiot she'd been? Probably not.

"I was eighteen," she reminded her mother. "Now I'm thirty-two, remember? I think I can keep myself from eloping again."

"Well, I certainly hope so. On the other hand, he was a good-looking boy. And always seemed so polite. I never thought anything would come of it, but you were happy. For a while."

"I really don't want to talk about this anymore."

"I don't want you to get hurt."

"It's not going to happen. Stop worrying. Go play golf. Go to dinner with one of your new boyfriends."

"Wait until you're a mother, and then you'll understand."

Meg let that remark go by without a comment, because if her mother started in on how much she wanted grandchildren, the phone call would last longer than Meg could bear. "So how's Aunt Joan?"

"She's good. Oh, that reminds me. We shipped you a crate of oranges."

"Why?"

"So you can pretend they're pumpkins."

"And I would want to do that because?"

"They're orange. It's almost Halloween. Sprinkle some black licorice around and you'll have a nice decoration for the counter. I saw it on HGTV, but with those tiny pumpkins. Except we couldn't find any. Just oranges." And now Loralee had turned into Martha Stewart.

"Thank you. I'll get to work on that as soon as they arrive." She checked her watch. Shelly was helping the Petersen twins this morning, but there would still be a lot to do. "I have to get to the café soon, Mom. The Sunday-brunch crowd, remember?"

"Just a minute. When were you going to tell me about the dating show?"

"How did you know?"

"Jerry, the mayor, has a blog. This morning he wrote about last night's lesson on dating. He sounded very impressed. Why didn't you call me? I could fill a book, *two* books, on what I know about men."

And that, Meg thought, was one of the truest things her mother had ever said. "Then you know it's for publicity."

"Publicity?" Loralee chuckled. "I'm not sure why you're sprucing up the local men and handing them off to other women. Don't you want to keep one for yourself?"

"No," Meg said quickly. "How's your golf game?"

"I'm taking lessons now. From the pro at the country club. You wouldn't believe how tanned he is. Your aunt and I tried one of those booths where they spray you with a tan, you know?"

"I know."

"It looked good at first, there on the beach, but then it started to streak. Two days later we looked like zebras. Well —" she paused "— zebras with a skin disease."

Now, there was a picture Meg didn't want in her head.

"Mom, I really need to go."

"Fine. Promise me you'll stay away from that man."

"No problem," Meg said, remembering kisses, longer kisses, hotter kisses. Kisses on horseback, kisses in the hay barn. Kisses in the cattle shed, kisses in the truck. Kisses under the stars. Her chest hurt just thinking about it. She didn't want to remember, didn't want to feel that pain again. She wished he'd go back to DC, to his city life and his big world. She didn't want him tromping around in her life.

"Good," her mother said. "You're a lot smarter now than you used to be."

CHAPTER NINE

Women baffled him. Jerry Thompson could no longer delude himself into thinking he knew anything at all about the opposite sex. If he hadn't pinned his hopes, dreams and substantial bank account on bringing more women to town, he'd cancel the whole thing, take some aspirin for his pounding head and go to an isolated black-sand beach in Hawaii.

"But I *really* want to stay in one of those cute little places by the restaurant," Tracy insisted. "For the local *flavor,* Jer. For the *atmosphere.* "

Jerry held the phone away from his ear and pressed the speaker symbol. Her whining made his headache worse. "My house has plenty of atmosphere," he assured her. "It's an old white Victorian monstrosity next to a park with a statue of the town founder's cow."

"Tell me you're joking about the cow."

"We also have an atmospheric bed-and-breakfast," he said, attempting to distract her from the idea of staying in one of Meg Ripley's hideous old cabins. He didn't remember taking pictures of them, but he might have. And he'd assumed Meg would have months to renovate them. "You'll love it. It used to be the town brothel."

"That's nice, and we'll use it on the fantasy dates perhaps, but you know I don't care for B and Bs. I feel as if I'm a guest in someone's home. The last one I stayed at had Madame Alexander dolls everywhere. I swore to myself, *never again*."

"You can be a guest in my home, sweetheart. It'll be like old times."

"With my assistant and cameraman? Surely you're joking again."

"I'm serious. I have four bedrooms. You'll love it." He heard ice cubes and the fizzing of liquid. Tracy was still addicted to pomegranate-mango seltzer water, he supposed. He'd have to get several cases of it before she arrived.

"I like my own space. You know that. Tell me more about Halloween. It sounds festive, in the local bar and all. Will everyone in town be there?"

"Of course. It's always a good time. There's a raffle every year to see who wins

181

the right to decorate the grizzly bear."

"And the bear doesn't mind?"

Jerry had to stifle a laugh. "He's dead. Stuffed. Not stuffed like a stuffed animal you'd buy a kid, but stuffed and mounted, like a trout." Jerry wondered if he was about to have a stroke. Every blood vessel under his skull throbbed. He wanted her here, in his town. He wanted to show her what he was in the process of building. Tracy had a thing for powerful men.

"You don't have to be so patronizing," the former love of his life sniffed.

"I apologize." He would never, ever repeat this conversation to anyone. He'd be dodging teddy bears for years. They liked their little jokes around here.

"I accept your apology, of course, babe," she said, her voice light and cheerful again. "And I'll see you on the twenty-eighth. What is that? In two weeks?" Knowing Tracy, she was centered in her enormous bed with all of her work spread around her on a 100-percent-organic-cotton duvet, surrounded by 100-percent-organic pillows. It was the L.A. way.

"Yes." He sat very still on the sofa in his living room, where tall windows looked out over the lawn, an iron fence and the streetlights glowing on an empty street. Nothing ever happened on First Street, not even on a Saturday night, unless Hip drank too much and took a walk over to the park to sing to the marble cow.

"And you'll book us into three of those cabins?"

"They're not what you're used to, babe. I really recommend —"

"I thought we were going to be able to use them when we filmed! You said there would be a motel for the crew, didn't you?"

"I did," he admitted. "I thought you might like something a little fancier for yourself, that's all."

"Not this time," she said. "It might be fun, like camping."

"Sure. Like camping." He knew when he'd been ground into the dust. There was no sense in trying to change her mind. So they exchanged a bit of gossip, he answered questions about the weather, she exclaimed over the wonderful photos he'd texted and that was that.

Now that he'd confirmed she was actually coming to Willing, he would take a couple of aspirin, make a few phone calls and figure out a way to make Tracy's latest demands come true. He had a feeling it wouldn't be the last time. She was high maintenance, as well as gorgeous, sexy, smart — okay, except maybe for her ignorance of Montana . . . and wild animals in general — ambitious and self-absorbed.

In other words, the perfect woman for him.

Owen didn't really think he needed advice about dating, but over his Sunday-morning coffee he read the various tips in the hand-outs he'd brought home from class Thursday night. Over the course of two hours, Meg had hit the stunned men with more advice and rules than they could comprehend. He'd heard the quiet groans, the swearing under their breath and an uneasy shifting of bodies in chairs. He suspected many of the guys wondered if this was going to be worth it.

The frightening thing he'd realized that night was that he'd missed her. All these years, with school and work and building a life, and he hadn't known he'd missed little Margaret Ripley. He had tucked his youthful memories away, under the category of Stupid Kid Decisions.

Eloping at the age of twenty was definitely at the top of that list. And thank goodness no one except his parents and Meg's mother had ever found out. Somehow his father had managed to keep it between the five of them.

But he and Meg knew they had a history together. She might want to ignore that. Actually, she seemed to prefer it. He preferred ignoring it himself.

But that didn't change the fact that the two of them had to work together on this TV thing. Oh, he could put the ranch up for sale and get the heck out of the county, but the thought made him feel sick. He simply couldn't walk away from the ranch again, not yet.

He needed more time. He told himself he needed to clean up the place, sort through four generations of stuff. Even if he wasn't going to live here again, he couldn't walk away from his history.

Clothes, blah, blah. Be clean. Look clean. *Make sure your fly is zipped.* Yada yada.

Don't talk about your ex.

Fair enough, since he hadn't dated anyone in seven months. He'd never been married. He'd had two long-term relationships that had gone on too long before he'd realized he was not going to make a real diamond-ring commitment.

He'd wondered if there was something wrong with him that way. Each time he'd attempted to look into the future, there'd been no one he wanted by his side. Unlike his parents, in love until his father's final, deadly heart attack, he'd never felt he needed a partner for life.

Well, only that once. At the foolish age of twenty. And with enough testosterone coursing through his body to fertilize a small nation. Owen forced himself back to the present, where the answers to dating success were in front of him, neatly printed and spread on his grandfather's Formica-topped kitchen table:

A good-night kiss may be appropriate, but do not jam your tongue down her throat.

Ask her questions about herself and then listen to her answers.

Boo sauntered over and plopped down at his feet. The dog groaned and tipped onto his side, gave one thump of his tail and closed his eyes. Owen considered heading to town for a late breakfast, but reconsidered when he looked around the cluttered kitchen. Stacks of newspapers, piles of plastic containers, empty cartons, plastic bags full of plastic bags and enough old Tupperware to fill a museum. He wouldn't toss anything he remembered his mother using or anything he recognized from when he was a kid. But junk was junk. If he was going to start somewhere, it may as well be here in the kitchen.

He'd have to get the junk out of here and into the Dumpster behind the old calf shed before he tackled the summer kitchen, which thankfully didn't look like an army of hoarders lived in it.

"We've got a real mess on our hands," he told the dog. Boo responded with a little snort but didn't budge. Owen rubbed his foot along the dog's spine. "I think it's about time I did something about it, don't you?"

But instead of getting up from the table, he looked at Meg's papers again.

He'd been rude to her last night.

He hadn't wanted to hear her apologizing for what happened between them. He hadn't wanted to sit across from her when all he did want to do was take her out of the café and kiss her until neither one of them could breathe. And that was pretty damn frightening.

All he had to do was look at her and he was back to being the lovesick college kid who'd thought he'd found true love.

He hated feeling like that. Hated the stupidity of it.

Hated remembering the consequences of

falling in love with Meg Ripley. She'd cost him the ranch. She'd taken his youthful dreams and tossed them back in his face.

Was it fair to hold a grudge? Well, sure. But it wasn't necessary. He was a man of the world now. He could certainly manage to deal with old feelings while he cleaned up an old house.

Besides, he felt sorry for her. She was still stuck in this town, after all of her dreams. He knew she'd gone to college. He'd heard she'd worked in five-star restaurants. But she'd landed back in Willing and was now involved with this dating school thing and trying to get her business going. If the town was in as bad a shape as Jerry said — and the figures he'd seen were grim — then Meg was fighting a losing battle. The woman had a lot going on. She probably needed help.

She'd said she wanted to spruce up the old cabins, rent them to the TV crew. She'd sounded as if she had high hopes for making some extra money during what he imagined would be a typically lean winter.

He could help with the dirty work, the heavy stuff, the hauling. He had time, a truck, a shed full of tools and a few handy skills when it came to fixing old things. Owen eased his chair away from the table so he wouldn't disturb the sleeping dog and carried his empty coffee mug to the sink. He'd spend a couple of hours clearing out stuff around here, then he'd shower and head to town.

Yeah, the sooner he got the ranch house squared away, the sooner he'd be free to return to his own life. There didn't seem to be much to go back to. He could lease out the condo, do some traveling, decide which offer to take for the business and do some consulting. Just because he was in the same town as Meg didn't mean he had to ignore her. He was a bigger man than that. They had a history. They could still be . . . friends.

He told himself that was the plan, anyway.

"You are amazing."

It was a little strange that Meg was smiling at Jerry Thompson when she said it. Owen couldn't stop himself from frowning. Had he missed something going on between the mayor and Meg? And what difference would it make?

"I still can't believe you organized this," she cooed. "And so fast."

"We have to stick together," the mayor grunted, struggling with an ancient television set. "All of us."

Owen had seen the closed sign on the restaurant door, had paid no attention to the trucks parked in the lot and only saw Meg, her arms loaded with blankets, stepping out of the middle cabin and tossing them in the bed of a red Ford F-150. He'd parked right beside it and hopped out to offer his services when the mayor had appeared.

Since when was Jerry Thompson amazing?

"Looks like you could use a hand with that," Owen said. He plucked the television from Jerry's grasp as if it were a loaf of bread. "Where do you want it?"

Meg waved her arm toward the truck. "In there, thanks. It's the last one. We're cleaning out the cabins!"

"I see that." He eyed Jerry, who had a guilty look about him. Jerry gave him a quick nod of his head. Sure enough, the man was hiding something. And here Owen thought the guy had it bad for the California woman, the producer. Was he really trying to impress Meg? *Good luck with that, buddy.* "Can I help?"

Meg looked adorably dirty and excited. "Did you come for lunch? Or did Jerry call you, too?"

"Neither. I was on my way to Great Falls and —"

"Hey, Meg?" Mike popped his head out

190

of the cabin next door. "You want me to rip out the carpet and the linoleum? Or just the carpet?"

Jerry answered for her. "All of it!"

The mayor was amazing and he was in charge. Interesting. Was Jerry the next man in a long line of frustrated men who'd been refused by Meg?

"They're coming in two weeks," Jerry explained to him. "They want to stay here."

They meant the Californians, obviously. *Here* meant at Meg's.

"The producer wants real Montana, small-town atmosphere," Jerry added. "I couldn't talk her out of it."

Owen studied the row of cabins. Meg lived in the one on the far end, closest to the café. Years ago she and her mother, along with her mother's fourth — or was it fifth? — husband, had lived in the largest cabin, which was at the other end of the L. Pink curtains hung from the window, giving it a weirdly girly look.

Boo stuck his head out of the open driver's-side window and whined for attention, which Meg gave him. She patted his head and told him what a good dog he was before she looked up at Owen again.

"I can't believe they want to stay here," she said. "I mean, the cabins aren't even close to being habitable and —"

"They're not that bad," Jerry said. "We'll have them fixed up in no time."

Owen ignored the man, though he hoped Jerry was right. "Show me," he said to Meg. "Maybe I can help."

"Really? You have the time?"

"I do." He'd allowed himself plenty of time to act like a hero, inspect the cabins, offer his wealth of knowledge and show her that he wasn't the least bit interested in her.

He told Boo to stay, turned his back on Jerry and followed Meg back into the cabin. They stepped into a pine-paneled room, empty except for an old dresser. A wide picture window on the same wall as the door faced the parking lot. Green paint peeled from its trim.

"A queen-size bed goes there." She pointed to the wall opposite the dresser. He followed her across dull blue shag carpet to a small kitchenette and a tiny bathroom in the back. Inside the bathroom, a metal shower stall, toilet and pedestal sink were crammed together.

"The bathrooms are the challenge," she said. "We're going to put new tile on the floor and hope that helps."

"If you take out this closet," he mused, examining the wall between the bathroom and the storage space. "You'd get more room for a bigger stall. Maybe even a small tub. We'd have to measure."

"That sounds awfully complicated."

"Not really." Here was something he could do. One-handed, almost. With flair and confidence. "Just tell me what you want."

She looked at his mouth and blushed. "Why?"

"You obviously need the manpower," he pointed out.

"Yes, but don't you have — never mind," she stammered. "I'm hoping for new toilets, shower stalls, carpet and tile. Jerry made a list."

"He's an organized guy, I've noticed. Are you dating him?"

Meg laughed. "Are you serious?"

He shrugged. "He's in the diner all the time."

"That's because he doesn't cook."

He reached out and touched a smear of dust on her left cheek. Her skin was as soft as his fingers remembered, smooth as satin and warm as summer grass. "Is he one of the men who proposed to you?"

"That's not fair."

"You've broken more hearts than mine," he pointed out.

"I'm sure you've done your share, too,"

she retorted, but the laughter had disappeared from her eyes and she moved away
from him, just enough to avoid his touch.
He dropped his hand.

"You wrecked mine pretty bad," Owen
admitted, keeping his voice even.

"That goes both ways."

His eyebrows rose. "It didn't feel like it.
When you're twenty years old and the
woman you're in love with changes her
mind and doesn't want to marry you . . ."

"I don't want to talk about this."

"Isn't that my line?" He looked through
the open door to the parking lot, taking note
of the trucks parked in front of the cabins.
"You have plenty of admirers now."

"So that's it. You wonder if I'm like my
mother. She wasn't promiscuous, you know,
no matter what everyone in town thought.
She picked men she felt sorry for, that she
could fix."

"But you have to admit, eighteen proposals is a little, uh, unusual."

"Nineteen," she reminded him again, as
she had a week ago. "And I only said yes to
one of them."

With that, she brushed past him and
stalked out of the cabin.

"Meg, wait —"

She didn't stop.

"Meg." He caught up with her in two long strides and grabbed her hand. Boo barked and whined from his seat in the truck, which caused Les to pop his head out of the cabin two doors down. Meanwhile, Jerry paced across the parking lot with his cell phone to his ear. Owen paid no attention to any of them. "Look, I didn't mean —"

"I have to go rip up carpet now."

"I'll help you."

"Don't. I'm all set. Mike's here. And Les." She motioned toward the far cabin, but Les had disappeared. "He and Shelly are scraping paint off the trim. And Hank Dougherty is coming later to check the wiring. We're in good shape."

"I could take some measurements," he offered. "See if there's room to expand the bathrooms."

"That's probably a bigger job than any of us have time for," she said, pulling her hand away from his. "But thanks anyway for offering."

She looked more hurt than angry, and the excitement over fixing up the cabins had faded. And all because he'd let his jealousy — and yes, he'd admit it was jealousy, pure and simple — get the best of him. He hesitated, wishing he could take back acting like a jerk.

He was left with the truth, though he felt awkward admitting it. He thought he'd show her that he was different now, a man in charge, someone who could help her without feeling the slightest attraction.

"Meg," he said, when she began to turn away from him again. "You said you only accepted one proposal." Her chin lifted; her gaze went to his. "I've only *made* one."

"What's he doing here?" Shelly, a scraper in her hand, perched on a wooden stool and attacked the peeling paint on the window trim inside cabin four. She'd watched Owen MacGregor, the grumpy guy who had gone through her things, follow Meg along the sidewalk. Neither of them looked too happy. "I thought he lived way out on a ranch somewhere."

"He does." Les stopped scraping the other side of the picture window to stare at her. "I sure wish you'd let me do that."

"Why? I can't sit around and do nothing." She wanted to help because it seemed real important to Meg. And as far as Shelly was concerned, Meg Ripley had her undying devotion. She'd given her food and a place to live, plus she let her work at the café. What better place to keep track of who came through town? Her secret little fantasy was that someday Sonny would walk in, ringing the bell as he swung the door open. It would be just like in a movie. She'd introduce him to Meg. Maybe they'd have their wedding reception right here. Meg would be her maid of honor.

But the groom had to walk through that door first, of course. Unless she could track him down through the library or . . . well . . . she'd come up with other ideas, too. She'd emailed the rodeo associations yesterday. And she almost had enough money to pay her phone bill. Boy, did she miss her cell phone.

"So are you sure you never met anyone named Sonny when you were on the rodeo circuit?"

"Is that his name? The guy who — you know." He glanced at her stomach and blushed before turning back to his work.

"Yes."

"I met a few guys called Sonny, I guess," he admitted. "I told you, I didn't know them. And that was a couple of years ago."

"So," she tried again, "do you think he likes Meg?"

"Who? Oh. Everybody likes Meg." Les concentrated on his work, reaching higher to the ledge above the window. "I heard you met Gram yesterday at the quilt thing. She wants me to bring you over for dinner some night. Wants to show you her quilts, I think."

"Okay."

"*Okay?*" He looked as if he'd expected her to refuse.

"Sure."

"When?"

"Whenever," she said, scraping carefully so she wouldn't scratch the wood. "It's not like I have a lot going on." She peered through the dusty glass again. "His truck is still here. The dog's barking again, but I don't see Meg."

"Quiet, Shell. He's coming over here."

Sure enough, the unsmiling rancher stepped in through the open door.

"Looks like you're making progress," he said to them. And then that dark gaze landed on Shelly and he asked, as if he actually cared, "How are you doing? Feeling better?"

"Yes," she managed to answer, and then Les showed him their assignment.

"It's not lead paint you're scraping, is it?"

"No, sir," Les answered. "Meg checked. She still had some paint left from the last time she touched it up."

"Well," he said, looking around the shabby room. Shelly noticed he held a tape measure in his right hand. "I need to take a few measurements. In case Meg wants to, uh, expand the bathroom."

"Cool." Les reached for some sandpaper. "You need help?"

"No, you go ahead with what you're doing."

"Mike's ripping up carpet," Les said. "Then we're going to the dump."

"The carpet really stinks in here." Shelly made a face. "Like old feet. I'm glad I get to stay at Meg's mother's place. Everything's pink, but at least it smells like roses."

"Loralee always did like the color pink," Owen said. He looked a little lost, like he didn't know what to do with himself. Shelly almost felt sorry for him. What if he did like Meg? And she didn't like him back? It would suck to be him if that was true.

"Do you see a broom anywhere, Les? One of my foster moms, one of the nice ones, always used to say it's good to clean up your mess as you work," she said.

"You had a lot of foster moms?" Les asked.

"Yeah. Between times with my mother. She, uh, had problems."

"Is that why you ran away?"

"Who said I ran away?"

Les shrugged. "Well, you do seem kind of, I don't know, lost?"

"Oh." She supposed it seemed that way.

And felt that way, too, sometimes. But this wasn't one of them.

Owen set his tape measure down and searched until he found a dustpan and brush in the cabinet under the kitchen sink. He seemed happy to sweep up paint chips and talk a little football with Les. And Les was all puffed up because the rancher was talking man stuff with him.

"Mr. MacGregor?" she said, cutting into the sports talk.

"Call me Owen."

"You must go to a lot of rodeos," she began. "Have you ever heard of a bull rider named Sonny?"

"We're almost done here," Les interrupted. "We could start tearing out the carpet."

"Sorry, Shelly," Owen told her. "I wish I could help you, but I haven't."

"It's okay. I found some rodeo forums, and my friends back home are looking on Facebook."

"Well, good luck," he said, sounding as if he really meant it, which was nice.

"Thanks."

Les cleared his throat. "What are you gonna do if you don't find him? I mean, before the baby —"

"I can't think about that," she told him.

Her heart gave a sad little lurch. "Because I love him, you know?"

She didn't miss the flash of pity that crossed Les's face or Mr. MacGregor's muffled curse. They just didn't understand, that's all.

"'Dancing at the Dahl,'" Lucia read from the poster on the café wall Monday. "Our mayor certainly believes in social activities these days."

"It's actually another dating class. To be combined with practice dating and conversation." Meg set a bowl of homemade chicken soup in front of Lucia's youngest child. "How are you feeling, Tony? A little better?"

"Yep. Thanks." Tony rarely had much to say. He let his two older brothers do the talking for him. Lucia said he used all of his energy to keep up with them and had nothing left over for communicating.

"Can you have crackers?"

"Uh-huh." He nodded, dipping his spoon into the soup. "Yum."

"Be careful. It it's too hot I'll put another ice cube in it."

"'Kay."

Lucia slid into the booth across from her son. "I don't think these men are into dancing that much."

"They're going to have to try. According to Jerry, Tracy, the producer, can't wait for the Halloween party. She expects dancing and general cowboy merriment."

"Merriment," Lucia repeated. "A little old-fashioned, isn't it?"

"Her word, not mine."

"Are the cowboys supposed to wear red bandannas around their necks and shout 'hee-haw' as they kick up their spurs?"

"Absolutely." Meg couldn't help laughing at Lucia's expression of horror.

Her friend sipped her coffee and considered it. "I'll ask Mama to watch the boys."

"You'll have to come up with a costume, too," Meg reminded her. "And don't forget the raffle."

"I don't especially want to decorate a bear," she said. "Getting three boys ready for Halloween is enough work." She glanced out the window. "Your boyfriend's back."

"Which one?" she joked.

"The one with the big shiny new truck filled with great big boxes."

Meg forgot about replenishing her customers' coffee and peered out the window. "That's Owen's."

"He's delivering stuff for the cabins? What'd you buy?"

"Not much. Yet. He's not supposed to be here," Meg said, watching Owen untie the ropes that kept the large boxes from falling. "I'd better go check."

"Yes," Lucia said, grinning at her. "I think you'd better get right out there and ask that man what he's doing."

Meg hesitated. She'd told him she didn't need his help. "I have no clue. Jerry must have asked him to get something, because I certainly didn't."

"There's only one way to find out. And don't forget your jacket."

Meg grabbed it on the way out. She didn't want him here, especially after yesterday. Okay, so she was a little overly sensitive about the number of proposals she'd received, but she didn't like Owen bringing it up as if she was some sort of heartless flirt. When she reached the truck, it took her only a few seconds to realize what was in the boxes. "You bought toilets?"

"I did," he said, not looking at her as he coiled the ropes, then tucked them in the truck bed.

"Three of them?"

"Yes." He lifted the tailgate down. "Did you need more than that?"

"No, but —"

"Would you rather have had flowers?"

Now his gaze held hers.

"Flowers? For what?"

"To go with my apology. I debated between practical and romantic," he explained.

"Your apology," she echoed. "Oh."

"Yeah," he said. "Oh. For yesterday. I guess we're both sensitive on that subject."

"Yes," she conceded. "I guess we are."

"So," he said, gesturing toward the boxes, "I went with something practical."

"Toilets? That's pretty practical."

Owen took a folded square of paper out of his shirt pocket. "Let me show you something." He unfolded the paper and showed her a diagram of a cabin interior. "All three have the exact same floor plan. There's the closet —" he pointed to a rectangle on the page "— between the bedroom area and the bathroom. It can be used for a decent-size shower stall. Now that we've taken the old metal stalls out, the walls can be taken down and extended. The closet door can be removed, the outside easily framed and paneled. It will look newer than the rest of the room, but still —"

"It's perfect," she said. "Jerry and Mike are coming over tonight to measure and figure out what can be done. They're going to love this."

"Look, I'm not here to make trouble for

you. I'm assuming we can be friends."

"Let the past stay in the past," she stated.

"Exactly."

Well, it was worth a try. And would make her life easier. Meg had a crazy urge to fling her arms around him, but she could blame that on the frigid wind. "You'd better come inside for something warm. It's freezing out here."

"I will, in a sec." He pointed to a spot on the paper diagram. "You have room over here, where the kitchen cabinets are, for a closet between the television shelf and the kitchen counter. Mike is going to install a shelf along the wall — one of those prefab counters — and you'll have room to put a small refrigerator underneath it. In each unit."

"Mike figured this out?" She hadn't expected the newspaperman was an architect, too.

"Yeah. He's a talented guy. Says he's a frustrated remodeler now that he's finished up his own house. He also suggested bifold doors for the closets so they won't take up much room. So what do you think?"

"I think I'd better sell a lot of soup today." She shook her head. "It's great," she grudgingly conceded. "All of it. Thank you."

He tipped his hat and grinned. "Just doing my part for the future of Willing, ma'am."

And that was the problem, she thought, returning to the warmth of the café after Owen told her that he didn't need any help, that he'd be along soon and yes, he liked chicken soup, especially the homemade kind with extra noodles. Owen MacGregor was bored and lonely. He'd told her so himself.

She preferred the young, passionate version of Owen, not this "let's be friends" business. When she fell in love next time — if ever — she wanted a man who would kiss her as if he never wanted to let her go, who would be by her side no matter what happened in their lives, a man who would support her.

He'd apologized and even stepped up to help her business, but she shouldn't take a gift of plumbing too seriously.

What the heck was he doing here? Owen followed his dog into the house but didn't bother to turn on the lights. The place was cold, empty and smelled like yesterday's bacon. Not the least bit appealing, and not at all where he wanted to be.

Well, that wasn't exactly true, either.

He'd never planned to be anywhere else.

Which was what he'd explained to

eighteen-year-old Meggie Ripley that long-ago August.

"I'm going to run the ranch with Dad," he'd said, omitting the fact that his father had looked pale and worn out all spring and summer and that he, Owen, was scared his dad worked too hard. "He needs the help," was what he told Meg.

"But what about school?" she'd asked.

"I just want to be here, you know?" He'd kissed her, wrapping his arms around her to hold her close. They were in the front seat of his old truck, parked on a small ridge above the river.

"I know," she'd said. "It's so beautiful."

"We can raise our family here," he'd said, full of confidence and pride. Full of all the optimism that first love brings with it.

"I'd like that," Meg had whispered, her big brown eyes staring into his before he'd kissed her again.

"We'll get married," he promised, sure it would be that simple.

CHAPTER TEN

"I'm in a real bind," Jerry confessed over a late breakfast Tuesday morning. He had waited for the rush to be over before he threw himself on Meg's mercy.

"Okay. How can I help?" Meg asked. "I definitely owe you big-time for Sunday."

"Yes, well, I had ulterior motives."

"I know. Tracy and her Montana atmosphere." She topped off his coffee and turned her attention back to her laptop screen. "What does she want this time?"

Meg hadn't experienced the whims of those in the entertainment business, but Jerry had. So he had no choice but to beg for help. "Remember how I told Tracy about the Halloween party? She and the crew plan to come. She thinks it will be a good way to get a sense of the town." He had his doubts about the wisdom of that, considering Aurora's cranky disposition. He'd also had experience with the raucous holiday celebrations of the past years. They were not for the faint of heart, but then again, Tracy could handle anything. Heck, she and Aurora might even become best friends.

"Good idea." Meg, huddled over the counter dividing the kitchen from the rest of the room, continued to type on her laptop. "Do you think white tile is too hard to keep clean or is it better to make the bathroom look larger?"

George, seated next to Jerry, lifted his head from the newspaper. "Too hard to keep clean. Trust me."

Jerry ignored him. "She's expecting dancing."

"Yes. You told me."

"I did?"

"In detail." Meg sighed and shut the lid. "I think you and Aurora had an argument over the band."

"Then you know what the problem is."

"The band?" She looked surprised. "They've been booked for months. It's just the local —"

"Not the band," he interrupted. "And all I asked was for some more modern country songs, you know, like what's on the radio. But no, we're getting classic country, Willie Nelson and Hank Williams."

"Nothing wrong with Hank," George muttered. "Or Willie, either, for that matter. He's almost eighty and he's still working, goin' around in that bus giving concerts."

"So what's the problem? Clothes?" she guessed. "It should be okay. Everyone will most likely wear the usual boots and jeans. And then some people will be wearing costumes, so you really don't even have to worry about —"

"Janet Ferguson broke her ankle last night," he said, ignoring the breakfast that sat half eaten in front of him. Who could look at cold fried eggs right now? "She was just walking down the steps — I guess she has stone steps to her garden — to see if she had any pumpkins left or something ridiculous like that, and *bam!* Cracked it like a chicken leg."

"Is she okay?"

"John took her to the hospital for X-rays last night. She has to wear one of those boot things for weeks. *Six* weeks."

"Thanks for letting me know. I'll call her in a couple of days and send over a couple of meals."

"Meals? You think I'm talking about *meals*?" He stood, stopping short of pacing up and down the room.

Shelly came over with a breakfast check and a credit card in her hand. "Machine's down again, Meg. You want me to keep trying or take a check?"

"Give it a few more minutes."

"Will do." The girl moved away, back to the register, and fiddled with the credit-card machine.

"You might want to cut down on the caffeine, Jer," Meg said. "You're a little wound up this morning."

Jerry felt himself twitching with impatience, and he didn't need Meg pointing out that he might be drinking too much coffee. "It's not the caffeine," he said, trying to sound calm and in control of his life. "I need your help finding another dance teacher."

"I'll make a fresh pot of decaf," she said, clearing away his dirty dishes. She gave the counter a quick wipe and removed his full coffee mug. "Just for you. Sit. It will only take a few minutes."

Patience, he reminded himself as he reluctantly returned to his stool at the freshly wiped counter. *Slow down. Breathe. Do not listen to George complain about Congress. Do not answer questions about the town's budget. Do not think about Tracy's —*

"I'm worried about you," Meg said, returning with a plate of English muffins spread with peanut butter, a dollop of

211

strawberry jam on the side in a little paper cup. "Here. Protein. You didn't eat your eggs."

"Thanks, Meg." He took a bite of the muffin, though he wasn't sure he could get it past the nervous lump in his throat. Fortunately Meg seemed to understand and provided a glass of water.

"Better?"

He nodded, swallowed and sipped some water. He'd need to see a gastroenterologist in Billings before this was over. He was too young for daily heartburn.

"Good. Now, start over. What kind of help do you need?"

"Janet is — was — our volunteer dance instructor. She was the only woman in town who ever actually taught dancing — two-step, swing, waltz, the real stuff — *profes-sionally.*"

"Ooh, now I get it." She walked over to the coffee machine and lifted the decaf pot. As she filled his cup, she said, "You really should switch to decaf full-time, Jerry. Your hands are shaking."

"I thought Tracy would stay with me at my house," he confided. "I made a guest room for her in her favorite color and I bought 100-percent-organic sheets. I thought it would be romantic, you know?"

"Organic sheets?" Now it was Meg's turn to look panicked. "I can't afford organic sheets! I thought she'd like a Montana country-western look, so I ordered a blue plaid sheet, comforter, dust ruffle and pillow sham set from J.C. Penney."

"Cotton?"

"Yes, but I don't think I read anything about organic."

"What's the thread count?"

"Are you out of your mind? How would I know?"

"I guess you could look it up. Or you could just lie. Tell her it's organic and really expensive." *Breathe. Focus. Dump the jam on top of the peanut butter and eat.*

"How would you know *what*?" This was from Shelly again, who carried a tray of dirty dishes. Jerry didn't mind the interruption this time, because he hoped Meg would be side-tracked and therefore stop shrieking.

"Thread count for the queen sheets," Meg muttered.

"Yep," George said. "And don't forget the organic part."

"Is that important?" She set the tray down and looked from Jerry to Meg and back again. "What's wrong with you two?"

"Janet broke her ankle," Meg replied.

"Yeah. I heard. That's why Mr. Ferguson didn't come in this morning. It's a small fracture, but they might not be able to go on their vacation now."

"Janet was supposed to teach the dance class tonight," Jerry managed to say with a mouthful of peanut butter. Yes, he was breaking the "don't talk with your mouth full" rule of dating, but he sure wasn't going to date either one of the women looking at him with pity in their eyes. "Who else around here can dance? There must be someone."

"Don't look at me," George hollered. "I need a hip replacement."

"Not me, either," Meg said. "I'm not the least bit coordinated, never was. You can ask my mother."

"Can she dance?" Jerry wiped a blob of strawberry jam from his lip.

"Probably, but she's in Tucson."

"Can you dance enough to teach the basics? I mean, I'm from California and I can do the two-step if I'm in a bar in Texas without embarrassing myself too much."

"You're way ahead of me. So *you* teach."

"I can't. It has to come from a woman to make the guys pay attention. They have to have someone who knows what she's doing so they can practice with her, to get the hang of it. Janet even bet me ten bucks she could make a dancer out of Hip."

"Okay." Meg thought for a moment. "There should be a dance studio in Billings, or maybe someone at Lewistown? We can call around —"

"I already did. Offered fifty dollars an hour, the going rate for group lessons. No one wants to come up here tonight, especially with the weather being as bad as it is."

They all looked out the window to check. Sure enough, it was gray and windy, with flakes of snow already beginning to swirl in the cold air. "We'll have to change the date, I guess, and hope I can get something scheduled before the twenty-eighth."

"I'll do it," a female voice said.

He turned away from the sight of snow and saw the determined pregnant girl, hands on her hips. "Huh?"

"I had to learn the two-step in gym class."

"Well, uh, thanks for offering, Shelly, but we need —"

"I can waltz. Fox-trot, too. I can do some swing dancing, but it can get a little tricky to remember the fancy stuff."

"Who taught you? Your parents?" Meg looked as if she'd like to ask a lot more questions, but Jerry didn't have time for delving into Shelly's mysterious past.

"Thanks, anyway," he told Shelly, hoping he wouldn't hurt her feelings. "But —"

"One of our neighbors had a school," she said to Meg. "I used to teach the little kids when she needed help."

Jerry didn't look convinced. In fact, his gaze drifted to the girl's stomach. "I don't know about this."

Meg lifted her hand. "It seems to me," she said slowly, "if Shelly could teach small children the basics of dance, she could teach our bachelors."

"That's right," the girl said. "On one condition. Someone has to take me to the rodeo." She took a folded piece of paper from the back pocket of her jeans. "Les's grandfather printed this out for me. NILE starts Thursday in Billings. This is the schedule of events."

"I think I heard about it on the radio," Meg told him. "Northern International Livestock Show, right? But it's a pro rodeo. Sonny wasn't on that level, was he?"

"Yeah, well, it's also the ranch rodeo finals. If he works on a ranch, and if he's any good, you never know. He could be there." The look on the poor kid's face showed exactly how much she hoped he would be. "I don't know how many ranches compete, but it's worth a try."

"Consider it a done deal," Jerry said. "Meg will make sure you get there."

Shelly's face lit up and she threw her arms around Meg's neck. "Thank you!"

Behind Shelly's back, Jerry shrugged at Meg's dismayed expression. "Hey," he said. "You can't dance and you can't sing, so you may as well hunt down a boyfriend."

"You don't need this class," Meg muttered.

"No?" Owen twirled her with effortless precision.

"Don't look innocent. I'll bet you could have taught it yourself."

"No, thanks. I think your students are happy with female instructors."

Meg didn't want to be in Owen's arms. She'd planned to look good and ignore him. She'd had the best intentions earlier this evening. Despite choosing to wear her skinny jeans and her favorite black Tony Lama boots, the ones with the red-and-purple feather stitching, and she'd told herself she didn't care if Owen attended the dance class or not. So what if she'd finally worn her fancy ivory ruffled top? She'd have worn it anyway, because it made her waist look small and had the rare Lucia seal of approval.

And she'd told herself it didn't matter if she wasn't coordinated and didn't have a sense of rhythm. And maybe she was just the tiniest bit tone-deaf, too. But she could still enjoy the music and have a good time. At least her awkward two-step would make the men feel better about their own dancing.

Jerry had personally begged every able woman in town, married or single, to serve as dance partners tonight. The Dahl had never seen so much gray hair. The place was packed, which kept Aurora and a couple of volunteer bartenders busy, but the crowded dance floor helped the students feel less self-conscious. Lucia had convinced the more talented Mama Marie to take her place tonight and had opted to stay home with her boys.

"I'm saving myself for the Halloween party," she'd said. Meg suspected her friend was much happier at home in her pajamas.

Shelly was patient and kept the instructions simple. She made them go over and over the steps without music, with music, slow, fast, alone and with a partner.

Meg thought she could *almost* two-step after forty-five minutes.

Shelly, satisfied with the progress of her students, switched to the waltz.

"One, two, three," she said. "Slow, quick, quick."

When it was time for partners, Owen scooped Meg into his arms. "Have we ever danced before?"

"You don't remember?"

"Shoot," he muttered, taking a few moments to think. "The county fair?"

She even remembered the song, but she would not humiliate herself by saying so. "It was a long time ago."

"That Tim McGraw song." His fingers tightened around hers. "And not so long ago, not really."

"We were stupid." That's what she needed to remember, not some silly love song. They'd been kids, thrown together on the ranch, hormones vibrating off their skin, with no idea what love really was.

"Maybe. Maybe not," he murmured. "But we're a lot older."

"Thanks for pointing that out."

"You know that's not what I meant." He chuckled. "And despite my advancing age, it still feels good to hold you in my arms."

"You're holding me a little too tight."

"It's a waltz."

"Yes, but —"

"And if I don't hold you like this, you'll step on my feet. You really don't have a knack for this."

"You were warned."

"We all were. I might be the only one who took it seriously, because I didn't have to knock anyone over to get to dance with you."

"Flatterer." She lost her concentration again and stumbled.

"Ouch."

"Sorry."

His arms tightened around her just a little bit. She wanted nothing more than to rest her head on his chest and close her eyes. He smelled good, unlike some of the others, who hadn't followed the rule about going easy on the aftershave lotion.

She needed to make a note about Irish Spring soap, too. Most of the men she'd danced with used it, and a little of that scent went a long way.

Fortunately for her, since she was practically glued to his chest, Owen smelled wonderful. She wanted to sniff his neck, but that would of course be too obvious. "What kind of soap do you use?"

"Hmm?" His chin was touching the top of her head. His body was warm and his chest was so wide. Meg sighed. She really did feel stupid, as if she was losing brain cells all over the dance floor. "What's the sigh about?"

"Soap," she murmured. "What kind?"

"Oh." He obviously had to think about it. "Ivory? It's white. Why?"

"Aftershave? Cologne?"

"Why?" He loosened his hold on her and looked down into her face.

"I'm taking a poll."

"Well, tell you what, you're invited to come on out to the ranch anytime you want to and go through my bathroom shelves. Bring a notebook, a camera, whatever. Now start counting. You've lost the beat again and Shelly is about to come over here and get us on track. Is it my imagination or has her, uh, belly tripled in size since last week?"

"It's not your imagination." She let her cheek rest on his chest for the tiniest second, just the blink of an eye, really, before the last notes of the old Willie Nelson song faded. "I'm glad we're friends again, Owen."

Gently released, she stepped out of his arms.

"Friends," he repeated, as if he'd never heard the word before. He kept hold of her hand as they waited for the next song to begin. It was silly to carry a grudge, Meg realized. They could be friends now. Older and wiser, she had no reason to fall in love again.

And no desire to. Her hand felt so warm and small inside of his.

No desire at all.

It irked him to be treated like every other man in this godforsaken town. *Friends? Friends!* That had been his own stupid idea — he'd actually said it to Meg when he'd been trying to protect himself. He was an idiot. Because he was the same as he was years ago: he wanted to kiss that smiling mouth, wanted to hold her in his arms and protect her. He wanted to tease her until that stubborn chin of hers lifted in defiance and then he wanted to kiss her until she laughed against his mouth.

Another song began, yet he didn't relinquish her hand and instead tugged her back into his arms for the next waltz. He glanced around the room to see if anyone would contest his monopolizing Meg, but the rest of the dancers seemed very preoccupied with their own feet. Shelly was attempting to teach Hip and Les at the same time, and the younger man looked self-conscious but determined. Hip looked more agonized, but watched Shelly's face instead of the simple steps she illustrated.

"What do you suppose is going on over there?"

Meg followed his gaze. "With Les and Hip?"

"I hope that girl is really eighteen, otherwise we're going to have trouble."

"Hip's too old for her."

"And Les is too young," Owen pointed out, at the same time realizing he'd been younger than Les when he'd tried to elope with Meg. Had he really ever been that young? That stupid?

"She's too young to be pregnant, too, but that doesn't seem to bother her."

Owen looked down at Meg. "Have you asked the county sheriff if there's a missing-person report on her?"

"No." She hesitated. "What if she's run away from an abusive situation?"

"What if she's run away from a family who's worried about her?"

Meg sighed. "I don't get that feeling. But she seems so lost."

"If she's a minor, she needs help. Obviously. For the baby's sake, if nothing else."

"You're right. I just don't want her to run away from here. At least here I know she's taking care of herself."

"Is she still looking for the boyfriend?" He drew her closer against him and she didn't protest, just leaned against his chest. He didn't dare point out that she was actually managing a simple box step without stumbling.

"Yes, but she doesn't say much. She's gone through the high school yearbooks. And she's on the internet for hours at a time, with no luck. In fact, I'm taking her to the rodeo in Billings next week. She has high hopes for that."

"She needs to find him. He needs to take responsibility for this, but I don't know, it doesn't look good." Shelly had been a foolish girl, seduced by a sweet-talking cowboy at a rodeo. She'd made a dangerous and foolish decision, and now a baby was going to pay for it.

"I hope she does. I worry about her," Meg said, snuggling just a bit closer as he pressed his hand gently against her back. She smelled like vanilla cookies. And cinnamon, too. "She knows where this guy is, one way or the other."

"That baby doesn't have much of a chance. Not without a home. Not without a father."

"Some kids don't have a choice," she said, pulling back to look up at him.

He realized he'd hit a nerve. "I'm sorry."

"I never met my father. He disappeared

before I was born. I have their wedding pictures in a drawer and that's about it." She lifted her chin, as if daring him to argue. "And I turned out fine."

"You did." He remembered how she used to change the subject whenever anyone at the ranch asked her anything personal. She'd willingly chatted about Loralee and the café but closed up whenever asked about her childhood or the rest of her family.

"I grew up with four stepfathers," she said. "Not that all of them were, well, fatherly. But they were all kind in their own ways, despite their troubles. They adored my mother."

"Everyone did," Owen admitted. Too much, he thought. Loralee attracted men as though they were fruit flies and she was a ripe peach. She'd never been involved with another woman's husband, according to the town gossips, but she'd had a knack for flirtation that put a twinkle in a man's eye. "She was very different from my mother."

"Your mother hated me."

"I wouldn't say —"

"I brought food," Meg said. "After the funeral. Macaroni and cheese, with sautéed onions and bacon. Your father's favorite."

"I didn't know that," he replied, but then

he hadn't been aware of a lot of things going on around him at the time.

"Your mother turned me away." She drew back in his arms and looked up at him. "She told me it was all my fault. My fault your father died. And she said you blamed me, too." She blinked back tears and attempted to leave his embrace, but Owen wouldn't let her go.

"I'm sorry," he managed to reply. He'd no idea back then that his mother was capable of such cruelty. In recent years he'd seen a different side to the woman he'd once thought devastated by the loss of her husband.

"But you did. Blame me."

"Not for Dad's death," he admitted. He'd blamed himself for that.

"But for everything else," Meg said. The music faded, then ended. Before he had a chance to deny it, Meg moved away from him and into the arms of some long-haired guy with a tattoo on his forearm. Owen felt like an idiot standing there in the middle of the crowd while Shelly, perched on a bar stool with a microphone in her hand, reminded everyone to feel the beat of the music and not look at their feet.

Yes, the truth was that he'd blamed her for a lot of things that happened that year, but she'd been the only woman he'd ever wanted to share his life with, the only woman he'd ever let into his heart.

And miracle of miracles, she was still single.

"I'll take you home," Owen said, helping her into her jacket.

"That's not —"

"Yes," he said, draping her wool scarf around her neck. "It is."

Meg shivered despite the crowded warmth of the Dahl. She recognized the look. She'd seen that "I want to be alone with you so I can kiss your socks off" look before. She'd spent an entire summer basking in the glow of that particular expression in his eyes.

"Come on." He took her hand and tugged her toward the door. She didn't have the breath in her to say good-night to anyone, to answer calls of "thanks" and "see you tomorrow" and "we did great, didn't we?"

That summer. That summer she'd learned to roast beef and fry steaks and slowly cook enormous slabs of pork ribs . . . build a fire, drive a feed truck and saddle a horse. That summer she'd also learned how to kiss and be kissed. How by simply touching Owen's hand she could make him grin. That rubbing the spot between his shoulder blades where his shirt stretched over his muscles could make him growl and laugh and tip her onto her back in the rough prairie grass.

"But Shelly —"

"Is all taken care of. I checked."

"But —"

"She's safe with Les," he said, guiding her through the door with his large hand on her back.

Memories of that protective, gentle side of him rushed over her. That summer she'd learned the power of his touch could make her body turn to jelly. And to trust him not to drop her when he lifted her in his arms and deposited her on the back of her horse.

She felt that intensity in him now. She didn't know whether to run or stop dead in her tracks and hope to freeze to death before her embarrassment grew any worse.

The wind, cold and relentless, hit her in the face the minute they rounded the corner of the building and headed north to his truck. A blessing, she thought, because it saved them both the bother of trying to speak. This was no warm summer evening by the Little Judith River. Thank goodness.

Owen put his arm around her and Meg was grateful for the warmth. Winter was coming faster this year, everyone said. Up until tonight she hadn't believed it. They hurried to the truck and Owen opened the passenger door and ushered her inside.

When he joined her, he quickly started the engine and pushed several buttons on the dashboard. "Heated seats," he said. "It will be warm in here soon."

"We're only going half a mile." She shoved her hands in her pockets and pulled out her gloves, which she'd forgotten about.

"It heats up fast." He made no move to put the car in gear. Instead he turned toward her. "I'd like you to come out to the ranch."

"Tonight?" Meg could hear the shock in her voice. She struggled with the gloves until she managed to get them on. "Absolutely not."

Owen chuckled softly. "No. . . . Not that I wouldn't like the company."

She attempted to make light of it. "The genetic hermit curse again?"

He shook his head. "No. The wanting Meg Ripley curse again."

She thought about that, especially since it didn't seem as if they were going anywhere at the moment. "Why?"

"I can't seem to stop." He reached over and tugged at her scarf, fingering the nubby material between his thumb and index finger.

"Then don't —" She stopped talking when he tugged her closer, caressed her face and ever so slowly leaned toward her.

"Don't what?" His lips grazed the left corner of her lips. Then the right. She lifted her face to his and his lips brushed against hers once, twice. "This?" he asked, sliding both large hands along either side of her face.

It was all so deliciously familiar. Meg closed her eyes and let herself remember, just a little, as the tempting kisses deepened into something more. And she welcomed them, tilted her head to make it easy to kiss him back. Her gloved hands went to his shoulders, but their bodies remained apart. The wide console of the truck saw to that.

His lips teased hers as if the past fourteen years had never happened. She kissed him as if she'd never stopped, and never would.

Owen eventually paused and took a breath. "I've wanted to do that for a very long time."

"Someone is going to see us," Meg said. The steamed-up windows were a dead giveaway if the partiers at the Dahl walked past. And they would know whose truck it was, and who Owen had left with. "It will be the gossip over breakfast tomorrow."

He paid no attention to her comment. "I

think you've wanted to do that for a long time, too."

"You want me to say I've missed you," Meg said, looking at his familiar face with affection.

He smiled and ran his index finger along her cheek. "Yes. Because I certainly have."

"It was fun," she admitted, silently willing her heartbeat to slow down to something less disconcerting. "Remembering."

"Come out to the ranch tomorrow. It's supposed to be a beautiful day. We'll take out a couple of horses and do some more . . . remembering."

"I have to paint," she said, pleased to have an excuse. It would be too easy to fall in love with this man again. Too easy to make a fool of herself. She'd thought he'd wait for her, had desperately counted on his understanding what she needed to do before getting married. "Mike and Jack are coming over after they get out of work."

"Jack?"

"Dugan. Town council, handsome, works at the feed store," she reminded him. "Jerry thinks he's going to be a big hit with the ladies."

"Then we'll be back before that," he said. "Put Shelly and Al in charge of breakfast and come out with me." Owen gave her one more hot, melting kiss as if she'd said yes, then turned away and put the truck in gear. Heat blasted from the vents now and Meg snuggled into her seat for the short ride home.

He walked her to the door of her little cabin. She wanted to ask him in; she wanted to keep him out. She could fall in love with him so easily, drop into the churning pit of emotions all too easily.

Why, oh, why did that sound appealing? She simply wanted Owen to kiss her, to keep kissing her, to wrap her up in those strong arms of his and take her back to a time when she'd felt beautiful and joyous and loved.

"I'll pick you up at nine," he said, taking her key from her and unlocking the door. One brief, toe-curling kiss and he was gone.

Meg switched on a light and closed the door behind her. Her cabin had never felt so cozy. Or so empty.

CHAPTER ELEVEN

"So," Lucia whispered, leaning over the counter to prevent anyone from overhearing. "When were you going to tell me?"

Meg didn't have to ask what her friend meant. She'd seen a few curious looks this morning, from the time she'd turned on the lights at 6:00 a.m. and three customers had followed her inside. Al, on the job by five, handed her a cup of coffee and said, "It's gonna be all over town."

She hadn't asked how he'd known, but since he lived right in Willing, she assumed he'd seen her in Owen's truck.

"I couldn't call you at ten-thirty last night."

"No, because you were too busy making out with Owen MacGregor, you little hussy." Lucia couldn't contain her giggles. "Come on, tell me everything. Don't leave out one single detail."

Lucia picked up Meg's coffee cup and her

own and walked over to a corner booth while Meg followed. She waved at Shelly, who gave her a thumbs-up sign.

"Sit," Lucia said. "Spill your guts. How did this happen? When did this happen?"

Meg slid into the booth and ignored the curious looks from those diners around them. "Does everyone know about it?"

"Probably. Mama saw you dancing together and said you looked pleased with yourselves. Body language and all that," Lucia explained. "You know how she is."

"Yes. And everyone's been talking about how Mama can two-step. I guess she dated a guy from Texas before she met your father-in-law?"

"She's a woman with many talents. I heard about Mrs. Lyons, too. Eighty years old and moves like Ginger Rogers, according to Mama."

"There are no secrets from that woman. How did you find out about the, uh, truck?"

"Esther was out with her dog. He took off after something and she followed him and there you were — or someone was — and when Mama went over to the Hut to bring Esther something for her dinner, meatballs, I think, well, that's how I found out." She took a sip of coffee and tucked her long hair behind her ears, where triple strands of coral-and-black beads hung on gold wires.

"Nice earrings."

"Thanks. Goodwill. Answer the questions, please. Or I'll make you play Monopoly with Davey."

"That's not funny." Meg fiddled with her coffee mug. She'd thought about nothing else but this until she finally fell asleep sometime after one. "Okay. I was eighteen —"

Lucia's mouth fell open. "You knew him then? Really?"

"Do you want to hear this or not? Because I have to go home and change in twenty minutes."

"Sorry."

"I'd graduated from high school and taken a job at the MacGregor ranch. Cook's help for the summer crew. Owen was two years older, so he'd graduated a month before we moved here. I wasn't getting along with my mother and I needed to make more money than I could working here so I could go to school. Loralee had been married to husband number five —"

"The one who died and left her this place?"

"Yes. Bill Smittle. We lived in Billings when she met him. He was a lot older than her. Loralee said he was lonely and needed cheering up. He needed more than cheering up, because he was as poor as a man could get without living under a bridge. No one could ever accuse Loralee of being a gold digger." She took a sip of coffee and set the mug aside. Lucia waited impatiently.

"And then?"

"Loralee worked in a Ford dealership, as a receptionist, which is where she met Bill, before he was fired for not selling enough cars. Six months later Bill told her he owned a place in Willing, and if she wanted to run it for him she was welcome to it. So we moved, and later on that year he was diagnosed with lung cancer."

"I remember you telling me about that part," Lucia said. "But you never told me about Owen MacGregor. I can't believe you left that out."

"It was embarrassing," Meg explained. "The whole thing. There I was, the daughter of a woman with five — *five* — husbands. Bill died a few months before I graduated and I couldn't stand watching her get ready to date again. I wanted to get out of here. So I applied for a job at the Triple M and got it. For the summer." She looked over at the cash register to make sure Shelly wasn't too busy, but the girl had everything under control at the moment.

"And you met the boss's son."

"I did."

"And you fell in love."

"I did. And so did he." She felt her cheeks grow hot. "It was a summer romance to end all summer romances. It was . . . special."

"How special?"

"We thought we'd be in love forever."

"Of course," Lucia replied. "You were a kid."

"And then Owen didn't want to wait. His father needed more help with the ranch and Owen didn't want to leave. He wanted to — well — we eloped."

Lucia was struck silent. She mouthed the word *eloped* and stared at Meg, so Meg continued with the story she'd never told anyone except her mother.

"His father caught up with us, took me home and that was that." She didn't want to tell Lucia about Mr. MacGregor's stroke right after the elopement or his death a few weeks later or the ugly scene after the funeral. She didn't want to remember Owen's furious attempt to make her see reason.

"Then what? And how come you never told me this before?"

"I wanted to move on . . . and keep my school life separate," Meg tried to explain.

She and Lucia, two strangers from Montana, had roomed together at culinary school. "I didn't want anyone to know about it."

"I thought you were crying because you were homesick," Lucia said. "So what happened after you couldn't elope? Did you try again?"

"His father got sick. And Owen still wanted to get married, but I was scared. I had a scholarship, remember? Just like you. I wanted to wait. He was furious because he didn't want to leave. His father died before we could make up. And I think he blamed me for everything going wrong."

The email address given to her by one of his friends in Willing no longer worked. She'd called his dorm but was told he'd moved out. She'd called the ranch to get contact information for him but the housekeeper had said she didn't have the authority to give it out. And apparently the woman hadn't given him her messages.

She'd waited every weekend for him to return to town, to drive up to the café and haul her into his arms. She'd planned to borrow Loralee's car and drive to Bozeman to say goodbye before she left for Rhode Island and the January semester at Johnson & Wales, but Loralee had convinced her that if he'd left the dorm he'd probably left the school, advising her to quit pining after someone who didn't want her.

"I cannot believe that you, of all people, *eloped.*"

"I know. I told you it was embarrassing."

"Anyone can do something crazy when they're eighteen, but you're so —" She paused, obviously searching for a word that wouldn't hurt Meg's feelings. "Cautious. And practical."

"And cold," Meg added with a wince.

"Well, only to men. I figured that was because of your mother. . . ."

"I'm meeting him this morning." Meg leaned back and watched Shelly refill coffee cups for the men stationed in their usual spots at the counter. "He's taking me out to the ranch."

"Did he ever say why he just dropped out of your life without a word?"

"No. He was grieving," she explained, wishing the lump in her throat would evaporate. "I always thought he blamed me for his father's stroke."

"Are you sure you want to do this?" Lucia looked at her with the worried expression she'd give little Tony when he had an ear infection. "Start the whole thing over again?"

"I won't get hurt," she promised, knowing she couldn't guarantee any such thing. Not after last night.

"Famous last words," Lucia muttered, then took a deep breath. "So I guess this is in the category of unfinished business?"

"The spark is still there," Meg admitted. The inside of the truck could have burst into flames.

"Spark or no spark, he left and never looked back. Because you wouldn't marry him. Could you try to remember that, please?"

"I got over that a long time ago, honest."

"We're not talking about a long time ago," her best friend warned. "We're talking about right now."

"And right now I have to go change. We're going riding."

"Riding," Lucia repeated quietly.

"Riding," Meg said. "Just riding, nothing else."

Lucia rolled her eyes and groaned. "Oh, *please.*" She pointed toward the pregnant waitress. "You know how cowboys are."

He was already rethinking this idea. At first he'd thought he would impress her if it killed him. And at this rate, with four hours' sleep and a nervous stomach from too much caffeine, it probably could.

Now, looking around his mother's kitchen, he wondered if he'd been too optimistic. Boo looked up at him, tail wagging in the hope that Owen would either feed him another round of breakfast or tell him they were going for a ride.

He didn't dare say the word *ride* in front of the panting dog. Boo wasn't going to town with him this morning.

It was supposed to be a clear day, but instead heavy clouds hung overhead and threatened rain. The wind was coming in from the north, but so far wasn't bad. They could still go out. He'd borrowed a couple of horses from Les early this morning. They were lounging in their freshly prepared stalls in the clean horse barn now.

He'd spent a couple of hours last night working on the living room. Meaning he'd moved stacks of newspapers, magazines and empty whiskey bottles into the Dumpster. Ed had never thrown anything away. Crossword puzzle books, jigsaw puzzles and worn decks of cards showed how his uncle had passed the time. They went into the Dumpster, too. The dust-covered books, mostly about military history, were now vacuumed and arranged neatly on shelves in the office that had belonged to Owen's father and which Ed had never used. He'd preferred to set up his computer on an old oak table in the living room.

Owen had dismantled that scarred table. The large room, once the scene of family gatherings and holiday parties, looked abandoned and old. The dining room felt the same way. Actually, the whole house, all six bedrooms, four bathrooms and a handful of other spaces, looked as if it had seen better days. Which, of course, it had.

Maybe the real-estate agent had been right to suggest taking a bulldozer to the place, but Owen felt sick to his stomach thinking about it. The old house was structurally sound and still beautiful. Surely someone would want to live here.

He didn't want to think about that, either. He was growing accustomed to this ranch again. Sometimes he woke up in the morning and forgot what year it was, how old he was, what he was doing and why.

Today there'd been no confusion. Today he was bringing Meg to the ranch. For all he knew, she hadn't been here since the funeral. If he had been twenty years old again, he'd be looking for an isolated spot in the barn so he could kiss his girl without interruption.

Now he was older and wiser. And he

wouldn't be sticking around the county or eloping again with his first girlfriend, so he'd better be on his best behavior. His laugh startled the dog and made him bark. The tail wagged faster, the eyes looked into his as if pleading.

"Sorry, pal," Owen said. "No dog hair in the truck today."

He made it to Willing in record time, pulling into the café parking lot ten minutes early. He parked in front of Meg's cabin and wondered if he should wait in the café. The Meg he knew was as punctual as an army general, a character trait that had amused and impressed everyone who worked on the ranch years ago. Sure enough, he saw the blinds twitch and then, seconds later, Meg popped out her door and locked it behind her. She wore jeans, boots and a heavy jacket, all of which were going to be important on a day like today.

He left the engine on and leaped out to get the door for her, but she'd already opened it by the time he raced around the car.

"Wait." He helped her climb inside, though she didn't need his assistance. He shut the door and went back to the driver's side.

"Good morning," was all he could manage to say now that Meg sat beside him. She wore her brown hair differently today, falling around her shoulders instead of pulled back into a tight ponytail. She looked radiant, and her dark eyes sparkled.

"I feel as if I'm skipping school." She glanced toward the restaurant as she fastened her seat belt. "Let's get out of here before there's a late morning rush or Al runs out of eggs."

"Yes, ma'am. I can do that." He had them out of the parking lot and onto the main road east of town within minutes.

"Tell me about the ranch," she said. "You're not running a cattle operation anymore?"

"No. Years ago we had to decide whether to hire people and make it profitable again, or lease parts of it out." Owen winced as a couple of raindrops hit the windshield. "Ed liked living there and my mother didn't want to have anything to do with it."

"I gathered that."

"Look, I'm sorry she was rude to you." He took a deep breath. "I love her, but she was a difficult woman."

"And now . . ."

"She doesn't remember who I am half the time. But back then . . . Well, she never was an easy person to understand. And she was determined to make her son into a success. And that didn't mean living on the ranch and having babies and sponsoring town projects."

"She didn't want you to marry the kitchen help."

"No," he admitted. "She made that clear at the time."

"She was grieving. It must have been awful for her to lose her husband like that. Your father was such a sweet man."

"My mother," he said, trying to keep his voice even, "was going to sell the ranch if I didn't go back to college."

"How could she do that?"

"She controlled my shares until I turned twenty-one, so she pretty much controlled everything for eight months after Dad died." He glanced at Meg, whose mouth had dropped open. "You didn't know that?"

"She told me I'd never trap her son, that you were destined for bigger things than herding cows and shoveling manure."

"That sounds like my mother," he said. "What I didn't know back then was just how miserable she was living on the ranch. She told me once that she never would have married my father if she'd known he wanted to go back to ranching. He'd been a banker," he explained. "And destined for 'great things.' "

"And that's what she wanted for you."

"Oh, yeah. That summer they were fighting a lot. Uncle Ed talked about it one time. He thought I knew she was leaving my father for another man."

"But you didn't."

He attempted a smile. "I was occupied with my own love life at the time."

It was time to change the subject, he decided. "Do you remember the dinner bell?"

Her face lit up. "Mrs. Hancock used to let me ring it."

"At noon. Exactly at noon." He chuckled softly. She hadn't forgotten.

"Why is that so funny?" She loosened her scarf and fussed with her hair before she turned back to him. "This heat feels good."

"My father was impressed with how punctual you were." He turned his windshield wipers on as the rain increased its noisy attack on the glass. "It's supposed to blow right over," he said, having no real idea since he'd had no time that morning to listen to weather reports.

They spent the next half hour talking about the weather, the TV show, how the cabin renovations were going, the producer's upcoming visit, supplies needed in Billings and the upcoming football game between rivals Montana State and Missoula's University of Montana. Owen put his blinker on and turned the car south onto another well-maintained gravel road. The rain continued, but it didn't come down hard. He drove through the open gates, wound around a stand of cottonwoods that lined a minor branch of Little Judith River and headed the last six miles home.

"I hope I made enough corn chowder for today." Meg peered through the windshield. "I told Al where I'd be in case of an emergency."

"Cell phone reception isn't always reliable out here, but I still have a landline."

"I'll call Al when we get there and let him know."

He pulled up beside the big house and wished he'd left some lights on. He could hear Boo barking from the living room as he turned off the engine. He opened his door and hopped out into the rain, then fumbled for an umbrella from the backseat. "I'll come round," he told her.

Instead of a casual stroll across the lawn to the front porch and wide door, they hustled quickly toward the side of the house and into the summer kitchen, a room that was damp and dark. He missed the scents of freshly baked bread and hot chili. Meanwhile Boo barked and whined like a maniac at the kitchen door, so Owen had no choice but to let the dog in.

"He's a rescue," Owen explained, anticipating some kind of bad behavior as Boo trotted toward Meg. "Sometimes it takes him a while to settle down."

"Ah, the bacon lover, right?" Meg patted his head and the dog immediately sat in front of her and impersonated a well-trained show dog.

"He's very sweet." She fondled his ears and the dog's tongue lolled out of his mouth. "Mrs. Hancock came in for lunch last year," Meg said, looking around the room very carefully. "With her grandson. She told some wonderful stories."

"She lives in Helena, near her daughter, now."

"Yes. She gave me her box of recipes. She said someone ought to have them so they could be used." She went over to the stove, ran her fingertips along the counter, peered at the thick white dishes stacked on the shelves and then turned to Owen, who was trying to decide how he'd gotten so damn lucky this morning. Meg was finally here again, in his home, and she seemed happy about it.

If that wasn't a miracle, he didn't know what was.

"Come on in the house," he said. "I'll make coffee and give you the grand tour."

"I'd like that," she said, and shivered, which was as good a reason as any to take her into his arms.

"Honey, get me a diet cola and a tuna-fish sandwich on white, toasted, with chips."

"Sure." Shelly tucked the unwanted menu back into its holder on the counter. She hadn't seen the woman walk in and take a seat on the middle stool because she'd been making her twentieth trip to the ladies' room. No one ever told you about that part of being pregnant. "Anything else?"

"No. I'd like something in my stomach before we go into the three-bears routine." She winked and then looked around the room. It was the quietest time of day, long after the lunch rush and well before dinner, so there wasn't much for the woman with the fluffy white-blond hair and rhinestone T-shirt to see.

"Okay." Shelly had no idea what the lady was talking about, but she wrote down the order and took it to Al, who was on the phone placing a meat order. She fixed the soda, set it in front of the stranger and carefully placed a straw and utensils along with it. "It will just be a minute."

"Sure. No problem. Margaret isn't here?"

"Meg? Uh, no. She'll be in later, around four." Was she fifty or sixty? Was she wearing a lot of bronzer or was she really tanned? Shelly thought the blue eye shadow was a bit much for a woman her age, whatever her age was. She kind of liked the T-shirt, with its pink smears and crystals, but no way would she wear those dangly earrings. But this older lady looked sophisticated, as if she traveled a lot and knew her way around. And she seemed friendly enough.

"So," the woman drawled. She unwrapped her straw, popped it into her drink and took a sip. "You're the mysterious pregnant girl. Have you found that boyfriend of yours yet?"

Shelly almost dropped her order pad. Who was this woman? "No, but —"

"Men are hard to find if they don't want to be found," she said. "But some turn up, whether you want them to or not."

Shelly didn't quite know what to say to that, so she settled for, "I hope so." She'd received lots of unsolicited advice in the past few weeks, but most of it had been about how to find a missing person. Les's grandfather had even offered to contact the state rodeo association, which she'd thought was awfully sweet of him. Les hadn't thought so, but she thought he might have a crush on her.

And she'd told his grandmother that a crush on a pregnant woman in love with someone else would ruin his life. They'd agreed on that, and then Mrs. Purcell had showed her how to make a piecrust. She doubted the woman in front of her would know flour from sugar.

"But you don't know much about this young man," the woman pointed out. "You don't know if he'll be a good father or a good husband. You don't know if he has fifty girlfriends or two wives or four children or any way to support a family."

Shelly didn't know whether to run, hide or fight back. "I don't think that's any of your business."

"It is when you're living in my house and wearing my clothes." She gestured at the yellow shirt Shelly wore. "I bought that in Austin on my honeymoon."

"You're Loralee? Meg's mom?" Shelly felt a little queasy. Did this mean she was homeless again?

"Bingo!" Loralee tapped pink-shellacked nails on the counter and looked off into the distance. "That was with husband number three," she said. "Sweet Gene. He drove truck and was gay as a two-dollar bill, but what did I know? That man loved to iron. We're still friends, of course. I keep up with him on Facebook."

"I'd better go see if your sandwich is ready," Shelly whispered, backing away from the counter. Al would know what to do. Shelly scurried into the kitchen.

"You can run, but you can't hide," Meg's mother called after her. "So take your time."

"We should probably stop and eat something," Meg said. She was out of breath and disheveled. She wanted to unlace her boots and fix her hair. She was starving and embarrassed and very, very warm. "Do you have food?"

"I do." He groaned as he said it, because Meg inadvertently elbowed him in the chest.

"Sorry." She struggled to get up from Owen's grandmother's green velvet settee. Her foot tingled uncomfortably as her circulation improved.

He reached out and caught her hand, planted a kiss on her knuckles and tugged her back down for a kiss.

"I'm going to faint if you don't feed me soon." When they were kids they'd fantasized about what it would be like to have the Triple M to themselves. To have the freedom to sit on that awful horsehair-stuffed sofa and kiss to their hearts' content, to hold hands at the kitchen table, to snuggle together on the big plaid couch.

This afternoon, with the rain preventing them from riding and hiking, they'd watched a movie and looked at the family photo albums. He'd shared some of the history of the ranch when she'd asked about his famous great-great-grandfather. He'd pulled her against him and they'd forgotten all about the enormity of the Triple M in 1887.

"It's still raining." Owen nuzzled her ear. "Please tell me you don't want to go riding in this."

"I don't want to go riding in this," she said. "Get up. We're going into the kitchen now. And we're going to stay, um, three feet apart, no matter what."

"You used to be shy," he grumbled, hauling himself to his feet. His shirt was untucked and wrinkled, his hair rumpled, and he looked gorgeous. Which he always did, she thought. She headed toward the kitchen.

"Tell me about cooking school," he said. He ran his hand through his hair and followed her down the hall. "That was your dream, right?"

"Uh-huh. I went to Johnson and Wales, in Rhode Island. That's where I met Lucia. We were roommates. She was from Wyoming, so we stuck together." She wished she'd thought to bring lunch. When she opened the refrigerator, however, she was surprised to find fresh vegetables and plastic pouches of deli meat.

"But you're back in Willing. Why?"

"I worked in New York," she said, stacking the food on the counter. "And Orlando. And Las Vegas."

"There's bread," he said, lifting a basket from the top of the refrigerator. "Sourdough and rye."

"Nice."

"Back to Vegas," he prompted, setting the basket on the kitchen table. "Then what?"

"Loralee was running the café into the ground, so I came home for a few weeks to reorganize it and I ended up loving the place. I liked being my own boss and creating the kind of food I'd always loved cooking — comfort food." She shrugged. "I stayed."

"And you're happy," he stated, not looking at her.

She didn't answer the question. Instead she fumbled with the plastic sleeve that held the roast beef. "What about you?"

"Happy?" He shrugged. "I'm not sure what I am. I haven't decided yet."

"Why aren't you married? Or were you ever?"

"I had a couple of close calls. You?"

"Afraid to make a mistake. Too independent. Never met the right guy. Take your pick."

"You met the right guy," he said. "Once."

She turned back to the refrigerator and pulled out mustard, mayonnaise and lettuce.

He stepped closer and wrapped his arms around her waist, exactly the way he used to when Mrs. Hancock wasn't around and they were alone for a few minutes in the summer kitchen. Owen kissed her neck and surrounded her with warmth. "You don't believe me."

She reached for the loaf of bread that sat between the telephone and the toaster. "Mustard or mayonnaise, cowboy?"

"Both. But —"

Meg jumped when the phone rang. Owen's arms tightened around her and he rested his chin on her shoulder. "Jerry calls me twice a day about getting the ranch ready for the TV people. He can wait."

But Meg saw the number displayed. "It's the café." She untangled herself and Owen moved away so she could pick up the receiver and find the right button to push. "Hello?"

CHAPTER TWELVE

"Well, that was a great big dose of reality." Meg hadn't said much during the drive back to town, despite Owen's attempts to distract her from her mother's surprise arrival.

"Yeah. Like a great big bucket of ice water dumped over our heads," he said, hoping to make her smile. She didn't. The rain had eased, but the skies were overcast and the wind had come up again. They'd made good time, even though he hadn't rushed. Despite his driving at five miles an hour below the speed limit, they were now pulling into the parking lot.

"I think you'd better just drop me off."

"No way." Owen parked the car on the far side of the lot, next to Jerry's 4Runner. "She won't see me from here if she's in the café."

"I'm sorry." Meg unhooked her seat belt but didn't move. "I wish I could sit here for a week or two."

"Sweetheart, say the word and I'll take you back home with me." He'd never meant anything more, but he suspected she didn't know that. He decided to keep the engine on, just in case.

"I'm such a coward. She makes me crazy. I mean, she's a good person and she'd never deliberately hurt me and she loves me, I know, and I love her, but she just makes me . . . crazy."

"Yeah," he said. "I plan to stay out of her way myself."

"Lucky you."

"In many ways." He reached for her hand and gave it a squeeze. "Thanks for the day, Meggie. I had a good time."

"Me, too." But she withdrew her hand as if she was afraid someone would see. "Are you coming to class tomorrow night?"

"Table Manners, Appropriate Conversation and Clothing Review? Wouldn't miss it."

"Try to avoid my mother."

"No problem." He looked past her. "I think one of your painters is already here." He turned the engine off and opened his door. "I'll see which cabin Jerry's working in and get started."

"You're painting?" She hopped out of the truck and stood under the eaves of cabin three with her hands in her jacket pockets.

Owen lifted a plastic bag from the back-seat and slammed his door shut. "Yes, ma'am, that's exactly what I'm doing. I even brought my own brushes."

"I'll see you in a little while, then. I'm painting, too."

"Keep Shelly away. The fumes aren't good for her."

"I know. But she wants to be helpful somehow, so I told her she could. I have a couple of high school girls coming in to wait tables." She smiled. "Or maybe I can get Loralee to waitress again."

If there was a way to run away, Shelly thought, she'd be out of here faster than you could say "bus." Loralee Smittle was just too scary, sort of a cross between a grandmother and a hooker, if there was such a thing.

Loralee wasn't a grandmother, though, because Meg was an only child.

Loralee was really outspoken and chatty. Not at all like Meg. And Meg didn't wear pink lipstick or tight T-shirts. She didn't have long fingernails with little rhinestones glued to them, either. The rhinestones were cool. No one in Willing had fingernails like them, and Shelly had seen a lot of fingers wrapped around a lot of forks and coffee mugs since she'd gotten off the bus.

Shelly didn't want to be here when Meg returned, but she was out of luck on that score. She'd seen Owen MacGregor's truck pull in a few minutes ago, which meant her boss would arrive with flushed cheeks and a sparkle in her eyes. She'd heard about what happened after the dance class last night — it was all over town — and hoped that Meg could keep that tall rancher to herself after the TV people came. He wasn't as grumpy when Meg was around.

Meg hadn't sounded too thrilled about her mother's surprise visit on the phone. She'd told Shelly not to tell her mother where she was or who she was with. And as far as Shelly was concerned, Meg's mom could stomp on her with those high-heeled Western boots — pink lizard wingtips — and Shelly would never talk. She didn't care if she had to sleep in Meg's car, though she knew her boss would never let that happen.

She hoped it wasn't time to move on. She wasn't ready. She sure hoped Loralee wouldn't mind a roommate, even though that seemed like a lot to hope for. Of course, she'd be happy to move to one of the cabins they were in the process of renovating . . . if the paint fumes weren't too bad. Her little bit of luck, that unfamiliar feeling that things were going her way, had evaporated, just the way it always did.

Now it was Loralee's turn to wonder about Meg. She'd switched from a stool at the counter to a chair at the table next to a booth. "She should be back soon, you said?"

"Yes, ma'am. Any minute." Kip and Kate, Mr. Petersen's twin granddaughters, were waiting on the four customers in the café. Shelly was officially off duty, but she wouldn't leave until she talked to Meg. So she stretched out in a booth with her feet up, which eased the ache in her lower back. The baby was growing faster than she'd expected.

"Did Margaret go into Lewistown?"

"Maybe," Shelly hedged. "She didn't actually say. Can I pour you another cup of coffee?"

"No, bless your heart. You'd better stay right where you are. If I want coffee I'll get it myself. How far along are you?"

"Twenty-two weeks."

"So you're over the morning sickness."

The bell tinkled and Meg stepped inside. "Mom?"

Loralee turned and gave her daughter a big smile. She jumped up and met her halfway across the room for a big hug.

Shelly swallowed the lump in her throat. Loralee might be loud and nosy, but she loved her daughter.

That counted for a lot.

"Here." Loralee produced a tube of lip gloss from her enormous pink handbag and handed it across the table to Meg. "Use this. Your lips are red. They're going to get chapped if you don't take care of them, and men don't like chapped lips. Makes them feel like they're kissing an iguana."

Shelly choked, and then coughed.

"Well, we can't have that." Meg did as she was told, but she didn't dare look at her waitress. She handed the gloss back to her mother, who told her to keep it.

"I'll get another one. The grocery store hasn't closed down yet, has it?"

"No. . . . Well, this is a surprise, Mom. You didn't tell me you were coming."

Loralee made a show of rearranging the inside of her enormous purse. "I thought I had some moisturizer in here, too. Your skin could use it. I thought I taught you to always apply moisturizer, especially in this kind of weather."

"Mom? I'll grease up my face, I promise. Just as soon as you tell me why you're here." Though Meg suspected she knew exactly why Loralee was back in town: she didn't want to miss out on the excitement.

"You know I've always loved Halloween here."

"Right. And . . . ?"

"I thought you would need help. With all the new people coming in."

"And . . . ?"

"I missed you."

"And . . . ?"

"You really should have told me about Shelly." She gave the girl a reassuring look. "Not that I mind, dear, but you could have knocked me over with a feather when I saw that someone was living in my cabin. It was a real 'who's been sleeping in my bed?' moment, let me tell you."

Shelly blushed. "I'll go somewhere else —"

Meg held up her hand. "Let's wait on that for a minute, okay? We'll figure it out, don't worry." And then she looked at her mother, who almost vibrated with excitement. Even the rhinestone earrings were twitching. "You're here for the TV show."

Loralee gulped, and then began to laugh. "Well, of course I'm here for the show! I left Joan with her yarn and her bridge group and got on a plane. Two planes. I've been following the news online, you know, just to keep up with what's happening, since you haven't had time to talk on the phone lately."

"The newspaper's online?"

"No, but the newspaper has a website. And Jerry likes to blog."

"Why am I not surprised?"

"And don't you worry about a thing," Loralee said to Shelly. "We'll be roommates for a couple of weeks. When are you due?"

"February twenty-seventh."

"Oh, my goodness. You still have quite a ways to go. Is it a boy or a girl?"

"Uh, I don't want to know. Not yet."

Loralee sighed. "I'm not going to ask how old you are. It would just depress me."

"Mom," Meg said, trying to distract her before Shelly slumped to the floor in embarrassment. "Let's go get you settled in."

"There's not much to settle," she said, but she sprang to her feet and picked up her empty cup. "I already put my suitcase in the cabin and I don't have much to unpack."

"How did you get here?"

"I rented a car at the airport. In Billings. It's too bad I wanted to surprise you, or you could have picked me up. Where were you, shopping?"

"There's been a lot to do to get three of

the cabins ready."

"I can't wait to see. Let me get my coat and you can give me a tour."

"Uh, not today." Loralee couldn't be counted on to be pleasant to Owen, and Meg hadn't had time to explain his part in the dating classes. "I'd rather you wait and see them painted. The new bathrooms are in, and the carpet comes on Friday."

"But —"

"Please? Let me surprise you," Meg insisted, using her sweet-daughter voice. Loralee's eyes narrowed, but she agreed.

"Come on, then, Shelly," she said. "Let's go home and talk about this boyfriend of yours. Have you talked to the police about helping you find him? He could be in jail, you know. Jail is always a possibility when a man disappears, though it's not likely, I guess. None of my husbands ever did time. Was he a lot older than you? Or was he young and —"

"Mom! Mind your own business and leave the girl alone." Shelly gave her a grateful look. "Let me check with Kate and Kip before we leave. Al's gone, but his nephew's cooking tonight and I need to make sure he has everything."

"What's the special?"

Meg had no idea, so she kept walking

toward the kitchen and the sound of Motown rather than admit she'd been too preoccupied to oversee menus. She couldn't remember if tonight was pot roast, turkey or meat loaf.

"Turkey, gravy, mashed potatoes and green beans," Shelly replied. "Ten ninety-five with coffee and dessert. And rolls."

"Perfect. I always say comfort food sells better than bean sprouts. We'll have Meg deliver our dinner to the cabin, then. Once I take these boots off, they're *staying* off," Loralee said. "Meg! Order three of those specials to go for six o'clock, will you? We'll have a nice little all-girl dinner and catch up! You can tell me what all you've been teaching the men around here."

It took another forty-five minutes to settle Loralee into the cabin and to assure Shelly that she didn't have to move out. Loralee wouldn't hear of Shelly moving into the spare room and Shelly tearfully refused to sleep anywhere else. They were still discussing it when Meg left to change into her painting clothes.

Amazingly, the men were halfway through the second cabin by the time she caught up with them.

"It's going real fast. Jerry's doing the trim," Les explained when she walked in.

"Mike and I are doing the walls with the roller." He held it up to show her. "Not the pine paneling, but the other walls."

"It looks great." And it did.

"Owen's making sure the plumbing is hooked up right. Where's Shell? Is she okay? She knows she can't come inside because of the smell, but I hoped she'd say hi."

"She's with my mother."

He gulped. "I heard Mrs., uh, Smittle was back. She's letting Shelly stay?"

"Absolutely."

"Oh, good. I was worried."

"I wouldn't let anything happen to Shelly, you know that."

Next door she found Hip and Owen deep in conversation about wood.

Owen's hands were covered in some kind of black grease and Hip, who had a flask in the front pocket of his down vest, was coated in a fine layer of sawdust.

"Hey," Owen said, smiling.

"Hi," was all Hip could manage to say.

"Hi," she said to both of them. She didn't know what else to add except, "Give me a job. I'm ready to paint something."

"Jerry's painting the bathroom," Owen said. "You and I can do the kitchen. How's that sound?"

"Okay. Oh, by the way, do either one of

you know anything about the rodeo in Billings?"

Hip looked trapped. "Uh, no."

"Sure. Stock show and a lot of other things going on. We never made it to the ranch finals, but it was fun to watch." Owen grabbed a roll of paper towels and peeled off a couple of feet. "Why? Do you want to go?"

"Maybe. Are you free this weekend?"

"Honey," he said with a big grin on that too-good-looking cowboy face of his. "That's a really easy question to answer." Hip fled, leaving the door open behind him.

She tried not to laugh when Owen kicked the door shut and stepped closer. "Do *not* touch me with those greasy hands."

"Did you just ask me out?" He carefully wiped his hands.

"Shh. Isn't Jerry in here?"

Sure enough, the mayor hollered, "I can hear every word! And yes, you did ask him out! Have you seen the bathrooms? They look great! Mike did the tiling."

"Hi, Jerry! I can't wait to see!" She took a step back from the man who looked very much as if he'd like to kiss her anyway, even if they weren't alone.

"There are enough rumors going around about us as it is," she whispered. "Now I have to bribe Jerry with extra pie or something."

"He already owes you. And me," Owen pointed out, gazing at her mouth. "But don't worry. He's a politician, right? I'll make him an offer he can't refuse."

"I've started a countdown." Jerry stared at the screen of his cell phone. "I need to call someone about better reception up here."

"A countdown for what?" Meg started setting a table for two. She carefully placed the silverware, napkin and wineglasses.

"After tonight we have four days. Four days," Jerry repeated, tucking the phone into the holder on his belt. "And on day five —"

"All hell breaks loose," Meg finished for him.

"Could we have a little more optimism, please?"

"I'm concentrating on getting this table right." Class would begin in ten minutes and the men had been trickling in, despite the fact that hunting season began in two days. It would be a busy weekend and she'd been working on new soup recipes all day.

"Sorry. Where's your mother? I want to meet her. Did I tell you that she comments on my blog?"

"She really loves her iPad." Meg refolded the white cotton napkin and set it neatly to the left of the forks. "She'll be here, don't worry. This is what she came here for. That, and decorating the diner with a crate of oranges."

"What?"

"Nothing." Meg had spent twenty minutes dumping oranges into bowls for center-pieces at breakfast. Whether anyone mistook them for pumpkins was a mystery.

"I'm glad she's here." Jerry scanned the crowd. "After five husbands, the woman's practically an encyclopedia of dating info. What's Esther doing here? She's eighty-five."

"Eighty-six." Meg studied the table and decided it looked beautiful. She'd used a round white cloth that dropped to the floor and topped it with a white-and-gold table-cloth she'd borrowed from Lucia. Mama Marie had provided the gold-rimmed china and the sterling silver utensils. The crystal glasses were Meg's, a matching set she'd bought in an antique shop in Bozeman last year. "And I have no idea."

"She's carrying a slide projector. Is she on the list for tonight?"

"Not that I know of. Lucia's doing a clothing review for anyone who wants to go over their shopping list, Shelly and Loralee will take them through the two-step again and I'm doing table etiquette, making small talk and how to make a good first impression."

"You know, the men are starting to look better."

"Grooming and makeovers still on for next week?"

"At the community center. I've made arrangements with a beauty school — Oh, hi, Lucia."

"Hi, Jer. Oh, Meg, the table looks so romantic!" She gave Meg a hug. "How are you holding up?"

"Actually, just fine. Mom spent the day visiting friends and annoying Shelly while I made soup. Business was slow."

"What's with Esther and the sex talk? She told me she found something at the library about the birds and the bees."

Jerry turned pale. "She emailed me something about fifth-grade gym class, but I didn't read it." He took Lucia's arm and pulled her toward Esther. "Come on. You can help me head her off."

Meg watched the door. She didn't want to seem as if she was waiting for Owen, but she didn't really expect him to show up for this particular session, not with Loralee around.

And here he was, walking through the door as if he'd been doing it for years. Meg watched Owen as he scanned the crowd. He smiled when he saw her, and then greeted Les and Hip and joined in a conversation with several of the younger men.

She noticed more than a few curious glances in her direction. She was supposed to be the most hard-hearted woman in town, Lucia had told her once. Lucia had been laughing at the time, because Meg had been rocking three-week-old Tony while Lucia was stretched out in bed with her two-year old and a stack of storybooks.

Meg liked her business. She liked her cabin, as small as it was. Her life was what she'd made for herself, by herself. Wanting Owen, needing Owen, falling in love with Owen? He'd been the man for her once, when he'd wanted the small-town life and she'd yearned to make something of herself. Funny how they'd ended up, both of them here in Willing, but this time she was the one who had cemented herself into a world she loved. And he was the one who didn't seem to know what he was doing. She could love him again. And maybe she'd never stopped loving him.

Did that mean they could make it work this time? Or should she start thinking about what she'd do after he left again?

CHAPTER THIRTEEN

"Forks? You're telling these men that their future love life depends on knowing all about *forks*?" Tonight her mother, although dumbfounded at tonight's dating-class subject, looked more rested than she had when she arrived yesterday. Her petal-pink top floated past her hips; her fashionable skinny jeans were tucked into pink-leather boots. She didn't look sixty. To Meg's secret amazement, her mother had stayed quiet during the first half of the class. But now, staring at the set table, she wasn't able to resist commenting on Meg's instructions to the hopeful bachelors, who gathered nearby after having demolished a large amount of corn chips and Meg's homemade peach salsa.

"We're getting them ready to make a good impression on the women they'll meet."

"There is no way Joseph Peckham is going to tell a salad fork from a dessert fork, no matter how many times he sits down at this table and practices."

"Do you mind? Everyone gets ten minutes and you're blocking the line."

"Jerry's cute," her mother said, ignoring Meg's not-so-subtle hint. "A little obsessive-compulsive, but charming. You dated him, I hear."

"Once."

"And?"

"Nothing." She rearranged the forks once again, hoping her mother would take the hint.

"He's a little tame for you, I suppose, but probably good husband material."

Behind her mother's back, Jerry grinned. He gave Meg the thumbs-up.

There were so many things Meg could have said in response, but she didn't want to hurt her mother's feelings. Loralee, whose tender heart could never resist a sad story, had decided to take Shelly under her wing and for that Meg was grateful. How Shelly felt about the unexpected mothering Meg didn't know, but the two of them were officially roommates and Shelly had worn a pink golf shirt to work this morning.

"Mom, it's Pete's turn."

"Oh." Loralee turned around and motioned for Pete Lyons to take the empty chair across from Meg. "Go ahead, sweetie. But with a handsome face like yours, I don't know why you can't find a girlfriend all by yourself."

"I'm working on it, Mrs. Smittle," he answered, giving her a cute grin. "But I sure don't mind picking up a few tips when I can."

"Call me Loralee, please. Why I ever married anyone named Smittle I'll never know. I think I'll change it back to Ripley. It's just easier to remember." She stepped away from the table and told Meg, "I'm going to go home, take Shelly with me and make sure she gets off her feet."

"Thanks, Mom. She did a good job with the dance steps tonight."

"It was the best part of the evening," she declared, eyeing the table again. "Pete, don't forget to ask the lady about herself, compliment her on something and listen. Listening counts for a lot. A lot more than knowing which fork to use. Don't belch, don't pick your teeth and you'll do fine."

"Yes, ma'am." Pete picked up the empty wineglass and set it down in the same spot. "I can do all that."

Loralee hesitated and leaned closer to whisper near Meg's ear. "I thought I saw someone who looked like *Owen* earlier. *He's* not involved in this, is he?"

"You'll have to ask the mayor," Meg hedged. Pete removed his napkin from the table and put it in his lap. He grinned at her as if he'd just gotten an A.

"Hmm." Loralee noticed Pete's gleeful expression. "Remember not to talk with your mouth full," she cautioned. "And no toothpicks!"

"Yes, ma'am."

"Watch him," Loralee said to Meg before she walked away. "Men are simple creatures, but they'll usually tell you what they think you want to hear and go off and do what they want to do."

"Maybe you should teach a class for women," Meg teased. Loralee hooted, her boots clacking as she toddled off to find Shelly.

After another hour and a half of teaching table manners and explaining which fork to use for which part of the meal to those who hadn't a clue, Meg ushered the last of the bachelors out the door, turned out most of the lights and opened a bottle of chilled white wine to share with Lucia. The two of them sat across from each other in a corner booth and clinked glasses.

"Your iron is your friend," Lucia toasted.

"No belching or slurping," Meg countered.

"Sort your laundry by colors."

"Eat to the left, drink to the right."

Lucia considered that one as she took a sip of her drink. "Clever. Your plates are always on your left and your glasses are on your right?"

"Yes. It was a novel concept to some, but they got the hang of it."

"Wait until next week, when some of them get haircuts." Lucia giggled. "I can't wait for Tuesday."

"Neither can Jerry. That's when *they* arrive in town."

"Are you in a panic yet?"

"A little." Meg thought of everything she had left to do on the three cabins this coming weekend. "Jerry wants me to stock the shelves with organic soaps and soy candles."

"Give me a list and I'll pick up what you need in town on Saturday. I'm taking the boys to the movies."

"Thank you. I'm going to Billings but there won't be a chance to shop. I could ask my mother, but I'm not sure what she'd come home with."

"Why Billings? Hot date with your rancher?"

"Right." She rolled her eyes. "With Shelly

as chaperone. The livestock show started today." She explained what the girl had told her about the ranch rodeo finals. "The mysterious Sonny could be roaming around there."

"Shelly still believes —"

"That she'll find her prince again, the same way she found him the first time, at the rodeo."

"I hope she's right, but you and I know the problems with princes. Speaking of royalty," Lucia drawled, refilling her wine-glass and gesturing toward the door with the half-empty bottle. "Here comes Ranch King now."

"Ranch King? I heard that," Owen said. "Which means you've never seen the ranch." He scanned the dimly lit dining room. "Is the coast clear?"

"You're safe," Meg answered. She thought he'd gone home . . . without saying good-bye. "Just don't turn the overhead lights on. She could be looking out the window to see if she's missing anything."

"I parked around the corner, in the alley next to the Laundromat," he said, approaching the booth. Meg scooted over to give him more room. "But she knows I'm in town, right? I can handle her when I meet her again, you know."

"Yes," Meg said. "I'm delaying the inevitable lecture. If I can get her back to Tucson without having an opinion on how I'm handling my life, I'll do whatever I can."

"Coward," Lucia said, then turned to Owen.

"Before you sit down, help yourself to a wineglass," Lucia told him. "We're recovering from the class and celebrating the rebirth of civilization right here in Willing."

"The wineglasses are over there, to the left of the sink," Meg added.

When he went behind the counter to find one, Lucia raised her eyebrows at Meg, who shrugged. "Want me to leave?" Lucia whispered.

"Absolutely not." Meg knew Lucia had looked forward to getting out tonight. Mama Marie had insisted on staying with the boys, along with providing dinner, so there was no reason for Lucia to rush home.

"I'd *like* to see the ranch," Lucia said, picking up the conversation when Owen sat down close to Meg and poured himself a small amount of wine. "My boys would get a kick out of the horses. My four-year-old is going to be a cowboy for Halloween."

"I have a couple of horses out there now, but they're not mine. They're gentle enough, though. How old are your sons?"

"Four, six and eight."

"Good ages to start riding," he said. He sat close enough for her to feel his warmth. His thick brown sweater smelled like the outdoors, and she wished she could lean her cheek against his arm.

"Oh, I didn't mean they needed to *ride,*" Lucia sputtered. "They'd just enjoy seeing horses, feeding them apples and carrots, petting their noses, things like that."

"If they'd like to get up on the horses, I'd be glad to lead them around in one of the corrals," Owen said. "Unless you don't want them to."

"No, they'd love it, but —"

"Hey." Owen, his voice low and gruff, stopped her protest. "I've heard good things about your husband. And I respect what he was doing. If his children want to ride horses and you want them to ride, then that's what will happen as long as I'm here."

Lucia's eyes filled with tears, but she choked out, "Okay. Thank you."

Meg swallowed the sudden lump in her own throat while Owen cleared his. "Les is going to bring over four more horses this weekend. His grandfather used to have a trail-riding business north of here, so the horses are used to beginners." He looked at Meg. "We're getting ready to impress the

Californians."

"You are?"

"I'm on the location committee, remember?"

"There are rumors you have a hot tub," Lucia said. "Is that true, Ranch King?"

He winced. "I hope you never call me that in front of anyone but Meg. And yes, I have a hot tub. My uncle installed it when he moved in, but I need to clean it up this weekend and get it running."

Meg touched his arm. "When did you decide to open up the ranch to the TV crew?"

"After the first class, I suppose. I'm not sure exactly when, but it's important to the town, right?"

"An excellent reason," Lucia noted. She widened her eyes at Meg. "And I, for one, want to see that hot tub."

"What do you clean the thing with?"

Lucia offered to look it up and call him tomorrow. After another twenty minutes chatting about the "boyfriend project," as Lucia called it, the three of them left the restaurant.

"So," he said to Meg, "when are we going to the rodeo to search for the elusive boyfriend?"

"Saturday?"

"What time?"

"If you're here at noon, I'll give you lunch before we leave."

"Sounds good." Owen didn't follow Meg to her door, though he watched as she unlocked it. He escorted Lucia to her car and then rounded the building to the alley where he'd parked. She had no business feeling disappointed. He could be rethinking their attraction, just as she should.

Meg quickly showered and tucked herself into bed, propping pillows against the carved oak headboard she'd bought one summer at an auction in Big Timber. She clicked the remote to turn on the television mounted on the opposite wall and found the local weather channel. Any kind of pending storm system would be a problem. All clear so far, she discovered, though there could be scattered snow showers on Saturday.

Whatever she and Owen were doing scared her half to death. She caught herself dreaming of a life with him, but those had also been her dreams as a teenager who'd assumed that love equaled happily ever after. And even though she had been the one to call off the elopement, she hadn't expected him to abandon her. She'd learned that love didn't always equal a happy ending.

But what if there was nothing wrong with that dream? What if, even though it hadn't happened for her once, it might this time? She was a woman attracted to a man. A decent man, from what she'd seen.

Or was she a complete idiot for even contemplating such a thing? He was a hot-shot businessman with a historic ranch and ancestors he could trace through five centuries in Scotland. Which he was going to sell, and then he was going to leave again.

Meg climbed out of bed and went into the bathroom to take a couple of aspirin. The question of love had given her a headache.

"The more the merrier," Hip said, standing awkwardly next to an enormous white Cadillac Escalade. Theo waved from behind the wheel. Owen stopped in front of the car, which was parked next to his truck.

"What the heck is Hip doing here?"

"I don't know." Meg hoped the man hadn't started drinking again. She waved to Theo.

"Hip wants to go, too," Shelly informed them. "They're going to help us look for Sonny."

"But they don't know what he looks like any more than we do," Meg said, hoping

Hip didn't have feelings for Shelly. She couldn't imagine that working out, not with the age difference, among other things. The man would only get hurt.

The girl shrugged. "If you see a tall, blond guy wearing a black hat, just holler, 'Sonny!' and see if he turns around." She gave Hip a wave and went over to say hello.

"That sounds easy enough," Owen murmured. "Because rodeos are so quiet and all."

"I'd thought more about studying the names on the program and going from there."

Owen shook his head and opened the truck passenger doors. "Sounds like a wild goose chase any way we do it."

"I know," Meg whispered, as Shelly joined them and climbed into the backseat. "Do they still have cotton candy?"

"Sure," the girl chirped. "And chicken on a stick. All sorts of good stuff." She fumbled in her bag and pulled out her cell phone. "Do you guys have your phones?"

"Yes," Meg said, and Owen nodded. He put the truck into reverse and followed the Cadillac out of the parking lot.

"I brought binoculars."

"I hope we get lucky," Shelly said, sighing as she looked out the window. "It's not supposed to snow, is it?"

"No," Owen assured her.

"Good thinking on the binoculars." Meg wished she'd thought of that, but she hadn't decided if finding a one-night-stand disappearing boyfriend was in Shelly's best interests. Was that the kind of man who would make a good father? Meg didn't think so.

"Are we sure this is a good idea?" she asked, turning around to look at Shelly. "What if —"

"Don't say it," the girl said. "Dr. Jenks said I had to keep positive and not get all worried and upset over things. Getting stressed out and stuff isn't good for the baby."

"Okay," Meg said slowly, glancing at Owen. He raised his eyebrows but didn't say a word. "Then we'll think positive."

Owen took his right hand off the steering wheel and reached over to take Meg's hand. He squeezed her fingers. "I'm positive we'll have a good time," he murmured. "How's that?"

"I like it." She liked the warmth of his skin against hers. "I like it a lot."

"And look at this." It was a lovely Sunday morning as Meg pointed out the carved elk head on the door of cabin four. "Hip made them for all three of the cabins. An elk, a bear and a Dahl sheep."

"That's talent," Loralee agreed, running her fingers over the outline of the elk. "I didn't know he was a real artist. I thought he carved tree trunks, not pretty things like this."

"He's making something for the baby," Shelly said.

"Lucky baby," Meg said. She looked exhausted, which made Shelly feel bad. They'd gotten home late after spending hours looking for someone who wasn't there.

Loralee opened the door to the last finished cabin. "Too bad Hip's a drinker. Never fall in love with a drinker, Shell. You can't fix them."

"Oh, I'm not —"

"Mom, what do you think of the colors in here? We picked out the blue for the walls to match the bathroom tiles. Mike got a deal on them on Craigslist."

"Just perfect," Loralee said, poking her head into the bathroom. "I like the new fixtures. We should have done this years ago."

Despite how exhausted she seemed, Shelly had never seen Meg so happy. She'd cried when the women from the quilt group had surprised her this morning with three bed quilts and six intricate quilted wall hangings to decorate the cabins. There had been other surprises, too. Lucia's oldest son's class had painted pictures of their version of Montana; the teacher chose the best ones and Mike matted and framed them to hang above the new towel racks in the bathrooms.

Mama Marie's specialty, Italian anise cookies, were packaged in cellophane and tied with ribbons to welcome the guests. Pressed-wildflower greeting cards said, "Welcome to Willing, Montana." Loralee had bought a trunkful of thick white towels and washcloths in Lewistown.

Owen had arrived this morning, after the new carpet had been installed and Loralee had gone to town. He'd delivered a truckload of furniture from his ranch and insisted that he had no use for it. Shelly had heard that he and some of the other men had had it all set up inside the rooms before Meg had known what was happening. It seemed as if the entire town was determined to impress their visitors.

A lot was riding on this visit, and the people in town knew it.

Shelly liked the quilts the best. She didn't know much about sewing, except for that quilt show Meg had taken her to, but she knew how pretty the quilts looked on the new beds. Like something out of the *Country Living* magazines in the clinic's waiting room.

"This is, um, unusual." Loralee turned to Shelly and made a funny face, but Meg didn't notice, which was good, because Shelly could tell she really liked the brightly colored quilt. It hung in the center of the wall that divided the bedroom from the bathroom and was bigger than the two in the other cabins.

"It's gorgeous," Meg said, stepping closer to study the stitching. "Aurora said she was learning to quilt, but I didn't know she was an artist."

"It's very modern," Loralee pointed out. "All those strips put together, no rhyme or reason, is very, uh, different." According to the tone of Loralee's voice, "different" didn't mean "beautiful."

"I like it," Shelly said, trying not to laugh. "I love the other quilts, too, because they look like quilts are supposed to look, you know? But I like this, too."

"Aurora told me she was inspired by Gee's Bend," Meg explained.

"What's that?" Shelly asked, but Meg didn't know any more about it.

"I'll look it up it on the iPad," Loralee promised. "After we eat. Is there any of that chicken-tortilla soup left?"

"Uh-uh." Shelly sat in one of the two chairs that flanked the round Formica-topped table. "It sold out."

"The opening weekend of deer hunting," Loralee said with a sigh, joining her at the little table across from the bed. "I should have known."

"I'll make it again next week," Meg promised.

"It's my new favorite," Shelly said, running a hand over her expanding bump.

The baby moved. Which made him — and she just knew it was a boy — real. Much more real. She'd studied the pamphlets the doctor had given her. She'd spent time on websites for expectant mothers. Shelly had tried hard to do everything right: getting enough rest, eating vegetables and fresh fruit, taking her prenatal vitamins and not stressing out too much when she messed up the kitchen orders.

Al never yelled, which was cool, but she hated screwing up and making more work for everyone else.

She'd been saving her money and she'd managed to pay the bill to keep her cell phone working. Sonny had the number. So did a couple of her friends from school, though they didn't know where she was. They'd promised to tell her if Sonny came looking for her, and they'd been trying to track him down online. But without much luck so far.

And she could take care of herself. Mostly. After all, she had a place to live and a job. Her roommate wasn't so bad. She didn't have boyfriends and she didn't smoke or drink or zone out on pot. She wasn't like Shelly's own mother at all.

The pink thing was a little weird, but Loralee looked good in that color. Shelly thought someone who'd had five husbands would be surrounded by men all the time, but so far Loralee settled for pouring coffee and chatting with her old customers. She remembered everyone's names. And so far she hadn't been to the Dahl for a beer. She was definitely more like a grandmother and a mom. Once you got to know her, she was just a loud person who liked pink and made people smile.

"Shelly? Are you okay?"

Shelly blinked and realized Meg was bending over her. "Sorry. I was thinking."

Meg sure looked worried. "I'm sorry about yesterday," she said.

"It was worth a shot," she said, echoing

Hip's one-sentence summary of the trip. It had been really weird at times. Hip had seemed nervous and his younger cousin had kept checking his cell phone as if he wanted to be anywhere else. They'd walked past barns and corrals and horse trailers, sat in the stands, strolled past the food trailers and watched the people. She didn't think Hip liked crowds. "Hip and Theo were really nice."

"Theo's still around? He used to drive kids to the prom in one of his old Cadillacs, remember?" Loralee laughed. "There were a couple of years when the high school seniors thought it was cool to get all dressed up and eat here, at the café. I'd set up tables with fancy tablecloths and candles. I don't think Hip did that, though. He was an oldest child, wasn't he?"

"Yes. He had younger sisters. Maybe that's who you're thinking about."

"We had pot-roast sundaes for supper," Shelly said. "And root beer. Hip didn't even drink a beer the whole time."

"I could use one of those now." Loralee scanned the room again. "The pot roast, not the beer. Where'd you find the beds? And these fancy dressers?"

"They're on loan," was all Meg said, but Shelly could tell by the expression on Loralee's face that she knew that explanation was a lie and poor Meg had walked into a trap.

"On loan from the Triple M," Loralee supplied. "Because I've heard that not only is Owen MacGregor on the location committee and the entertainment committee, he's also on the *renovation* committee. I suppose this whole thing was his idea?"

"Uh, no. He was reluctant at first." Meg smoothed the blue-and-yellow quilt across the queen-size mattress. "Can you believe they even had dust ruffles? Janet ironed all of them. And the shams, too."

"You could have told me he'd come back here," Loralee said. She eyed Shelly. "You, too, missy. You could have said something."

Shelly played innocent and widened her eyes. "About what? Mr. MacGregor? Is he the guy with the old black Jeep? Does he have a beard?"

"Nice try," the older woman muttered, but she looked at her daughter when she said, "Fool me once, shame on you. Fool me twice, shame on me. That ring a bell?"

Meg blushed and went back to fussing with the quilt.

"He's avoiding me, I suppose." She stood and smoothed her coral sweater over her hips. "Which means he's smarter than he used to be."

"Let it go," her daughter said, sounding tired. "You can't hold a grudge forever."

"No?" Loralee motioned to Shelly. "Let's go eat, girlfriend. I'll tell you all about grudges and then we'll watch *The Amazing Race.*"

Shelly, knowing Meg would be happy for the break, followed Loralee out the door. She'd rather listen to the woman's chatter than worry about what she'd do if she couldn't find her baby's father.

Yesterday she'd been filled with hope. She'd seen so many jeans-clad young men in black Stetsons and worn leather boots, but none had come close to looking like Sonny. He wasn't tall, but he was wiry and muscled. Lean and strong. With a confident swagger and a sweet smile, he naturally caught the attention of women.

She'd tried so hard to look pretty. She'd straightened her hair into silky smooth sheets. She'd borrowed Loralee's red boots with the blue butterfly pattern and a red-and-pink-patterned blouse that flowed over her growing belly. She still wore a belt to hold up her unzipped jeans, but the blouse went all the way down past her hips and covered the gap. Her favorite gold hoop ear-rings and pink lip gloss made her look trendy and cool. Loralee advised her not to use any makeup because she'd spoil the "ripe peach" effect.

It had all been for nothing. She was trying so hard to do the right things for her baby, but so far she couldn't do the one thing that was the most important: find his daddy.

"No to an official welcoming committee. While most of you will be at the grooming session tonight, I'll be waiting for Tracy and her group to arrive, which should be between seven and eight. Meg and I will get them settled in. As far as tonight goes, yes to Marie Swallow's pizza being served during class tonight. I'll pick up the tab for that. Yes to cookies, as long as they're homemade. Gluten-free or not, doesn't matter." Jerry read silently for a moment while the members of the town council — minus Les — enjoyed their lunch.

Meg and Lucia were at the far end of the long table, but Meg had eaten earlier so she only had a cup of coffee in front of her. She'd expected to see Owen earlier on his way home from visiting his mother in Great Falls, but he hadn't stopped for breakfast. He probably had a lot to do at the ranch to get ready, she told herself, but she was disappointed. He wouldn't be at the grooming class tonight and he'd be busy playing tour guide for the rest of the week.

Shelly, who looked distracted, managed the few stragglers at the counter by herself. It was after two o'clock, so the small lunch rush was long past. Loralee was down the street at the Hair Lair for highlights and a mani-pedi.

"Yes to horseback riding Thursday morning. We'll take a picnic lunch. Tomorrow morning we'll scout locations and they'll get a sense of the town. Tomorrow afternoon at three there will be a tea and a brief history of the area given by the historical committee."

"Where is that again?" Meg checked her notes.

"At the community center. If the weather holds, we'll walk through the cemetery and point out the more historic grave sites."

Meg and Lucia exchanged horrified looks. Lucia raised her hand.

"What about shopping?"

"They'll have Friday afternoon and part of Saturday," Jerry assured her. "Tracy is bringing two technical advisors and her assistant, all women." He grinned at the men around the table. "We'll have ample opportunities to practice making a good impression. Make sure you dress with a little

Western flair, remember?"

"I've definitely worked with the guys on flair," Lucia assured him.

"Great. Meg, are you all set with the menus?"

She held up a large notebook. "Al and I have come up with daily specials I think they'll like. We're having elk roast Thursday night and venison tacos Saturday, before the party. I'm going all out on soups and stews during the day, along with artisan breads and Lucia's pies. Tomorrow Marie is catering an Italian dinner at your house. What's happening on Friday night? Have I missed something?"

"I'm leaving that open for now," he said. "We have the high school football game in Lewistown — go Wildcats — Friday night. We can grab something at Chili Dawgs or even have drinks at the Dahl later that night, after the game. Aurora usually has live music on Friday nights, doesn't she?"

"Sometimes."

He looked around the table. "Any questions?"

Pete raised his hand. "How do we get to meet them? Before Friday night and before the thing on Saturday?"

"Good question. I was about to get to that." Jerry flipped to another page in his notebook. "Shelly and/or Loralee will send out a group text to every bachelor on our list when our guests are in the café. That will give you time to get over here and have coffee or whatever, as if you didn't know they were here."

"Genius," someone exclaimed.

Meg tried not to laugh. She didn't dare look across the table at Lucia.

Jerry continued. "Aurora will do the same at the Dahl, as will Joey Peckham at the Gas 'N' Go gift shop. I want our visitors to see a lot of men. *A lot of men,*" he repeated, though Meg was certain everyone got the message.

"Even if they're the same men over and over again?" Meg couldn't help asking.

"Damn right. We want to look like a town bursting at the seams with bachelors."

"Speaking of bachelors," Lucia said, looking past Meg. "I see two heartthrobs right now."

Les stopped to talk to Shelly, but Owen made a beeline toward Meg and pulled out a chair at the end of the table. He smiled and sat down. "What'd I miss?"

"Do you know about the text list?"

"Oh, yeah. But I live too far out of town to participate."

"I had another idea," Jerry announced,

only this time he looked nervous instead of organized and bossy. "What do you think of asking all noncrucial available ladies between the ages of twenty-three and thirty-five to avoid downtown for the next four days?"

"Noncrucial?" Lucia looked at Meg. "What does that mean?"

"I'm not sure," she said. "I'm working on 'avoid downtown' and 'available.' "

Owen raised his hand. "You want the TV people to think we don't have any single women here at all? What do you expect them to do, stay in their homes with the blinds shut?"

"Well." Jerry hesitated, because clearly that was exactly what he'd had in mind. "It was just an idea."

"Patsy is standing by to do last-minute haircuts," Meg told him. "Iris plays drums in the band on Saturday. I don't know about the others, but no one misses the Halloween party. Ever."

The mayor held up both hands in a gesture of surrender while his town council members stared at him as if he'd suggested they run naked down Main Street.

"He's gone completely crazy," Meg whispered. She turned to Owen and Lucia. "Maybe we all have. Maybe this whole idea is insane."

"Of course it is," Owen replied. He leaned closer to whisper, "Will you please go out with me tonight? We could have dinner in Lewistown —"

"Company's coming," she reminded him. "I'm on duty."

"After this is over," he said, "could we do something *normal* together?"

"Like what?"

He gave it some thought. "I'm not sure. But if we work at it, we might end up doing something traditional and boring."

"Wow, you sure know how to seduce a girl, don't you?"

"We could invite your mother over for Sunday dinner."

"Aw." Lucia sighed. "That's just like being married."

"I don't think," Meg said, ignoring her friend, "you should put anything to do with my mother in the 'traditional and boring' category."

CHAPTER FOURTEEN

"She's the skinniest person I've ever seen."

Meg didn't disagree. She and Shelly stared at the four women who stood talking to Jerry by the front door of the restaurant. Tracy, the birdlike blonde with a spiked pixie cut, was obviously the one in charge. Dressed in tight black leggings, a form-fitting black turtleneck top and high-heeled patent leather boots, she was the only one of the women who held the mayor's attention as she spoke. The other three looked hungry, tired and bored, but at least two were wearing the right kind of clothes — jeans and vests — to look as if they'd fit right in with the locals. The third, at least a foot taller than the other three, with jumbled red hair down to her waist, was built like an Olympic volleyball champion. Meg guessed she was the camera operator.

"He doesn't have a chance with Tracy," Meg muttered. "Poor guy."

"I thought *I* was thin." Shelly absently stroked her round belly. "Wait until Marie Swallow sees her. She'll want to feed her meatballs and lasagna and garlic bread three times a day. The others look okay, though. Maybe a little cranky."

Jerry proudly guided the visitors over to Meg, who met them halfway across the room. One lone customer sat nursing his last cup of coffee at the counter and the Fergusons occupied the corner booth, where they were finishing dessert. Meg planned to greet her guests and show them to their cabins after the introductions were made.

She'd guessed correctly. The little blonde was Tracy, the producer.

"Do you serve quinoa, Meg? And fresh, raw vegetables? Please don't tell me that everything is fried." Tracy liked giving orders, it seemed. "Aside from the menu, I love the authenticity of your little café."

"We aim to please," Meg said drily. Lin, a shy young woman with sleek black hair straight to her chin, was Tracy's assistant. Amy, a dead ringer for Taylor Swift, was in charge of casting the show. The tall redhead with the impressive shoulders introduced herself as, "Cane, the woman behind the camera," and asked where all of the cowboys were hiding.

"They're in class tonight," Shelly explained.

"Class?" Tracy looked at Jerry, whose guilty expression would have had a busload of lawyers going after him. "The cowboys go to school?"

"Not exactly," he stalled.

"Our bachelors wanted to look their best when they met you," Meg explained. "That's all."

"They're getting makeovers," Shelly added, thinking she was being helpful. "It's grooming night."

"Get your equipment," Tracy cried, waving her hand at Cane. "Hurry! We don't want to miss this!"

Jerry managed to block the door before Cane opened it. "Wouldn't you rather have something to eat? And see your rooms? Tracy, hon, let me show you your cabin. You wanted Montana atmosphere? Well, you've —"

"What I *want*," she told him, "is Montana *men*. And if your Montana men are all in one place, right now, then that's where I want to go. You can drive us." She didn't wait for an answer. Instead she stood on tiptoe, kissed Jerry on the mouth and gestured to her crew to follow her out of the restaurant.

"Sorry," Meg mouthed.

"It's okay." He paused by the door. "You're coming, too, aren't you? I could use the, uh, support."

"I wouldn't miss it," Meg assured him before he scurried away.

"Me, either." Shelly hurried over to the window and flipped the sign to closed. "I want to see Les get a haircut and I want to see if they'll really shave off their beards. Lucia said some of them were even going to wear their new shirts, just in case the TV crew showed up."

"What I *want,*" Meg said, imitating Tracy, "is Montana *men.* And if Montana *men* are at the center, then that's where I want to go."

Shelly giggled. "You already have Owen."

"I'm not sure he's staying in town.

"But what I *want,*" Meg whined again, watching John Ferguson help Janet to her feet, "is Montana *pizza.*"

"Me, too," Shelly said. " 'Cuz I don't ever want to be skinny again."

What she wanted, Meg thought, envying the Fergusons, was a marriage and a love just like that.

"Anyone but him," Loralee said, having

finally and inevitably noticed Owen's presence next to her daughter.

"Mom," Meg said, keeping her voice low. Tracy and her minions would surely pounce on any morsel of drama and her mother was anything but discreet. Case or Cane or whatever her name was had spent the past hour walking around the community center's meeting room with her camera on her shoulder. She'd filmed interviews with freshly shaved members of the council, she'd filmed Patsy's demonstration of how to use gel and she'd eaten quite a lot of pizza.

Meg thought Pete Lyons had better pick his tongue off the floor and stop panting. Reminded her of Owen's dog.

"Anyone else," Loralee repeated, waving her hand toward the crowd of bachelors. "Just pick one of them. Because *he* will break your heart. He will stomp it into little pieces and then drive over it in his fancy truck, and if that's not enough he'll shovel cow manure on top of the whole mess that *was* your heart and he'll ride off into the sunset. Laughing all the way, of course, just like last time."

"You've gotten real descriptive in your old age," Owen drawled, having stepped to Meg's side. "Have you been taking writing classes in Arizona or just watching a lot of television?"

Meg's mother narrowed her eyes. "All she wanted was for you to give her time. She wanted to go to school."

"Mom, not here," Meg hissed.

"You *are* a bit over-the-top," Tracy said, eyeing Loralee as if she were a particularly interesting animal at the zoo. "But dramatic in a country-western, redneck way. Has anyone ever told you that you look like Dolly Parton?"

"Sweetie, I may have a figure like hers, but I can't sing a note. Runs in the family. Ask Meg, she's the same way."

"Loralee's talents run in a different direction," Owen drawled, managing to hold his temper. "She's very good at getting —"

"Married," Meg interjected. "Good at getting *married.*"

Owen took a deep breath. "I was wrong, Loralee, but what's between me and Meg is nobody's business."

Loralee didn't look convinced, and turned to her daughter. "Meg?"

Tracy sniffed and looked Meg up and down with obvious disapproval. "Are the *women* in town getting makeovers, too?"

"Unlike the women of today," Loralee retorted, giving Tracy a disapproving glance,

"I didn't sleep with every man who bought me dinner. I married them. *M-a-r-r-i-e-d.*"

"And how many men did you *m-a-r-r-y?*" The producer clearly enjoyed proving she could spell, too.

"Five, sweetie." She held up one hand to display a beautifully manicured thumb and four fingers. Her nails were neon pink. "Five."

"What happened to them all?"

"One disappeared on me, just walked out right before Margaret was born. One annulment. Two divorces, I won't go into the sordid details, but we're still friends, believe it or not. And the last one, my Bill, died of cancer. I've been *single* for *fifteen* years."

"S-i-n-g-l-e," Shelly said, standing close to Loralee. Meg wondered why everyone was spelling all of a sudden.

"I know a lot about men, but I've learned my lesson," Loralee said. "There will be no more husbands for me, not at my age."

"And how old *are* you, exactly?"

"Not old enough to brag about it." With that, she turned on her aqua-booted heels and marched back to her seat.

"Let's go see how the haircuts are coming along." Jerry's face was flushed above his new navy Wrangler shirt.

"Yes. Let's." The producer shot one last

look over her shoulder at Loralee Smittle. "That woman sure has a mouth on her."

"*That woman* is my mother." Meg wanted nothing more than to haul Miss California out the door and into her rental car.

"My bad," Tracy said quickly. "But we might be able to develop a character for her. Amy? Make a note of that."

"We have a *lot* of interesting characters around here," Jerry said, pulling her away from Meg and toward the pizza. "That's what makes the West so colorful. Wait until you meet Mrs. Swallow, our own Mama Marie. Have you tried the pizza?"

"I don't eat carbs," the woman sniffed. "Is there any salad?"

"Of course." Jerry hustled her over to the tables against the wall. "I'll show you."

"It's not that I don't want her to get married and give me grandchildren," Loralee explained, stretched out on top of her bed. Her pajamas were satin and covered with pink flamingos. "It's that I don't trust him."

Shelly perched on the foot of her roommate's bed and listened. She liked Owen, and she really liked Meg. But according to Loralee, Owen had broken Meg's heart when she was eighteen. His father had caught them trying to elope and his mother had taken Owen away after the father died. Shelly had a hard time picturing Meg eloping. "Meg likes him."

"He was her first love," Loralee said. "That mother of his wouldn't even let her in the door after the funeral. She cried for weeks."

"Then what?" Shelly couldn't picture Owen letting Meg cry. He looked at her as if she was the most special woman in the world. He came for breakfast every morning, didn't he?

"I'm not sure. Meg was determined to go away to school, so she packed up and headed east. She wanted to get out of town, get her education."

"He didn't come back?"

"Once," Loralee admitted. "But Meg was back east, settled in college."

"Owen seems nice. I didn't think he was at first, but now I do. He helped her a lot, you know. With the cabins."

Loralee didn't seem impressed. "She went to the post office every day, waiting to hear from him. He never called her, either. He was angry, I think, because she went along with his father, stopping the elopement. She was scared and very, very young and I don't think Owen understood anything but that he wasn't getting what he wanted."

"That's really awful." Shelly knew how Meg must have felt. It was a lonely, sad story and she hoped she wouldn't have to wait fourteen years to find Sonny again. She couldn't wait fourteen weeks. "It's hard to love somebody when they're not there."

"Oh, sweetie, don't I know it." Loralee scooted over and wrapped Shelly in her arms. "I'm sorry about your boyfriend. And you're so young. Too young to be going through this."

"It'll be okay." She absolutely, positively refused to cry.

"What about your family?" Loralee sat back and looked as if she wouldn't go along with any kind of fib, so Shelly told her the truth. Part of it, anyway.

"I was in foster care," she admitted. "My mother wasn't around that much."

"And your father?"

Shelly shrugged.

Loralee sighed. "I want you to think long and hard about what kind of life you can give your baby, sweetie. Even if you find Sonny, that doesn't mean everything is going to be roses and blue skies. I've been in your shoes and I know how hard it is."

"Don't be hard on Meg."

"I'll try," Loralee said. "Especially since I'm the only one of the three of us who has any sense."

Shelly couldn't stop laughing, not even when Loralee threw a pillow at her.

"Man plan alert!" Lucia carried two more pies into the café and set them on the counter. "They're heading this way for breakfast."

Loralee and Shelly stopped working, grabbed their phones from their apron pockets and started texting furiously. "What are they doing?"

Meg opened the lids of the boxes and inhaled the scents of apples and cinnamon. "They're keeping score — who can send the message first. I think there's a prize involved, but I'm not sure. It's been going on for days."

"How does anyone get any work done around town?" Lucia sat next to George. He was working on a stack of pancakes and reading the paper. "Hi, Mr. Oster."

"Good morning, Lucia. Where are those hooligans of yours?"

"With their grandmother at the moment, so you can eat in peace."

"They're not that bad," he said, turning to page three. "I've seen worse."

"Do they know about their future horseback-riding trip?" Meg poured her a cup of coffee and placed a pitcher of half-and-half next to it.

"Horseback riding? Yep. I've been using it for a bribe for days. They've been the best-behaved little hooligans ever."

"Owen's looking forward to it, too."

"He'll need the patience of a saint," She swung her stool to face the door. "Speaking of patience, the Wicked Witch and her Three Musketeers have arrived."

"Cane isn't so bad. At least she eats pie."

Conversation in the restaurant quieted, allowing Trace Adkins's new song to be heard loud and clear. Men sat up straighter. Their wives looked to see what the Californians wore this morning. A table of four young men put their heads together and planned their strategy.

Tracy had made it known Wednesday morning that she preferred the large corner booth, though Meg had reserved a large table in the middle of the room between the counter and the door. The original plan had been to allow plenty of space for the bachelors to walk past and, if encouraged, stop for a chat.

But Tracy wanted to be in the corner, where she could sit with her back to the wall and watch the counter, the door, the cash register and every single person in the room. She couldn't see around the corner to the back of the other dining area or the restrooms, but that didn't seem to bother her. The table at the booth was large enough for paperwork, iPads, a notebook computer and various cell phones. The mass of technology discouraged visitors.

"I wonder what they thought of the football game."

"I'm sure Jerry will tell us," Meg assured her. She set the pies on stands and covered them with glass-domed lids.

"I can't believe he's not here already."

"He fell asleep during the game. Right there in the bleachers. Kate Petersen — she and Kip are cheerleading this year — put a blanket over him. I think he's just worn out. Owen said the game went into overtime."

"Owen said?" Lucia took a sip of coffee. "What else does Owen have to say these days?"

Meg blushed. "He calls every night, tells me about the day. Sometimes in the morning, too."

"Hmm. Is this getting serious?"

"We talk. We're getting to know each other again."

"What does he say about selling the ranch?"

"Nothing," she admitted, watching as

313

Shelly hustled over to the booth to greet the latest arrivals. Men would start coming in any minute and the place would be busy for at least another hour. Business was good. Business was *very* good. She could only imagine how good it would be if they actually filmed a television show here. "They loved their cabins. Lin and Amy took the larger one with the double beds, and Cane and the Witch each have their own."

"That could be good," Lucia said. "He's coming to the party tonight, I assume. I mean, no matter what kind of fit Loralee throws?"

"She's been pretty quiet the past few days. She and Owen have managed to avoid each other."

"He's a really good man," Lucia said with a sigh. "And you look happy. Is this getting serious? From what I see, the man's in love."

No one but Lucia heard her admit in a low voice that she was, too. George was in a deep discussion about the federal budget with Martin and Mr. Fargus. Loralee chatted with Hip, Theo and Amber at their table, while various other customers were intent upon their own meals and conversations. "In love, I mean. But I don't want to rush into anything, you know? He may still intend to sell the ranch and move back to

Washington. He could meet someone else and —"

"And he could die," Lucia said. She stared down at her coffee for a long moment before raising her gaze to Meg. "If you love him, let him know it. Let yourself love him back. Because there are no guarantees, Meg." She slid off her stool and slung her purse over her shoulder. "I'd better go get my cowboys ready for the ranch."

"You'll be at the party tonight?"

"Wouldn't miss it."

"Lucia?"

Her friend paused.

"I know you're right. Thank you."

She'd dressed as the Bride of Frankenstein again.

Loralee had dumped her box of treasured possessions, which consisted mostly of wedding memorabilia, in the middle of the bed, showering the pink bedspread with various tulle concoctions and dusty silk daisies.

On the other hand, it could be worse: Loralee could have talked Shelly into wearing one of the veils and ringing her eyes with black shadow. Meg could see it now, Frankenstein's ex-wife accompanied by the newer, fertile model.

Now, that was a truly horrifying thought.

She was almost glad she was running late. She'd been the last one to leave the café, but even closing early for the party hadn't given her much extra time to get ready. Especially not when there were costumes involved.

She'd only wanted to borrow eyeliner for her Annie Oakley freckles. A fringed leather vest, braided hair, her seldom-worn ivory Stetson and Davey Swallow's toy holster made a good Annie Oakley. Lucia had insisted that she wear a short denim skirt, black tights and tall, black, vintage Tony Lama boots — which only just fit — giving her what Lucia called flair. Meg hoped the freckles would erase the naughty impression.

Meg set the plastic box upright and, since it was second nature, cleaned up after her mother. She tossed the mess of lace, flowers, a pair of white satin gloves, two shawls, a miniskirted bridal gown, a beaded headband, two wedding guest books, a set of his and hers guest towels and Meg's baby book — a faded pink Hallmark edition stuffed with report cards and school drawings — back where it had all come from.

Those things reminded her of a different lifetime. She wondered if she'd ever have her own wedding. After all, the closest she'd

come to that was with Owen.
She'd never wanted anyone else.

CHAPTER FIFTEEN

"You look like an idiot in that outfit."

"What?" Jerry patted the ace of spades sticking out of his vest pocket. Aurora's hostile comments had stopped bothering him months ago. "You've got something against Wyatt Earp?"

"I've got something against someone who won't sell me a worthless parking lot." She grudgingly slid the beer he'd ordered in front of him.

"Nice costume," he said, pointedly noting the oversize witch's hat she wore. Her platinum hair looked like a wig. "Looks good on you. Almost natural."

Content to have the last word, he turned his back on the bartender. The crowd never looked better. None of the town's bachelors had opted for naked chests painted with the colors of their favorite football teams. No one had draped fake vomit on their shoulders or on top of their heads, a real crowd pleaser last year. The younger, good-looking men had taken his advice and wore their best Western wear. Why look like Sasquatch when you could be Brad Pitt in *Legends of the Fall*?

Meg strolled past. She looked a little lost without Owen hovering over her. The guy had it bad, but Jerry couldn't blame him. The two of them had some kind of history, he figured. Even Owen MacGregor couldn't have won over the previously hard-hearted Meg Ripley in a matter of weeks. "Hey, Meg! What do you think about a Willing Western-wear clothing line?"

"Great idea. Maybe I'll print up some 'Willing Westauwant' T-shirts, you know, to sell in the café."

"Ha, ha. At least that sounds better than the Dirty Shame," he said. "Wasn't that the original —"

"Please," she said, holding up her hand. "Sometimes history is best left buried. Trust me on that."

"What do you have all over your face?"

"Those are my Annie Oakley freckles."

"It's not your best look." He turned back to the party while Meg asked Aurora for a glass of seltzer water. "Your mother's outdone herself tonight."

Loralee wore a vintage 1950s waitress

uniform, complete with a red-striped apron and matching ruby lipstick. Her blond hair was sprayed into some weird sort of thing on top of her head. Shelly, growing more pregnant by the minute, was at her side and dressed as a Beatles-era hippie with strings of beads and feathers. The flowing calico dress covered her belly.

"Shelly looks so authentic it's almost scary," Aurora said to Meg. "The tie-dye headband must have been Lucia's idea."

"It's obvious who won the raffle," Meg said, looking grimly at the bear, whose enormous head was topped with a fluffy white tulle bridal veil. Jerry had never seen anything like it. The crown was beaded, rhinestones sparkling in the light of the beer signs on the wall behind it. A bouquet of white silk roses drooped from its menacing paw. And since the bear was in attack mode, the expression on its face looked as if the groom would be eaten alive if he appeared within three feet of the bride.

Tracy's people had probably taken three hundred pictures of the beast. Now they were posing with it while Cane filmed them.

"Who?" Jerry shot her a puzzled look.

"It's not going to be announced until midnight," Aurora said. "We have hours left to guess. You mean you know already?"

"I forget the two of you have only been here a couple of years," Meg said.

"Three and a half," Jerry corrected her.

"And how could anyone forget?" was Aurora's dry comment.

"My mother, you know, the woman who has been married five times? That's her veil. One of many. The bear has worn wedding gear before."

"Poor bear," Aurora said. "Especially since it's a male grizzly."

"It's inspired," Jerry said. "Brides, bachelors and bears. We could have the image on coffee cups and aprons and coasters." He thought harder, recognizing a brainstorm when it hit him.

"Beautiful brides, bashful bachelors and badass bears," Aurora drawled. "Catchy, isn't it?"

To his own embarrassment, Jerry didn't reject it immediately. Aurora snorted and turned away to wait on three over-the-hill cheerleaders. Loralee bounced over and grabbed Jerry's hand. "Come on, you promised the next fast one."

"Sure." Jerry turned to ask Meg to join them in the crowd warming up to the introductory notes of "Save a Horse, Ride a Cowboy," but she'd joined a butcher, a baker and a candlestick maker in conversa-

321

tion at the bar. He saw Owen, dressed as a mountain man, arrive and head over to Meg. Now there was an interesting couple.

"Just exactly who — or what — are you supposed to be?" Meg ran her hand up the sleeve of Owen's rough leather jacket. "I've never seen you in fringe before."

"I'm a grizzled old trapper," he said, rubbing his hand over his day-old beard. "Isn't that obvious?"

"Like Robert Redford in *Jeremiah Johnson,* I suppose?"

"Yeah." He took her into his arms and eased into the crowd of dancers. "Didn't we watch that movie together?"

"Yes. With Mrs. Hancock. She was a big Robert Redford fan back then."

"You look pretty cute, Miss Oakley," he murmured into her ear. "I doubt Annie ever wore that short a skirt, but it looks good on you."

She laughed. "Lucia thought you'd appreciate it. She's my fashion advisor." Meg leaned back a little to look up at him. "You've been a big help to the town through all of this."

"It wasn't —"

"Yes," she said, stopping his protest. "It was a big deal and you made a big difference. Once the show gets started, everyone will see what a great place this is. And Tracy loved the ranch. I think she might have a crush on you. Jerry told her you wouldn't do the show, but —" She stopped as he winced. "What?"

"You can't count on the show," Owen said, looking at the dancers two-stepping their way around the room. "It might not happen."

"I realize that," she said, sensing there was more. "What else?" He didn't answer, but the guilty flash in his eyes was easy to read. "The rumors are true?"

"Which ones?"

"You tell me." She stopped dancing and let him lead her to the side of the dance floor where the bear stood ready to attack. "Golf course? Engaged to the daughter of a senator? What?"

"Nothing so dramatic."

"You're selling out? Some movie star make you an offer you can't refuse?"

"Not yet. I hadn't planned on living here," Owen said. "I hadn't planned on anything."

"I thought this was what you always wanted."

"It was," he admitted. "A long time ago, I wanted the ranch. I wanted that life."

The music faded, and the sound of a

fiddle vibrated one last sad note.

"Well," Meg said. "It's yours now."

"It's too late," he countered.

"So I'm not to be forgiven after all," she said, seeing past his career issues, knowing full well that with his family money he didn't need to work — never had. "Do you remember what you said that day you came to my house, when your father was in the hospital?"

"Yes, as a matter of fact, I do." His words were clipped, and a muscle tensed in his jaw. "You wouldn't go away with me. And I asked you what you wanted."

"And I said, 'I want you, but I don't have the rest figured out.' "

"I did," he said, ignoring the people around them. "I wanted you, the ranch, a family, a life there. And you said no."

"That's right. I said no. Was that the first time in your life you couldn't have what you wanted?"

"Pretty much," he said, but she was already moving away from him. He felt like an idiot standing there on the edge of the dancing crowd.

Shelly hoped there'd be a prize for the best costume. Lin, Amy and Cane had talked Al into letting them borrow three of his chef jackets. Lin held a tinfoil butcher knife, Amy wore an old metal muffin tin as a hat and Cane had shaped a long, tapered candle so that it fit over her head and stuck out on the sides. She looked like a warped Statue of Liberty. Shelly couldn't figure out what Tracy was supposed to be. Maybe a black cat. Her drawn-on whiskers hadn't survived the evening.

She wanted to go home and crawl into bed. Les had been flirting with the baker for the past hour. Hip hadn't shown up, though he'd told her he was coming as Paul Bunyan, complete with beard and overalls, just to aggravate Jerry.

Shelly didn't think anyone would notice if she left really early. Well, no one but Loralee. Shelly waved at Loralee and mouthed the words *going home* when she caught her eye. She exchanged her sandals for winter boots and dug through the hooks by the door until she found the down jacket Loralee had given her. With her purse slung over her shoulder and her new gloves on, she set out for home.

She hoped the walk would get rid of her headache and the fresh air would help the sick feeling. She felt as if she'd eaten a large plate of fries for supper. Which she couldn't do, not with Loralee and Meg constantly supervising healthy prenatal meals.

Snowflakes, big fluffy ones, hit her cheeks and caught in her eyelashes. They were few and far between, but Shelly loved the chill they left on her face. Tracy had worried about a storm coming in tomorrow and fretted about getting to the airport in the morning, but Meg had assured her that snow flurries weren't as bad as they sounded. Shelly knew the last thing Meg wanted was a storm that kept Tracy and her gang in town a few days longer. Despite enjoying the increase in business, her boss was tired.

Later Shelly would realize that if she had taken the shortcut through the alley she wouldn't have seen the familiar jacked-up truck with the splash guards and the distinctive bumper stickers waiting at the town's only red light, just a couple of blocks from the café and what had become home. The driver was looking down as if checking his phone. Otherwise she doubted he would have sat at the light, patiently waiting for it to change, when there wasn't another car to be seen.

She waved, walked faster along the sidewalk, called out his name and hurried toward the intersection. But the light turned green and he turned south on the empty road. She recognized Sonny's profile, the tilt of his cap, the casual way he draped one arm over the steering wheel.

But Sonny didn't notice her. Trying desperately to memorize his license plate, she ran alone in the dark watching her baby's father drive away.

"Leave her alone," Les snapped. "You're too old for her."

Hip blinked. "Man, you don't —"

"What?" the younger man asked. "I don't understand. I know I'm too old for her, too, I guess. Maybe. She's just a kid."

"A pregnant kid," Owen interjected. "What's going on?" He'd never seen Les lose his temper or Hip look so miserable. He was sober, too, and ignored Aurora's offer to get him a beer.

"I need to talk to Shelly about something," Hip said slowly, keeping a wary eye on Les. Owen was surprised. The kid looked as if he wanted to punch someone, all right. "Is she here?"

"She went home quite a while ago." Which was where he should have gone after Meg had left, but he'd been hoping to knock on Meg's door and try to explain. Then he'd wonder exactly what it was he wanted to explain. Did he love her? Or had the trip down memory lane finally come to a screeching halt?

But at the moment he felt sorry for his old friend, a man who looked as miserable as he himself felt. He took Hip's arm and led him over to a corner where there were empty chairs around a table piled high with beer bottles and glasses. It looked as if everyone in town with two working legs was on the dance floor, whether or not they could dance.

Les took the hint and stayed where he was, next to two of the Californians.

"What's going on?"

"I needed to talk to the girl, that's all. There's something —" He glanced at the pager hooked to his belt. "Darn."

"What?"

"Accident."

"Where? Who is it?"

"Not around here. North of Great Falls, up by where my sister lives, but she's here for the weekend."

"Do you have to go?"

"No. The info goes out to every — Sorry." He studied the message. "Gotta call in."

"Stay away from Les until I get him to cool off."

"Yeah." He pulled his cell phone out of his jacket pocket and headed for the door. Owen saw Loralee leading Les around the dance floor. So at least his attention wasn't on Hip. The party was winding down and Owen thought he'd better head straight home and leave Meg be tonight. He'd retrieved his jacket and gloves when Hip came back inside.

"Get Loralee," the man said.

Owen froze. "What's going on?"

Hip looked distraught. "Come on. Gotta go."

Owen did as he was told, hustling Loralee off the dance floor, with Les following them. Aurora handed the woman her coat and managed to get a few details from Hip before they left. He explained there'd been an accident north of Fort Benton, on Highway 87. Three vehicles, one of them belonging to Meg, were involved. Two women had been transported by ambulance to the hospital in Great Falls. *No fatalities.*

"But why — That doesn't make any sense," Loralee sputtered. "She can't be —"

Owen hustled her out the door, Les promising to follow. Theo waited at the curb in front of the bar, and once they were inside he put the car in gear and peeled out of the lot. His conversations weren't any more extensive than those of his cousin.

"Theo, turn the heat up," Owen said. Theo fiddled with the buttons. "Take deep breaths, Loralee. We've got a couple of hours to go."

Hip was on his phone again. "Shelly's in Benefis. There's a neonatal intensive care unit there."

"The baby. Not even six months —"

"Breathe," Hip said. "We'll handle it." He punched numbers on his cell phone. Loralee leaned her head back against the seat and stared out into the darkness while Theo made short work of the drive to Lewistown. From there they'd head west.

Loralee took a deep breath and asked what they all wished they knew. "What was Meg doing so far away from here? Where were they going?"

"They must have seen Sonny," Theo replied.

Owen swore under his breath. "It's the only thing that makes any sense."

It was two before they reached the hospital. There, in the waiting room inside the emergency center, they tried to find someone who could tell them how Meg and Shelly were.

Owen would have stormed past the reception area and into the E.R., except Loralee clung to his arm as though she was strapped to him. Not even Hip could coax information out of anyone at the hospital, and thirty minutes passed like thirty hours.

It was nearly three before a nurse could give them an update on Meg's condition. She was going to be fine. She'd had an X-ray. There were stitches on her forehead. She'd be released shortly.

Then Loralee told the woman in charge that she was Shelly's grandmother and only living relative. Owen doubted the nurse believed her, but she shared the most recent information, anyway: Shelly had a broken ankle and some bruising. There was some concern about the baby. There'd been an ultrasound. She was hooked up to a fetal monitor and would be admitted to the maternity ward shortly, where they would be able to see her. A doctor would be out soon to give them more information.

"Would one of you gentleman be the father?"

The nurse sighed her disapproval when none of the four men replied. "Does anyone have her medical information? Health insurance?"

"She went to the clinic in Winifred, and at the center in Lewistown," Hip answered. The nurse handed her a clipboard with a thick layer of forms attached to it.

"Fill these out the best you can, please."

"What about the others?" Hip leaned forward, his face a study in misery. "In the accident. There were two other cars."

"You can talk to one of the deputies, but as far as we know there have been no fatalities. The driver of the truck has a broken nose and facial cuts. We have four banged-up teenagers from the first car, but nothing life threatening, from what I've heard. And as they say on the news, alcohol might have been a factor."

"Thank you for letting us know," Loralee said, weeping softly.

Owen thought he'd pass out from the relief.

Meg wanted to weep right along with her mother. She wished she could feel the warmth of Owen's chest under her cheek and be comforted simply because he was there with her.

But instead she felt cold and distant, as removed from Owen as she'd been when he'd walked into the restaurant for breakfast weeks ago. Meg followed an aide into the waiting room, where she joined her mother on the vinyl sofa. She felt so isolated, despite the people surrounding her who were also worried about Shelly. The waiting area was large, its wide doors admitting distraught fathers and tense, pale mothers. But no matter how many people filled the room — arriving, leaving, returning with coffee, pacing — Meg had never felt so alone. She kept worrying about Shelly and her baby. She couldn't let anything else in.

"What were you *doing*?" Loralee looked at Meg. "What on earth possessed you?"

"She saw Sonny at the stoplight. I'd just come home when she ran into the parking lot and wanted to borrow the car. I couldn't let her go by herself, so I drove her."

"The boyfriend," Owen replied. "I knew it had to have something to do with the boyfriend."

"Hip," Theo said quietly, "you want me to tell it?"

Hip shook his head. He sat, his elbows on his knees, his large hands holding his head as if he was in terrible pain. "Here's what happened. I have three younger sisters. Youngest is Portia. She's married to Sonny. Sonny Nance."

Meg leaned forward. "Sonny? *The* Sonny?"

He nodded. "Yeah. Shelly showed me the picture of her so-called boyfriend. It wasn't real clear, but I could tell. Plus, he's a player."

Owen leaned forward. "How long has he

been married to your sister?"

"Two years. They have a kid. A little boy. Almost two."

"Married," Loralee muttered. *"Married?* Where is he? Where does he live? Does your sister know what a creep she's married to?"

"Yeah. She left him. Got here last night. With the boy."

"And Sonny?" Meg waited for Hip to look at her. "He was in town tonight?"

"He followed her home. To Willing," Hip admitted. "That's how I know it's the same Sonny. He made a big scene at the house, but he left the house after Portia said she'd call the sheriff. I guess he was hanging around hoping she'd change her mind and talk to him."

"Jail would be a good place for that guy," Les muttered.

Meg agreed. If he was behind bars, he'd be safe from Loralee, Lucia and a number of other women whose hearts would break for Shelly and who would want to inflict revenge and pain on the man who'd hurt her.

"Shelly must have seen him leaving town. Maybe they talked, maybe she couldn't let him go, I don't know," the big man said. "I didn't know what to do. I figured it was him — who Shelly was looking for — all along.

But my sister . . ."

"You didn't want to hurt her."

"Thought she might make it work, you know?"

Meg could understand. But Hip's sister was married to a man who cheated on her. That wasn't the kind of thing that went away just because no one talked about it.

At first she wondered if she was back on a bus. She was sick and shaky and everything hurt, especially her right foot. And her chest felt as if Al had fallen over and pinned her to the kitchen floor.

"You're going to be all right," she heard someone say, but she kept her eyes closed because that was easier than trying to open them.

"We'll take you home in a couple of days," another woman promised, but Shelly couldn't focus on whose voice was next to her head. Warm fingers held her right hand.

"Try to rest." The voice belonged to Meg. She recognized it now. "Everything is going to be all right. You're safe. You're in the hospital."

Shelly heard the murmur of male voices, too. The sounds grew more and more familiar. Meg, Loralee, Hip, Les, Owen. What were they doing?

And then she remembered. It all came flooding back, the cold, the stoplight, the long drive trying to keep up with the speeding truck. Meg screaming to hold on. The crash.

"The baby? The baby!" She untangled her hand and ran her palm over her abdomen. "Is the baby —"

"So far so good," Loralee replied in a soft voice meant to be soothing but that instead scared Shelly so much she could barely breathe.

"The baby," she insisted. "What about the baby?"

Loralee stroked her arm. "Can you open your eyes? Just a little bit?"

"The baby is fine," Les assured her. He stepped close to the bed and touched her shoulder. "You've had all the tests and she's okay."

"She?" With that, she forced her eyes open and attempted to focus on the man talking to her. Les, sweet Les, looked anxious.

"Yeah," he said. "It's a girl."

"A girl," she murmured, running her hand once again over her stomach. "There was . . . an accident," she said, looking around the room. Meg, Loralee, Les, Hip and Owen sat or stood close to the hospital bed. "Meg? You're okay?"

"I'm good," she said, but Shelly saw a bandage on her forehead.

"Is Sonny — ?"

"Has a broken nose, that's all," Hip told her. "They fixed him up and let him go home."

"Where's that?"

Les winced, and Hip responded, "Near Havre, north of Fort Benton, where you had the, uh, accident."

Her eyes filled with tears as she looked at Meg. "Your car! Is your car okay? Did it get wrecked? I'm sorry. I mess everything up."

"Please don't worry about the car," Meg said, blinking back tears. "It's not what's important now."

"Shelly," Hip began, looking as pained as a man could get. "There's something I have to tell you." He took a deep breath. "Sonny is married to my little sister. He was in Willing to try to talk her out of leaving him."

"I . . . I am so sorry, Hip. I mean . . . I knew — Oh, not about your sister. But . . . I didn't know he was married, I swear. . . . He didn't even recognize me," Shelly said. She blinked back tears and ran a shaking hand over her stomach. "He didn't even recognize me. He helped me out of the car and he didn't even know who I was. He told me he was on the phone with his wife —

337

his *wife* — when the other car stopped and he couldn't stop fast enough and then —"

"Don't think about the accident," Meg said. She handed her a tissue. "Hip is going to explain a little more about Sonny. And the rest of us are going to step outside and let you get some rest."

"He kept saying he was sorry," Shelly whispered. "That it wasn't his fault. And he didn't even *know* me."

"I'm sorry, sweetheart," Loralee said. "But you have to put him out of your mind and concentrate on that baby now."

Much later, after Hip told her the rest of what he knew, Shelly lay quietly in her hospital bed. Loralee dozed in an oversize chair in the corner while Meg had gone to find coffee. They'd both offered to call her friends in Boise, but Shelly knew she was better off with the family she had right here.

"I'm sorry," she whispered to her unborn daughter. "I was stupid and you're the one who will suffer for it."

But, she silently promised her child, from now on she would do the right thing, no matter how difficult. She would stop building fantasies in her head, stop thinking about herself all the time. Sonny had a child who needed him and a wife he'd made vows to. She wouldn't interfere with that, and her daughter wouldn't grow up being charmed by a man who would never really be there for her or her mother.

It was long past time to grow up.

She was so *young.*

That was the first thing Owen had realized when he'd walked into Shelly's room. He'd stood by the back wall, he'd heard the explanations, he'd watched Meg hold back tears and comfort the teenager.

Meg was very pale. Owen saw her hands shake and he wanted to cover them with his own and tell her it was going to be okay.

But he didn't know that.

She'd been so young. And he'd been so wrong to pressure her into marriage. They'd both been too young. His father had been right to stop him. Oh, he'd always known that, but someplace deep inside he'd resented having his life controlled.

He'd expected Meg to give up her own dreams to make his come true.

And now was he truly older and wiser?

Chapter Sixteen

"It's just us again," he told the dog. "And we've got a lot of work to do."

Boo panted his agreement and whined for the scrambled eggs Owen clearly wasn't going to eat.

He'd turned his leave of absence into a resignation, walking away from the business of environmental law once and for all. He could not only have the life he'd wanted, but he could also have the life he should have had. And the only woman he'd ever wanted to share that life with was still here. Still single. Still able to look at him with those big brown eyes and drain every sensible thought from his head. Still able to drive him crazy when she smiled.

He wanted her as much as he ever had. More, even. Yeah, she'd said they were older and wiser. He was old enough to know what he wanted now, and smart enough to figure out how to get it.

He cleaned out more rooms in the cluttered house, painted ceilings and tossed trash. He left the summer kitchen alone, telling himself he'd get to that next spring. He hired Les for as many hours as the young man could spare from his grandparents' place and talked to him about setting up a horseback-riding business on the Triple M. Television or not, Owen assumed there was business in tourism.

Jerry agreed, but in the two weeks following the Halloween party at the Dahl and Shelly's accident, the mayor had convinced himself that Willing was still ready-made for television and certain fame.

"We're on the verge," he told Owen when he'd arrived on his doorstep. "I can feel it."

"Can you also feel this storm coming?" Owen looked at the darkening sky and motioned the mayor inside. "Come on in. Coffee's on," he said.

Jerry settled himself at the kitchen table as if he'd been doing it all his life. He scratched Boo's head and leaned back in his chair. "Haven't seen you at the café in a while."

"I'm cooking for myself these days."

"Just as well," Jerry said, as if blissfully unaware that Owen and Meg had been a couple and now weren't. "Dating classes have been put on hold until I hear from Tracy." He continued as if he thought Owen actually wanted to hear the local news. "Meg keeps trying to send Loralee back to Arizona, but she won't go until Shelly is on her feet. Which she is, by the way — just about as good as new. Except for the boot on her foot. Meg won't let her work, so she's moping. She's going to rent one of the cabins when the baby's born and Loralee's making noises about moving back to town to help her."

He took a sip of his coffee, winced and reached for the sugar bowl in the middle of the round table.

"Al's threatening to quit," he continued, "though he won't, and Lucia — I ran into her at the clinic at Lewistown when they were getting their flu shots — wouldn't say much except to warn me about Meg's new Mexican soups. I guess she's gotten creative with jalapeños lately."

"Sounds as if the café is a quiet place to eat now."

"Not really. You know how people gossip." Owen didn't reply, so Jerry pressed on with his version of the news. "Jack Dugan, you know, Jack from the town council? He's going to California for the winter. He and Tracy's assistant, Lin, have something going."

"Good for them." Owen put what he hoped was a pleasant and interested expression on his face and drank his coffee.

"And what about you?"

"What about me?"

Jerry gulped down some coffee and cleared his throat. "You and Meg. What happened?"

"If I told you that was none of your business —"

"I'd shut up," Jerry answered. "I'd shut up after I told you that I was your friend and if there was anything I could do, I'd like to help."

"Thanks. But there isn't anything anyone can do."

"I could call an emergency meeting. Get the two of you in the same room."

"Thanks, but no thanks."

Jerry nodded. "She dumped you, huh? Well, she's got a reputation for doing that."

Owen switched the subject back to the weather. They both agreed it was going to be a long winter.

When in doubt, ask her best friend. That advice had come from Jerry, an unlikely source of romantic advice, but Owen didn't have any better ideas of his own. When the three Swallow boys were tossing balls for

Boo to chase across the backyard and the horses had been ridden and given enough apples to bake a couple of pies, Owen stopped Lucia before she could round up her kids and head back to town.

"I have my grandmother's sapphire engagement ring," he said, bending over to retrieve a wayward, sticky tennis ball. None of Lucia's boys could throw straight. He tossed it far past Boo so that the dog would have to run fifty yards to retrieve it while the kids ran behind him. "Maybe you know I gave it to her once before. I'm not sure she'd want it again."

Lucia didn't have to ask who he referred to. "You don't know if she'd want that ring or any ring at all?"

He winced. "Both."

She grinned before calling for her boys to turn around and come back. "I thought you were selling and going back to the big city."

"I was," he admitted. "And then I came to my senses. Do you think she'll believe me?"

"I think you can figure out how to convince her," Lucia said, "and I'll help you any way I can."

"Thanks." He cleared his throat. "She's not taking my calls."

"She's hurt. You've been making yourself

pretty scarce since the accident."

He shoved his hands in his pockets. "Do you think I still have a chance? I'll be in Great Falls this afternoon. I thought about going shopping for something new, you know, something that looks more like an engagement ring. To let her know I'm serious."

"And you're asking for an opinion." Lucia was silent for a minute. She wrapped her jacket tighter around herself, as the wind had begun to pick up in the past half hour. The air smelled like snow, the skies overcast and gray. "Did she love the sapphire ring?"

"Well, she cried. I remember that. She cried both times. When I gave it to her and asked her to elope and then when she gave it back to me."

"I'm not sure I'm going to be much help," Lucia said, but she was smiling up at him. "Meg has never seemed to care much about jewelry. So whatever you decide to do will be the right choice."

He chuckled. "Here I thought you were going to make it easy for me."

She gave him a quick, surprising hug before rounding up the boys. "Don't worry, Ranch King. When the biggest problem you have is deciding between sapphires and diamonds, you really can't go wrong."

■ ■ ■ ■

"What is this?" Aurora asked, following Meg and Lucia to the Dahl's isolated corner table. "Another meeting to bring love and romance to Willing?"

"No. This is a private emergency," Lucia clarified, sitting with her back to the room. Meg ignored the bear, now sporting only an MSU baseball cap. A pumpkin perched near his toes on the new stand.

"No mayor?" Aurora dared a smile.

"No mayor," Meg assured her.

"Then the wine is on the house. What'll it be?"

Meg let Lucia decide, and soon a chilled bottle of pinot and two wineglasses appeared on the table. Aurora uncorked it and half-filled their glasses.

"Thank you." Meg took a sip. She wouldn't have cared if it was hot chocolate or ice water. What mattered was that her friend had dropped everything this evening, as had Mama Marie, to be here for her. Loralee was packing for her morning flight to Tucson and Meg couldn't avoid Shelly's teary-eyed looks any longer.

"Anytime," Aurora said. "I don't know what happened, but I wish you luck."

"Thanks." She and Lucia waited for Aurora to return to her place behind the bar, where two men sat watching *Monday Night Football.* The volume was high, so Meg wasn't concerned about being overheard.

"How's your little family?" Lucia asked.

"Doing well, except my mother thinks she's moving back to town to be a grandmother." Meg couldn't stop Loralee from staying and fussing over Shelly, whose recovery had been amazingly swift, despite the worries over the baby she carried.

Shelly had soon been pronounced healthy by the experts, who'd released her from the hospital and turned her care over to the center in Lewistown. The ankle boot would come off in three more weeks, but Shelly insisted she was in no pain. She refused to speak about Sonny, except to say that she'd been stupid and now had to be smart.

"And what about you?"

"I'm fine. I miss him, you know?"

"He's still here."

"Not for long," Meg said. "I don't think he knows what he wants."

"Maybe," her friend said. "And maybe not. But what do you want?"

"The same thing I wanted when I was eighteen. Him." She wiped her eyes. "But I'm so scared. I'm not the kind of person who jumps into things with both feet, you know?"

"So what?"

Meg stared across the table at her friend. "What?"

"So what?" she repeated. "There's *always* something to lose, you idiot." Lucia smiled. "That's the way it works. It's *all* a risk. You're going to let a man you love — a man you've loved so much that you never fell in love with anyone else — walk away?" She leaned back in her chair. "Wow."

"I'm an idiot? That's what you're trying to tell me?"

Lucia raised her glass. "Absolutely. Here's to the biggest idiot I've ever been friends with."

Meg clinked her glass against her friend's. "Cheers."

They were silent for a long moment until Lucia said quietly, "He's planning to stay here, you know."

"I heard rumors. But he hasn't told me himself. I keep thinking he'll walk into the café, you know?"

"Maybe he's giving you time."

"Maybe he hasn't decided what he wants." She took another sip of wine. "And maybe I haven't decided what I want."

"Give him another chance," Lucia said.

She hadn't talked to Owen for more than three weeks, since he'd walked out of the hospital. For all she knew, he'd packed up his house and moved back to DC with his dog.

Lucia leaned forward. "Sweetie, everyone needs a second chance at least once in their lives."

"We gave it everything we had," Jerry assured the members of the council. The first Monday of the month found the men gathered around the table at the café. They'd finished their breakfasts, they'd each enjoyed at least three cups of coffee and now it was time to move on to business. What was going to happen with the television show was uppermost on everyone's minds.

"And?"

"We wait. Tracy is very enthusiastic, very optimistic." She'd also hooked up with a producer at the Food Network, according to Jack. The former councilman kept him updated on the news from California. "As far as business goes, I'm officially appointing Owen MacGregor to the town council to fill Jack's empty seat. All in favor?"

"Aye," they said.

"Ayes have it." He nodded toward Owen. "Thanks for filling in."

Owen nodded back, but Jerry saw his attention wander to Meg. She'd stayed away from this part of the restaurant, letting Shelly handle the orders, but now she approached their table. She looked uncharacteristically nervous, he thought. Which made him want to pick up his papers and run out the door.

Owen looked as if he wanted to escape, too. But to give the man credit, he ignored her presence, picked up his coffee cup and drank from it as if he hadn't a care in the world.

"Could I have a minute?" She carried a large manila envelope. "If you don't mind?"

"Uh, sure." Jerry scooted his chair back. "Have a seat."

"No. This won't take long." Her cheeks were flushed and she didn't look at Owen, who sat silently at the foot of the table. "I thought you deserved — Well, here." She slid out official-looking papers with gold seals. "I made diplomas," she explained. "For the men who took the classes."

"Seriously?"

"Sure." She smiled. "You wanted to know what women want, and you listened. That deserves some kind of award."

Meg handed a diploma to each man at the table. She'd saved Owen for last, Jerry noticed, watching to see what would happen next. The rancher didn't look the least bit impressed. Meg fumbled with the papers and handed Owen his diploma. The man stared at it for a long moment, pushed back his chair and hauled Meg out of the restaurant.

"Meeting adjourned," Jerry called and joined the rest of them hurrying across the room to the windows.

"Is this some kind of joke? A diploma from The Husband School?"

"No," she sputtered, shivering in the cold. Owen looked down at her, took off his vest and wrapped it around her shoulders. "You deserved your diploma. After all your hard work and all. And besides, I thought it was a catchy title."

He looked up at the sky as if he was praying for patience, then back to her. His hands tightened on her shoulders. "I guess this means you're talking to me again? I've been calling you for three weeks."

"I know." She hadn't wanted to hear excuses or explanations. "I wasn't sure I wanted to hear what you had to say."

"I figured I'd given you enough time, so today I was going to sit outside your door until you had no choice but to hear me out."

He tucked the collar against her neck.

She took a deep breath. "That's why I'm here. You're the reason I've never fallen in love with anyone else. You're the reason I never said yes to any of those foolish proposals —"

"Except mine," he reminded her, a smile beginning to crease his face.

"Except yours."

"I did come back to Willing on my twenty-first birthday. You were gone, of course."

"You could have found out where I was."

"I did." He grimaced. "But by that time my uncle had moved to the ranch. The place was safe and I wasn't in any hurry to live there. The dream wasn't the same without you in it."

"And now? Have you figured out what you want?"

"Oh, I sure have." He dropped a gentle kiss on her mouth. "I love you," Owen said. "I loved you when I was a kid and I love you now. I want to rebuild the ranch. Fix up the house. Get married. Have kids. I wanted to do that with you. Heck, I *still* want to do that with you. If I propose to you right now," he said, glancing over her shoulder, "in this very public place, with about twenty people looking out the win-

dows, it will be, what? The twentieth proposal?"

"I stopped counting."

"Reach into the right pocket of my vest."

"Why?"

"Just do it," he replied, so she slid her
hands from his neck and fumbled with the
Velcro closing until she retrieved a small
jewelry box. She held it in her hand.

"Are you serious?"

"Open it," he urged, his voice husky.
Inside the box lay the sapphire ring, the one
she'd worn so many years before.

"You carry this around, in your pocket?"

He slipped it onto her finger. "Just for the
past few days. I thought it might bring me
luck." He pulled her closer. He brushed a
tender kiss across her mouth. "Meggie, will
you finally, once and for all, marry me?"

She looped her arms around his neck and
kissed him long and hard. "Yes, once and
for all."

ABOUT THE AUTHOR

Author of more than forty novels for Harlequin, **Kristine Rolofson** divides her time between Rhode Island, Idaho and Texas, where her handsome and brilliant grandson entertains her with drum solos. When not writing, she quilts, bakes peach pies and plays the fiddle in a country blues band. Her love of vintage cowboy boots is the stuff of legends.